*Never let down your guard. . . .*

"Acari Drew." A mellow voice spoke from behind me.

*Oh God.* Too late, I noticed the shadow that had fallen on me. My skin rippled with goose bumps, as if a chill breeze were at my back instead of a vampire.

I looked over my shoulder and had to force myself not to startle when I saw how close Alcántara had managed to come behind me. *Stupid.* Things like that could get a girl killed in my world.

He stood there, tall but not towering, with bottomless dark eyes and smooth black hair that brushed the collar of his black leather jacket. He looked like a beautiful indie rocker . . . carved out of marble.

I hopped to my feet as reverently as one could when wearing damp, sand-encrusted gym shorts. It struck me that all the other Acari had grown quiet around me, and even Tracer Otto was standing in respectful silence. They knew as well as I did how the sudden appearance of a vampire could mean somebody's imminent evisceration. I only hoped it wouldn't be mine.

ALSO BY VERONICA WOLFF

*Isle of Night*

# VAMPIRE'S KISS

## the watchers

VERONICA WOLFF

 NEW AMERICAN LIBRARY

NEW AMERICAN LIBRARY
Published by New American Library, a division of
Penguin Group (USA) Inc., 375 Hudson Street,
New York, New York 10014, USA
Penguin Group (Canada), 90 Eglinton Avenue East, Suite 700, Toronto,
Ontario M4P 2Y3, Canada (a division of Pearson Penguin Canada Inc.)
Penguin Books Ltd., 80 Strand, London WC2R 0RL, England
Penguin Ireland, 25 St. Stephen's Green, Dublin 2,
Ireland (a division of Penguin Books Ltd.)
Penguin Group (Australia), 250 Camberwell Road, Camberwell, Victoria 3124,
Australia (a division of Pearson Australia Group Pty. Ltd.)
Penguin Books India Pvt. Ltd., 11 Community Centre, Panchsheel Park,
New Delhi - 110 017, India
Penguin Group (NZ), 67 Apollo Drive, Rosedale, Auckland 0632,
New Zealand (a division of Pearson New Zealand Ltd.)
Penguin Books (South Africa) (Pty.) Ltd., 24 Sturdee Avenue,
Rosebank, Johannesburg 2196, South Africa

Penguin Books Ltd., Registered Offices:
80 Strand, London WC2R 0RL, England

First published by New American Library,
a division of Penguin Group (USA) Inc.

First Printing, March 2012
10  9  8  7  6  5  4  3  2  1

REGISTERED TRADEMARK—MARCA REGISTRADA

LIBRARY OF CONGRESS CATALOGING-IN-PUBLICATION DATA:

Wolff, Veronica.
Vampire's kiss/Veronica Wolff.
p. cm.—(The watchers; 2)
ISBN 978-0-451-23572-5 (pbk.)
1. Vampires—Fiction. 2. Undercover operations—Fiction. 3. Kidnapping—Fiction.
4. Torture—Fiction. I. Title.
PZ7.W8185546Vam 2012
[Fic]—dc23          2011044646

Set in Bembo
Designed by Ginger Legato

Printed in the United States of America

*To Martha Flynn,*
*for bringing the awesome*

# ACKNOWLEDGMENTS

I owe a tremendous thank-you to the amazing team at Penguin. Everyone's enthusiasm, support, and smarts makes my otherwise isolating job a real pleasure. In particular, my heartfelt gratitude goes to Cindy Hwang, who is an editor without parallel. I'm also grateful to my superhuman publicist, Rosanne Romanello, and to the art department, which always designs such rocking covers. Thanks also to the remarkable Robin Rue, for giving me a shot in the arm, and to Beth Miller, for her help on everything up to and including music recommendations.

I'm blessed with some dear friends who double as early readers. Drew wouldn't be the same without the feedback and encouragement of Kate Perry, Martha Flynn, Monica McCarty, and Connie O'Donovan.

Finally, this book wouldn't be in your hands—not to mention, I'd be a great big wreck—were it not for the extraordinary love and support of my husband, Adam, and our two fabulous kids.

# VAMPIRE'S KISS

# CHAPTER ONE

As my friend Yasuo the vampire Trainee would say . . . *Headlines*. As in, here they are:

1. Girl Genius Flees Crappy Home Life; Discovers Vampires over the Rainbow
2. Army of Females Vows to ~~Beat~~ Mold Girl into Vampire Operative
3. Girl Finds Success and Friendship and *blah blah blah*
4. Girl Pledges to Escape at All Costs
5. Girl ~~Accidentally~~ Kills Classmates to Survive
6. Girl Wins Massive Competition; Will Participate in Mission Off-Island (repeat #4)

I sat with Emma on the sand, contemplating my situation, but my uncharacteristically optimistic outlook was squashed as I realized my butt was getting wet. I shifted, peeling the cotton shorts away from my skin. "Dammit. Are you *sure* he said the beach?"

Today's gym class was to be held outside, and my friend and I had shown up early—partly because we took every chance we could to hang out, and partly because the new gym teacher totally freaked us out.

Ronan had been our instructor last term. *Sigh* . . . Ronan. Talk about hot for teacher. But file that under Never Gonna Happen. He was a Tracer—meaning one of the guys responsible for tracking and retrieving girls like us to this sorry island—and that chilling detail kept my all-out schoolgirl crush at bay. Okay, that and the fact that he has some crazy hypno-voodoo-mojo where he can affect what I think just by touching me. Not exactly the foundation for a trusting relationship.

But Ronan was currently away to God knew where—just as well for my generally overwrought teenaged faculties—and some guy named Otto was his replacement for the summer semester. He was a Tracer like Ronan, only this particular guy didn't strike us as someone to mess around with. Definitely not crush material.

"He said beach." Emma gave me one of her signature flat stares, and I rolled my eyes. I knew the saying went *Still waters run deep*, but did she have to be so damned still *all* the time? Sometimes a little expression was called for.

Sadly, I often had expression enough for the both of us. Like, just the thought of which bizarre oceanfront punishments might await us that morning had me getting surlier by the minute. Not to mention I was hyperaware of the damp sand now—it stank like dead sea creatures and it was lumpy with pebbles and jagged bits of shells that were digging into my skin.

"I hate beach days," I grumbled, not ashamed that I probably sounded like a four-year-old. But Tracer Otto had a thing for doing sit-ups while thrashing in the freezing surf, and I wasn't the biggest fan of swimming. I'd recently learned how, and I doubted I'd ever get used to the sensation of water whooshing into my nose and ears.

I thought of our new teacher's sharp, austere features and well-combed blond hair. "Or maybe it's just that I hate *Otto*. Him and that German accent. It's like he's auditioning for the role of Evil Nazi Number One in a remake of *The Sound of Music*."

Emma looked nervously over her shoulder. "You should hush."

"Yeah, yeah, farm girl. I'm hushing." I straightened my legs in the sand—even with the vampire blood to speed my healing, they were looking ugly, my knees mottled yellow and pale green with fading bruises. I scraped a shell from where it'd stuck to my calf and began snapping it into tiny shards.

Other girls began to drift in, wandering along the sand while waiting for class to start. Our numbers were fewer now—fighting your peers to the death had a way of trimming the student body—and I noted some were doing their best to conceal limps and other injuries, some fresh, some still lingering from the recent Directorate Challenge. It may have been summer term, but the vampires weren't about to let up on our physical trials to give us a chance to heal. Only the strongest and the fiercest survived.

Emma sidled closer in the sand, reading my thoughts. She pitched her voice low, knowing as well as I that none of the other girls could be trusted. "Not many of us left."

"And we'll lose more this summer." My words were a harsh whisper, but they were true. Our numbers would dwindle each semester, until only a handful of our original group remained. I thought of the girls who'd died so far, and I tried not to consider what it might mean that I'd already forgotten so many of their names.

"I imagine more will arrive in the fall."

I gave Emma a sour look. "More of *these* people?"

"Well, now that Lilac's gone, they'll need to give you a new roommate."

I shuddered. "Is that your way of putting a bright spin on things?"

It chilled me, but Emma was right, and I studied the other Acari, which was the creepy name they had for us girls. It was clear the vampires had a penchant for good-looking teenagers—everyone here was pretty in some way, if not outright gorgeous. It was annoying and sexist and gross. The vampires weren't exactly enlightened—they were a bunch of guys in power, some of whom had been around for hundreds of years—and I guessed it was no surprise that, in training an army of agent/assassin/guardian Watchers, they'd select girls who were easy on the eyes.

Other than that, we were a mixed bunch. Farm girl Emma, accustomed to hard work and solitude, was fairly unique on the island. Lilac had also been a rare breed—of the rich-bitches-gone-bad variety. We all had our individual talents, too. Mine was being a girl genius who knew how to take a punch *(thank you, drunken, no-good dad)*. And Lilac had been a pyro—witness, for example, my shaggy, burnt-off hair.

But there was one distinctive characteristic each of us shared: We were all outcasts. Gang girls, runaways, you name it—we'd all fled our homes, and not one of us was missed.

Emma eyed the other Acari along with me. "I noticed some of the Tracers are gone. They must be out gathering new girls."

Her comment got me thinking. Was *that* where Ronan had gone? He was rounding up new candidates for the next incoming class?

As was the case for all good Tracers, his job was to identify, track, and retrieve fresh batches of Acari, doing whatever it took to convince girls that leaving life as they knew it for some distant rock in the middle of the North Sea, where they were either good enough to become Watchers for a bunch of vampires or they *died*, was a good idea. I didn't know how other Tracers did it, but Ronan had special powers of persuasion at his disposal.

So was he out there right now, looking at some other girl with those mysterious green eyes and touching her with that melting, hypnotic touch? I scowled.

Emma guessed where my mind was. "*That's* probably why you haven't seen Ronan," she said in a gentle, understanding tone that annoyed me.

"I wasn't thinking of Ronan." I frowned, because I was *totally* thinking of Ronan. His complete hotness aside, he was one of the few people on the island—hell, he was one of the few people in my *life*—who'd ever shown concern for me. He'd managed to weasel his way into my consciousness, the dream of having a guy to look out for me like a thorn in my heart that wouldn't leave me be.

And, of course, I was also remembering how he'd duped me. When he'd approached me in a Florida parking lot, I'd thought he was just a hot college guy giving me some deeply soulful looks, but it turned out he'd been trying to hypnotize me. *Hypnotize*, for God's sake.

But my mind wasn't that easily swayed—being a kid genius had to be good for something, I guess—and he'd had to use both eyes and touch to persuade me to follow him onto the plane bound for *this* rock. *Eyja næturinnar*, they called it. The Isle of Night. Which at the moment was a laugh, because summertime, or *the Dimming*, as the vampires so annoyingly referred to it, meant zero hours of dark per day—just unending gray, gray, gray sky pressing down on us.

Once, I'd been afraid of the dark, but Ronan had warned me I'd miss the black of night. He'd *known*, just as he seemed to know and understand so many other things about me. Really, if I'd thought about it, I could've said he was one of my first friends.

So I tried not to think about it.

Instead, I stared out across the roiling gray sea, pretending I didn't have any use for hot guys and soulful looks. And who was I kidding? I missed Ronan. Like, really missed him. Not just as a teacher, though I'd have traded just about any other Tracer for *Otto*. But something was—I don't know—missing without him around.

Like Ronan's steady forest-colored eyes, always so focused on me.

"Okay, so you're *not* thinking about Ronan," Emma said,

and I heard the skepticism in her voice. She shifted, considering. Long speeches weren't her way, and she spoke slowly, choosing her words with care. "It just seems like you've been . . . distracted since the Directorate Challenge. I used to see you and Ronan talking a lot. But then there was the competition, and you won, and then I didn't see you two together anymore, and I thought maybe . . ."

Emotion stabbed me—so sharp and sudden, I had to scrunch my face against it.

She thought maybe I might miss him? She thought I'd taken him for granted? She'd guessed I was planning to make a break for it, but the prospect of never seeing him again made my chest feel as if my internal organs had somehow drifted out of place?

She'd be right on all counts.

I cut her off, saying, "I just have some questions for him, is all."

Like, a *bunch* of questions. Questions I'd never ask, of course. I'd won the competition, beating Lilac and winning a trip off-island and a shot at escape. But afterward, I'd caught him watching me, and something about the look in his eyes— regret? grief? longing?—haunted me.

What had the look meant? Did he know I planned to escape?

"Do you think he's jealous of *Alcántara*?" Emma's voice was barely a whisper, which was the wisest course when discussing a vampire—particularly Hugo de Rosas Alcántara, of the fourteenth-century Spanish royal court.

"Jealous?" It would imply there was something between Alcántara and me. Though I *did* suspect he'd had something to do with my winning. And then there was the way the vampire had scooped up my broken body to hold me close after my victory. But if Ronan was *jealous*, it'd mean he was interested in me. My belly churned. "No way. Ronan's not jealous."

He'd probably just been disturbed by the glimpse of my dark side, perceiving the secret, savage pleasure I'd taken in beating my rival. Because even I had trouble considering *that*. "Maybe the whole fight-to-the-death thing weirded him out more than he let on."

Emma solemnly shook her head. "He's more used to that than we are. You two are friends. He wanted you to win."

"Friends?" I inhaled sharply. *Friends* was a dangerous word. Alcántara had warned me about *friends*. And besides, it wasn't very friendly how Ronan had gotten me here in the first place.

I scraped my sandy fingers through my hair, cursing the jumble of thoughts in my head. I finger-combed some more, this time cursing my hair—*such* a hassle since Lilac burnt off my braid, leaving me with a shaggy, shoulder-length do. "Stupid hair."

What I really wanted to say was *stupid Ronan*.

Although he and I had forged a sort of alliance, the memory of his initial betrayal made me surly. When we first met, he'd touched me, and I still felt his fingers hot on my skin. And yet the reason he'd touched me wasn't because he'd wanted to— not because he was a guy and I was a girl—but because it'd been his *job* to touch me. It'd been his job to make me so warm and gullible and *dopey* that I'd found myself on an airplane bound for nowhere.

I thought of the new girls Ronan was out there gathering. And *touching*. Every one of them a total teen hottie, no doubt.

*"Great,"* I said. "Either way, he's out there, finding new friends for us to spar with, snipe at, stab in the back, and eventually kill."

Emma stared at me. If it weren't for her blinking, I swear she could've been mistaken for a sphinx.

"Spit it out," I told her.

"I still think it has to do with Master Alcántara."

This time I was the one glancing around nervously. "Please stop saying his name. I'm scared you might summon him or something, like Voldemort."

But I worried she was right. It did seem Alcántara had taken a liking to me. Whenever I caught the vampire looking at me—and I seemed to catch him a lot—it was as if he was plumbing the depths of my soul, puzzling through some sort of master plan written there.

It was hard not to feel disturbed by the whole thing, and not in an entirely unpleasant way. I mean, Alcántara was young and he was hot . . . or at least he had been several hundred years ago. But he was a bit like a panther—darkly seductive, and yet a predator nonetheless. To be feared and, according to Ronan at least, avoided.

"Yes," Emma agreed, "best not to call attention to yourself."

"I'll say. But there'll be no avoiding him when the time comes for our mission."

"Do you know yet what you'll be doing?"

"I don't know where we're going, I don't know what we'll be doing, and I don't know why we'll be doing it. All I know is I have to wait till the end of summer term to do it. Alcántara insists I need more training."

What I didn't tell Emma was that if all went according to plan, I wouldn't get too much of a chance to consider our mission anyway, since I'd be too busy *getting the hell off this rock.*

That's right: escape. It was all I thought about now. I'd begun considering it pretty much the moment I arrived, but then I got lulled into a sense of security, of family. I had smart teachers, was learning cool things, and making a couple of the closest friends I'd ever had in my life. I'd begun to believe that being a part of something—being a Watcher—might give me a sense of belonging, like finding the family I'd never had.

Until the Challenge, when I'd seen what the Isle of Night was really about, which was kill or be killed. I'd triumphed, and sure, partly it was because I was smart, but I wasn't as strong as some of the other girls, and I suspected it was only Alcántara's help that'd pushed me over the top. I'd triumphed over Lilac, and she'd disappeared, and now I'd begun to worry that maybe I should cut my losses and find a way out of here before the vampires changed their minds and decided *I* should be dead, too.

I tried to think proactively about it all, but my mind kept wondering what might've happened to Lilac's body after I beat her, and how mine might suffer the same fate if any escape attempt were to fail.

There was movement around us, and we followed everyone's eyes up the beach. Tracer Otto was approaching, carrying burlap bags.

My shoulders sagged. "*Crap.* Adolph brought the sandbags." Sandbags were a pleasant little pastime wherein we scooped handfuls of sand into bags, and proceeded to run around in circles, carrying them over our heads. "Arduous *and* pointless."

A half smile quirked Emma's lips—the equivalent of a belly laugh from my redheaded friend. But then Otto turned our way, and she bristled. "Shh. Here he comes."

I tucked my head toward hers, quietly singing, " 'The hills are aliiiiive . . .' "

She shot me a panicked glare. "You, hush!"

I smiled placidly as the other Acari joined us to sit in a row on the sand. I leaned over again, pitching my voice to the barest whisper. " 'Viss ze sound of muuuuziiic . . .' "

Tracer Otto stormed up the beach and proceeded to pace up and down the line, dropping the empty bags at our feet and instructing us in his best drill sergeant impression. "You will fill the bags," he said, in a decidedly German accent—all he was missing was a little whistle around his neck. "Without delay."

He reached the end of the line, and as he turned, I couldn't resist murmuring, "Vizout delayyy."

"Acari Drew." A mellow voice spoke from behind me.

*Oh God.* Too late, I noticed the shadow that had fallen on me. My skin rippled with goose bumps, as if a chill breeze were at my back instead of a vampire.

I looked over my shoulder and had to force myself not to startle when I saw how close Alcántara had managed to come behind me. *Stupid.* Things like that could get a girl killed in my world.

He stood there, tall but not towering, with bottomless dark eyes and smooth black hair that brushed the collar of his black leather jacket. He looked like a beautiful indie rocker . . . carved out of marble.

I hopped to my feet as reverently as one could when

wearing damp, sand-encrusted gym shorts. It struck me that all the other Acari had grown quiet around me, and even Tracer Otto was standing in respectful silence. They knew as well as I did how the sudden appearance of a vampire could mean somebody's imminent evisceration. I only hoped it wouldn't be mine.

I cleared my throat, speaking slowly enough to ensure avoiding any tongue twisting. "Master Alcántara."

One side of his mouth crooked up in a wicked half smile, and I didn't understand how it was possible to feel cold on my skin but so hot in my belly, all at the same time. "Acari Drew," he repeated, stretching my name out on his tongue. "You have no taste for sandbags?"

*Crap crap crap.* I racked my brain. What, exactly, might the correct answer be? *No, sir,* and I'd be a troublemaker; *Yes, sir,* and I'd be an intellectual dullard.

"So silent all of a sudden?" Though Alcántara addressed his next words to Otto, he held my gaze, speaking slowly as though imparting his message with significance. "Tracer Otto, it appears young Miss Drew doesn't relish the gritty futility of your selected workout." His smile grew broader. "I think perhaps Acari Drew craves more of an intellectual challenge."

Alarms shrilled in my head. Had he read my thoughts? Or was it just a weird coincidence that he'd spoken my mind?

"I . . . Yes," I stammered, second-guessing myself. *What's the right answer?* It came to me, and I buried my nerves with a bravado delivery. "And no. The challenges I crave are of both the mental *and* physical variety."

Alcántara barked out a satisfied laugh, and I felt a hot blush creep from my chest to my hairline. How was it his laughter made my words echo in such a naughtily suggestive way?

Eager to change the subject, I glanced to the limp sandbag at my feet. "Is it time for the . . . for *these*?" At that moment, I'd have traded running up and down the beach with a sandbag over my head for Alcántara's uncomfortable stare any day.

"Yes—"

"No," Alcántara said, speaking over a visibly shaken Tracer Otto. "I am finding this exercise too . . . *vulgar* for Acari Drew." The vampire's voice was smooth as brandy, with a faint, sultry Spanish accent, his murmured *vulgar* managing to make sandbags sound like the crassest endeavor ever conceived by man.

I snuck Alcántara a tentative look, uncertain whether to feel thankful or terrified at just what other activity might be in store for me. The glint in those black eyes decided it, telling me the appropriate emotion was definitely *terror*.

"There is a different assignment for Acari Drew. Today Acari Drew begins an . . . *independent* study."

# CHAPTER TWO

—————⌘—————

*B*reathe in, breathe out, foot up, foot down. We wound along the trail leading from the beach back to campus, and it was taking all my concentration not to make an ass out of myself.

Why vampires didn't choose to drive was beyond me— instead they just seemed to *appear*, and usually at inopportune times. Or, as I was currently discovering with Alcántara, they simply glided from one place to another, as though navigating a dinner salon instead of a rocky, rugged, *uneven* isle.

Stumbling a little, I amped up the mantra looping in my head. *You are not an ass. You are sophisticated, graceful, and bright. Watch the rock—*

While my eyes were on one rock, I tripped on another, stubbing the toe of my sneaker hard and toppling to the ground, looking pretty much as *un*sophisticated and *un*graceful as a girl could get.

"Shi—" I swallowed my curse, quickly correcting myself. Vampires were old-school in every sense of the word, and Ronan was constantly warning me about my swearing. "Sh-shoes. My feet are sandy in my *shoes*. That's why I tripped."

*"Cuidado, querida."*

I dusted off my hands, as embarrassed by my lame excuse as I was by my epic fall. Picking the sharp pebbles from my knees, I mumbled, "So much for graceful."

I heard a low, rumbling chuckle overhead. The shadows shifted, and Alcántara came into view, squatting before me. "If you but relax, the legs will be as supple as the mind."

I felt his deft hands on my knee and elbow, and before I knew it, he'd arranged me so I was sitting before him. I was horrified, sprawled there in my damp cotton shorts and oversized sweatshirt—my legs seemed extra pale, the flesh extra mottled with bruises. But it got worse, because he took one of my sneakers in his hand, unlaced it, and slipped it free, and then the other, until both my feet were pale and naked before him.

I felt as if he'd bared more than just my pruny toes.

I'd lied—I didn't trip because I had sand in my shoe; I tripped because my nerves made me clumsy. But if he sensed my excuse, he didn't show it. Instead, Alcántara took turns cupping each heel, gently sweeping away every last bit of sand. The sensation of his hands rubbing rough sand over the delicate arch of my foot sent electric shocks zinging up my body.

I couldn't have budged if I wanted to, I was so paralyzed watching his every move. He worked in silence, eventually lacing me back up, and as I came back to myself, he was sliding his hand over mine, his grip cool and firm on my buzzing skin.

He stood, pulling me with him, and I became aware of his nascent power. Hugo de Rosas Alcántara might have been lean, but he was *strong*.

Those dark eyes met mine. "Better?"

"I'm feeling much more . . . uh . . . supple now, yes, thank you." I felt the blood dump into my cheeks.

*Great.* First Alcántara witnessed me stripped of dignity, and now my violently blushing cheeks would make him so thirsty, he wouldn't be able to fight the urge to bite me and drink me dry. *Well, maybe he'll make it quick. . . .*

But instead he smiled. "You must have a care," he told me with that devil's grin. He bent over the rock that'd tripped me and easily pried it from the dirt. He held it before him in his outstretched palm. "We cannot have the best fighter on this island downed by a simple stone."

And then he crushed it to powder.

He dumped the dust from his palm, his fingers sprinkling it into the breeze. "You are working with me now, and we must let nothing stand in your way."

It was a kind thought, and yet menace had infused the words. I got the sense that Alcántara would allow nothing to distract me—not obstacles, not fear. And especially not people.

"Thank you," I managed. If I'd known winning the Directorate Challenge would mean *this*, I might've rethought things a bit.

He gave me a courtly nod in reply, strolling on, and I did my best to keep up, despite my trembling legs.

We walked, and time passed, and despite our little foot interlude, his features remained as still as marble. I imagined that, to an immortal, fifteen minutes of quiet was like the blink of an eye, but to me, the silence was excruciating.

I distracted myself by carefully scanning the path as we went, all the while trying to discern whether Master Alcántara breathed and wondering if his heart beat. Would I ever feel comfortable enough to ask?

Not daring to look straight at him, I snuck a peek at his legs and feet. Black denim. Thighs that were not too skinny, not too muscle-y. Simple ankle-high boots in a leather that wasn't too shiny, nor too weathered. This vampire might've looked the part of an indie rocker, but his attention to detail struck me as studied. He'd have been just as pitch-perfect in the seventeenth century, or the nineteenth, or forty years ago for that matter.

I stifled the nervous laugh that threatened to bubble free, picturing Alcántara in a seventies leisure suit and paisley shirt.

Surely he sensed my shifting gaze—nothing escaped the vampires—but still he remained silent, until it began to scare me, certain as I was that I'd start giggling at any moment. Unable to bear it any longer, I asked the question that'd dogged me since I won the Directorate Award. "So, what's my, uh, independent study, anyway?"

I knew our assignment would take us off-island, and my mind raced with all sorts of James Bond possibilities. Would I learn to fly a plane? Ski while balancing a rifle over my shoulder? Hack into state-of-the-art computer systems?

His black eyes went flat. "You really must work on your diction, Acari Drew. You are lovely, your wit amuses, and your mind has great potential, but your language betrays a certain lack of sophistication."

"Umm . . ." I began, earning a sharp look from the vampire. I swallowed hard, trying again. "I mean to say, what will be my independent study this term?"

We reached our destination, and I'd been so preoccupied, I hadn't noticed we were standing in front of my most detested spot on campus—the Arts Pavilion. It was a ridiculous name, and I was sure *he'd* named it, the head of the arts department and my least favorite person, dead or undead: Master Alrik Dagursson.

"Wait. What are we doing *here*?"

"I am delivering you to your independent study."

"I thought my independent study would be with you."

Embers smoldered to life in those coal black eyes. "I am deeply flattered, *querida*." He stroked a finger down my cheek, and I held my breath, vowing to guard my words more carefully from now on. "We shall have many hours together, you and I. But first you must begin with Master Dagursson."

I cleared my throat, focusing on the matter at hand and not the silken feel of his cool finger on my hot skin. "But he's my decorum teacher."

"And so the obvious choice to delve deeper into topics of manners, dining, and dance."

"But I'm in my *gym* clothes." I squirmed. My shorts were almost dry, but a thin layer of sand was caked to my chilly butt cheeks.

"And so an Acari learns to adjust."

I'd registered the warning in his tone and tempered my voice. I had yet to figure out who these vampires were and what their goal was. I'd gathered that they were fighting some unnamed foe, which was why they needed to train us Watchers in the first place. But *dancing*? "I'll need to know . . . manners for our mission?"

He brushed a wisp of hair from my eyes. "Yes. Among other skills."

My heart leapt to my throat. Had he meant to give the word a double meaning, or was I just a hormonally overactive teenager?

"When you blush so, you resemble a cat caught with the cream." He pressed the backs of his fingers to my cheek as though fascinated. "Such an innocent you are. Yours, such peculiar circumstances. You have been touched by man, yet you remain unsullied. Tempered like steel, with what wisdom you possess hammered into you."

To call getting smacked around *hammered with wisdom* seemed a stretch, but I had no choice but to play along. Besides, it beat analyzing his other subtext, namely the whole unsullied-virgin thing. "My dad as blacksmith—that's one way to interpret it."

He chuckled at that. "Yes, a very pretty reading of an ugly childhood." Cupping my chin, he added somberly, "Such a pretty creature demands no less."

His hand migrated to my hair, twirling a lock between his fingers. "It's a shame, really, what Acari Lilac did to your hair. *Tan rubia*. So very pale and fine. But it shall grow back, no?"

I managed a nod. Always the damned hair attracted attention. "I'm told blondes have more fun, though I'll believe it when I see it."

But instead of looking amused, he stared blankly. When he spoke again, his voice was subdued. "Do you know a vampire's hair does not grow? This notion that our hair, our nails, grow on after death—sadly, it is a myth."

But then his voice strengthened again, his tone stern, laser focused, and back on topic. "I know you dislike topics in decorum. As I also know, I've shown you favor that some might deem unacceptable. And so I tell you now, Acari Drew, you shall dance because *I bid it*." He still held a swath of my hair between his thumb and finger, and he gave the merest tug, holding it taut from my scalp. "You shall focus on topics in decorum because our mission requires it. And the first of these topics is dance."

I tried to keep my face stoic but must've failed, because he added, "You *can* dance, Alrik has assured me." He let go of my hair, and with it went the edge from his voice. "The key to elegance on the dance floor is to believe you are beautiful."

"Beautiful," I repeated tonelessly, wondering what sort of mantra I'd need to withstand a summer full of *elegance*. With *Dagursson*.

"You can say it, you can repeat it"—he paused long enough to make me once again question how many thoughts of mine he knew—"but you must *believe* you are beautiful. You must feel it, *here*." He grazed a finger just above my left breast.

I held my breath, and my heart thumped to meet his touch, as though beckoned.

Alcántara let his hand linger, his fingertip gently pressing down on the soft swell of my flesh. My skin always felt cool in his presence, but this time flames licked up my legs, dancing into my very core.

I didn't want him, though. Not in a sexual way. Not precisely.

The yearning I felt was more for the glimpse of something

dark and forbidden. I wanted to go there in my mind, but never could I ever imagine going there in *body*.

The strains of some cloyingly classical tripe drifted through an open window. I fought the urge to grimace. How was it I found myself in this preposterous situation? I had to leave one vampire because another awaited me.

Alcántara took a step back. Without dropping his gaze, he tilted his chin in an elegant nod of farewell. "Until we meet again, *querida*."

He turned and walked away. Leaving me to wonder at the mess I'd gotten myself into. And how I might get myself back out again.

# CHAPTER THREE

I stared at that bizarrely skinny back and steeled myself. Master Alrik Dagursson—the creepiest of the creeps. As far as I could tell, he'd been some sort of Viking in his time— but weren't Vikings supposed to be all big and brawny? If anything, Dagursson looked like an aging rocker after several hard-lived decades of sex, drugs, and rock and roll. Except maybe not the sex part.

He turned in that felt-you-looking sort of way, and I darted my eyes away. A few other students were there, all in their standard uniform—girls in gray leggings and tunics, boys in black denim and wool sweaters. I became acutely aware of the wedgie my damp cotton granny briefs had deposited between my sandy cheeks. I forced myself to stand tall and ignore it, but I felt like a moron.

I scanned the dance studio for a familiar face. And find one I did. I felt my face explode into a smile, because pretty much one of the only things that could make a special seminar in decorum palatable was my friend Yasuo.

"Yo." He gave me a huge grin, apparently as happy as I was that we were in this together.

I made a beeline straight for him, and he scanned my clothes, cocking his head in amusement. "What's with the outfit, Blondie?"

I crossed my arms in front of my chest, feeling exposed standing there in my shorts and sweatshirt. "Alcántara pulled me from Tracer Otto's gym class."

Yasuo raised a brow.

"Don't ask." I stole a surreptitious glance at the other students. "Don't get me wrong—I am totally thrilled that I'm not in this alone, but what's everyone doing here?"

"Remedial dance." He showed off an impromptu—and awkward—box step, and I saw immediately why *he* had to put in extra time on the dance floor.

I smiled. "Yas can fight, but he can't dance?"

"Oh baby, Yas can dance. He just don't do . . ."

"Ballroom?"

"Yeah. That one." He extended his arms, combining a fluid wave with a little step-step slide. "And they won't let me pop and lock for extra credit."

"Go figure." I shook my head and had to admit he looked pretty awesome—like a chiseled, tall, and taut Japanese pop star. I gave him a playfully snarky smile. "So, do the smooth moves come naturally, or is hip-hop part of the Los Angeles public school curriculum?"

"Oh, Blondie, this is all one hundred percent natural, Yasuo Ito vampire mojo. All the better to wow the ladies."

"Yasuo Ito vampire *Trainee* mojo," I corrected him. Like the girls aspiring to become Watchers, a bunch of teenaged guys on this island were training to become vampires. The vampiric process was kept pretty secret from us Acari, but it seemed to me that a lot of the guys didn't survive it. And though Yas wouldn't give me any clues, every once in a while I could sense his anxiety about the whole thing. "Seems to me you're still a long way from vampiredom."

He raised his hands in surrender. *"Ouch."*

I sensed a shift in the energy around me, as if class was getting ready to start, and I stifled a giggle, whispering, "Yeah, because *you're* so sensitive."

"Attention." Dagursson stood at the front of the studio, clapping his bizarrely long, bony hands. His eyes swept the room, pausing on me for the merest second. If I knew Master Dag, he'd hate the sight of cotton, particularly damp, sandy cotton.

I shuddered, and Yas leaned down to whisper in my ear. "Dude looks like the Crypt Keeper's ugly cousin."

I concealed a smile, glad he was there to share my pain. "Sucks that the whole vampire-mirror-reflection thing is a myth." The mirrored walls at the front of the room made it seem as if there were ten thousand Master Dagurssons standing before us.

"You will each choose a partner," Dagursson said.

Yas and I simultaneously stepped closer to each other's side. Make that *beyond glad* he was there.

"Today we shall perfect the Viennese waltz."

We simultaneously took one step apart, and at the look of horror on my friend's face, I had to choke back a laugh, which unfortunately ended up sounding more like a snort.

"Viennese waltz?" I glanced up at Yasuo. He was so tall, and I was so *not*. "How, exactly, is that supposed to work? You're too big."

He put a hand to his heart. "I never knew you cared."

I gave him a piercing look. "Shut up. It wasn't supposed to be a compliment."

"Get into position." Dagursson's voice bounded off the walls.

Yas and I obediently faced each other. He shook his head regretfully, taking my right hand in his left. "D., you slay me."

"I think I know who slays you, and it ain't me." I'd seen how close he and Emma had gotten by the end of last semester, leaning closer than necessary to talk and catching each other's eyes in little private jokes.

His right hand gripped my waist hard. "Stop right there, baby girl."

The music cut out, and we shut up in the sudden silence, waiting as Dagursson fiddled with his iPod. The sight was so weird, my mouth smiled, but my brows frowned. Apparently vamps liked cool tech toys, too—though, for all I knew, it was the iPod that'd been confiscated from *me* last semester. They'd never consider letting *us* have any gadgets, and they kept the computer lab under lock and key.

The music started, and some standard-issue Strauss piped into the room.

*Ugh.* Not on *my* iPod.

"Listen carefully." Dagursson began to clap those freaky hands again, beating in time. "One-two-three, one-two-three. Do you hear the triple beat? Gentlemen, you'll step with your left foot on the first beat. Ready?" He zipped back to the beginning of the song, shouting, "Four, five, *six* . . ."

Yas stumbled on the very first step, and it took a moment for us to find our rhythm. "I feel like the freaking sugarplum fairy," he grumbled.

"That's *ballet*, not ballroom." Yas took too big a side step and earned a snarly look from me when I tripped on his foot. "That you're almost a foot taller than me doesn't help."

Yas waggled his eyebrows. "Not my fault I'm such a fabulous specimen."

"Spare me." I really was losing patience, and it wasn't just because of Yasuo. I wondered whether I'd be able to dance with *any* partner, or if I was just that lame. Was that why Alcántara insisted I take this class? Not because of our mission, but because he'd somehow found out I sucked so royally?

But then I remembered that last weird exchange of ours. He'd told me to believe I was beautiful. That the key to dancing well was *believing* my own elegance, my own grace.

I concentrated hard, and we danced in silence for a time, Yas mouthing the words *One-two-three, one-two-three* as he did a fairly clumsy job of a box step. "So why do we need to know how to dance, anyway?" he finally asked. But talking messed up his rhythm, and we both had to do a quickstep back into time with the music.

I shrugged in answer, which seemed to throw Yasuo off again, and so I snickered. "Maybe we'll have vampire prom."

He shot me an appalled look. "What is this, *Twilight*?"

"How should I know? I'm still getting over supposedly needing this for my mission."

"Maybe you'll have to dance with Alcántara," he teased.

The prospect gave me the chills. "Don't even say it.

Seriously, Yas. Literally, don't say it. Last time Emma mentioned his name, he appeared."

"One-two-three," he whispered, then added distractedly, "Hey, the guy saved you from gym class."

I guessed he had a point. "Yeah, and that creepy Herr Otto."

"Tell me about it," Yas said. "He's the dude who brought me in, you know."

My brows shot up. "Seriously?"

Yasuo had lost his mind when he saw his Yakuza father kill his mother. And then he'd lost his options when he turned around and killed his father. But I hadn't realized Tracer Otto was the one who'd found and retrieved him, and somehow I had a hard time picturing Otto trawling Hollywood Boulevard for prospective students.

I was about to comment, when I noticed Yas was doing strange things with his mouth as he concentrated. I shoved a little space between us. "*What* are you doing?"

He gave me a blank look, and so I mimicked the look of his tongue pulsing beneath his closed lips.

"Ohhh," he said with a grin, and then he bared his teeth, wiggling his canines with his tongue. "I'm gettin' my fangs, Blondie."

"Eeesh." The sight of it took me aback. I'd never known how the vampires got their fangs, and here was the explanation right in front of me. The canine teeth became loose and fell out; then shiny new fangs grew in their place—we'd been administered regular doses of vampire blood since arrival, and it looked like this was one of the side effects for the boys. "Crazy. Wonder if the tooth fairy will come for you?"

We shared a smile that froze as we realized Dagursson stood at our shoulders. "It is my turn to dance with Acari Drew."

Yas gave my hand a quick squeeze, then with a respectful bow of his head, stepped back to let Dagursson cut in.

I tried to clear my face of expression, because I had a big picture of what happened to Acari who displayed revulsion in the face of vampire greatness. But instead of thinking about the ritual of the dance, I was concentrating too hard on looking calm, steeling myself for the moment his skin would touch mine, and so when Dagursson took one big side step, I didn't think; I just instinctively mirrored his action.

His beady eyes narrowed to slits. "No, Acari Drew. This is the time at which a man bows to his partner. I step like so"— he swept his hand, repeating the elegant side step—"and *you* curtsy."

I did my best curtsy, feeling like a total moron. Dagursson made an indistinguishable *mmph* sound, which I assumed wasn't complimentary.

He stepped closer and took me in his arms, and the proximity so freaked me out, I had to look away. To my surprise he praised me. "Very prettily done, Acari. Partners do not gaze into each other's eyes. A lady should tilt her chin up"—he pinched my chin between his bony finger and thumb to adjust my head—"up, up, up. Look over my shoulder."

He scowled at my hand resting on his upper arm. "That is all wrong. Your fingers are like little sausages. Extend them." I stretched my fingers out as long as they could go, listening to him drone on, "You are small. Compactly made. You must try to elongate your body as much as possible."

*Jerk.* He made me sound like a minifridge, when really I was just petite, *thankyouverymuch.*

The song was ending, and a new one was beginning; I braced myself for whatever saccharine musical history we were to be subjected to next. I needed to hear only a few notes before I knew. God help me. It was "Edelweiss."

I bit my tongue not to laugh. And then with the effort of not laughing, I needed to laugh even more. I thought I must've been turning purple from the effort.

To make matters worse, Dagursson began to sing under his breath to the music, but rather than the lyrics, he chanted, "Onnne, twooo, threeee . . . onnne, twooo, threeee . . . back, side, together . . . forward, side, together . . ."

I tried to focus, but I was only aware of the feel of his cold skin, one hand holding mine, the other a gentle touch on my back. He was close enough to smell, too, and it was a strange, blank scent, like paper, or powder.

He knew my thoughts were elsewhere and scolded me. "You must empty your mind, Acari Drew. The Viennese waltz is the most classic, the most elegant of dances, but you must feel it, not think it."

But rather than take his advice, I considered the creature holding me. Despite his hollow-cheeked and generally cadaverous looks, his movements were graceful and smooth. It blew my mind to think he'd been alive when society had danced its first waltz—had already been alive for hundreds of years when ladies were donning tall white wigs for the first time and pasting black beauty marks on their white-powdered faces.

My mind was whirring away, and I was on autopilot.

But Dagursson was getting his groove on. "Now you will turn and open your body," he was saying, and then he *spun* me.

I was *so* not prepared to spin.

I tripped. And I was unable to stop the words that burst from my lips. Two crisp, clear pops of sound. "Oh shit."

Dagursson turned to ice and froze me with him, holding me apart as I balanced precariously on one foot. His hand at my back was firm now, the only thing preventing me from tumbling to the floor. But his other hand darted out, and a long, razor-sharp fingernail slashed my lip.

I swallowed my gasp, then licked my lower lip, tasting blood.

"A reminder, Acari Drew, to speak like a lady."

He pushed me away from him, and I stumbled a few clumsy steps backward, miraculously managing to stay on my feet. "You must master your change step if you ever wish to dance proficiently." Dagursson stared for a moment at my split lip. "Attend to that. We cannot allow facial scarring."

And with one last clap of those freaky Crypt Keeper hands, he dismissed class.

Yasuo and I bolted for the exit, and I burst ahead of him, gulping the cold, fresh air. Only then did I realize that my thundering heart felt ready to bruise the inside of my chest.

Yas caught up to me, uncertain what to say. "*That* was . . ."

"Yeah." I shivered. "Weird."

We headed a ways down the quad path, and although I was eager to put the whole episode behind me, Yasuo was still clearly uncomfortable.

I elbowed him. "What? Did you think he was going to slice

up my belly instead of just my lip?" Because we'd all seen that happen—I'd seen it on my first day here.

He nodded to my mouth. "It's a little . . . uncomfortable."

"Whaddya mean *uncomfortable*? I'm the one who got slashed by Dag's pinkie."

"You know, D." Yas was nearly writhing with discomfort now, staring at my mouth. "The *blood*."

"Is it that bad?" I licked my lip to see if it was still bleeding. Yasuo darted his eyes away. "Don't *do* that."

"What is your problem?" I stared at his profile, and then it hit me. "Ohhhh. Is it hard for you to see blood?" *Duh*.

"Yeah. I'm only a Trainee, but already we can . . . We have . . . There's a hunger, you know?"

I grabbed his arm and playfully pursed my lips. "Want a taste, big boy?"

Yas recoiled, flinching away from me. He looked angry and just a little disgusted. "I said don't do that."

I stared blankly, totally confused now.

Yasuo sighed, sounding pained. "Listen, D. It's a hunger, but with the blood, it's more than a hunger. Like, it's a little . . . It's kind of—I don't know—sexual."

Floored, I was unable to say more than, "Oh." I mean, how does one go back to normal after a statement like *that*?

But then he made it worse by trying to dig out from his hole. "And you know I think you're pretty and all, but I just don't feel like that—"

"Stop." I put my hand up. "Seriously. Stop. *So* not an issue, okay?"

He drew in a sharp breath and let it out. "Okay."

We were such a lame pair, both of us blushing furiously now, and we upped our pace, walking briskly to the dining hall. The silence was uncomfortable, and I felt how both of us were racking our brains to come up with some genial, plain-vanilla chatter.

Yasuo braved it first, though his voice was tight when he spoke. "So. You swimming later?"

"Why?" My answer was automatic. Ronan was MIA, and swim lessons with him were the only reason I'd ever get in the water. That, and maybe a gun to my head.

*Ronan.* Damn the little pang I felt in my chest. I wondered if *Ronan* ever had hungers. . . .

I shrugged away the thought, quickly adding, "There's no way I swim if I don't have to."

"But didn't you hear? Ronan is back."

# CHAPTER FOUR

Ronan was back?

I told myself it was no big deal. He hadn't been gone for long. He was nothing to me, just as I was nothing to him. He'd helped me last semester, and we'd gotten a little chummy, but I figured I was just his special project. I figured Tracers got brownie points the longer their Acari survived.

Besides, he'd gotten so aloof after I'd won the Directorate Challenge, just as Master Alcántara was beginning to pay me *more* attention. I thought maybe I was shifting from Tracer Special Project to Vampire Special Project, as terrifying as *that* was.

Running into him would be no big deal.

So why did my chest tighten as I walked up the steps to the dining hall? Not because of Ronan, I told myself. It was because it was noon and time for lunch, and meals were always a good excuse to freak out. Because *everyone* went to meals. All the Tracers, the Acari, the vampire Trainees, and the Watchers, too—though there were only a very few of them. All the cliques, all the drama . . . and it seemed the more I tried to keep a low profile, the more I became a magnet for attention.

Yeah, that was for sure the only reason I was feeling stressed. Not Ronan at all.

I screwed my eyes shut tight for just a moment, preparing myself and thinking of the older girls who'd also be in the dining hall—the Initiates and their more advanced Guidon sisters whose job it was to keep us in line. The dorm Proctors would be there, too—they were kinder, like my Proctor, Amanda, but it didn't make up for the casual cruelty of the rest of them.

I paused on the landing. "This always wigs me out."

Yasuo opened the heavy oak door, shooing me inside. "Nah. You just feel stressed because it's time for you to feed."

I put a hand on my belly. "I'm not *that* hungry."

"No, Blondie. I mean *feed.* Your body has gotten used to the blood. It knows it's time."

I shuddered at the thought, even though I knew he was right. I found myself licking my split lip again, perceiving that metallic taste, this time in anticipation.

I felt Yasuo grow still, and I slapped a hand over my mouth. *Can't go* there *again.* "Dude, I am so sorry."

But this time he laughed it off, and when he noticed a table of fellow Trainees, he shot them an easy nod. They looked like a bunch of former Disney Channel stars—super attractive guys who seemed too old to be teens, yet not old enough to be men.

I spied Yasuo's friend Josh and looked away, studiously avoiding eye contact. Josh had gotten a little flirty with me last semester, and I was *not* the girl guys flirted with, so of course

I'd distrusted him immediately. I had yet to talk to him since Lilac disappeared, and you can bet I was going to postpone *that* encounter for as long as I could.

"You go play with the guys," I told Yas. I'd spotted my Proctor, Amanda, anyway, and needed to find out where exactly a girl went to "attend" to a split lip.

"Will do." He gave me a broad smile. "Later, Blondie."

I caught Amanda's eye, and she gestured to the empty seat beside her. I nodded but pointed to the salad bar line, mouthing, *Food*. Fresh produce was scarce on this isle, and unless you were a big turnip fan, you had to shovel something onto your tray before all the good stuff was taken.

I made my way to her table, my tray laden with a salad that looked alarmingly weedy for my tastes, a bowl of carrot soup, a big hunk of crusty bread, and, of course, the requisite glass of blood. It was chilled and the consistency of cough syrup, and it was *blood* for crissake, but you'd be surprised at how easily it went down, particularly when your body craved it as mine did now.

"Acari Drew." Amanda shot me a wink, and something in my chest loosened. My Proctor was a statuesque black woman, with an open, heart-shaped face and shoulder-length dreadlocks, and even though she was seated and she was smiling, still she commanded respect. Though I hadn't built up the courage to ask about her background, she struck me as far wiser than her twenty years would suggest.

I thought her the most fabulous person I'd ever met.

"Cheers, dolly," she said in her thick Cockney accent. She scowled at my tray. "Mind the salad, aye? The greens are a bit turned."

"Thanks." I plopped in the chair beside her, happy that the table was still empty. It was the only reason she was being so friendly—she wouldn't dare this sort of easy chatter in front of other Initiates, but ever since Ronan asked her to look out for me, she'd been startlingly warm.

In proof of my theory, another Initiate walked by, and Amanda sat a little straighter, making her features a little sterner. They shared a cool nod.

The girl passed, and though Amanda's shoulders relaxed, when she spoke again, it was in a whisper meant for my ears alone. "How I'd love me a trip to the rub-a-dub right about now."

I frowned, not sure what the hell she was talking about. "Is that, like, a London bathhouse or something?"

She rolled her eyes. "Pub, Drew, a *pub*. Don't be such a fookin' Muppet." Pulling her tray closer, she began to pick at a salad that looked more brown than green. "But, aw yeah, what I wouldn't do for a pint and a packet of crisps."

"Ohhh," I said, getting it now. "That game's easy. For me, it'd be a salad that didn't suck, with feta and black olives maybe, and a vanilla shake from Mickey D's." Faced with her blank look, I clarified, "McDonald's."

She grimaced. "Salad *and* a shake? And don't that defeat the purpose?"

I slathered some butter on my bread. "A girl needs her calcium, you know."

"That tripe's not real food." She gave a toss to her dreads. "Disgusting."

I gave her a shrug and a smile as I chewed a big mouthful

of bread. It was still warm from the oven, and I had to hand it to the cooks—they didn't get salads right, but they sure knew how to bake. I put my hand in front of my mouth and said, "Oh, but disgusting in the tastiest of ways."

Her eyes went sharp, looking at my hand. "Talking while chewing, dolly? Don't let the vamps see you do that. They'll attach you to Master Dagursson's side, where you'll spend the next two months minding your manners."

I swallowed and made a grumpy face. "Would someone please tell them this is the twenty-first century? And anyway, I think I already *am* signed up for that. It's decorum for me all summer. Why I need to learn how to dance, and curtsy, and know the ins and outs of table seatings and settings for my upcoming mission is beyond me."

"Don't question." Her succinct statement hung, and I wondered if she'd meant it to be as foreboding as it sounded.

I changed the subject, and fast. "Hey, speaking of disgusting, when do I get my next roommate?"

She shook her head, making an exasperated sound.

"Charmed by my sass, are you?" I asked nonchalantly, stirring my soup to let it cool.

She crossed her arms over her chest. "What am I supposed to do with you?"

I met her eyes and saw the amusement she was trying to hide. I smiled wide and felt my lip split back open. I licked it, tasting blood. "Ow."

The vampire blood tended to speed up healing, so I grabbed my glass for a sip of my drink. But I couldn't help my convulsive swallowing, and my sip turned into a chug.

"That's the way," Amanda said. "You're young to be going on a mission. You'll need all the strength you can get."

The taste of chilled blood mixed with the taste of blood on my lip, like metal on metal, and a shot of pleasure shivered over my skin in goose bumps. So weird. If I managed to escape while I was off-island, would my body miss the drink? Would I crave it after I'd gone? I tried not to think about it.

I slammed the glass down in pretend triumph. "Now, about my new roommate?"

Surely I wouldn't be so lucky as to get a single room for much longer. And, in a strange way, I kind of wanted a new girl to move in. The room felt empty, and it creeped me out to see Lilac's stripped bed in the corner. That stark, gray mattress ticking. The gray and white bed linens, cleaned and folded on top. It was a constant reminder that I'd killed a girl.

*Girls*, rather. I'd killed *girls* to survive.

"Well, dolly," Amanda said, "you won't get your new roomie till the next crop of recruits arrives."

"Nice word choice." I nodded sagely, thinking how the vamps devoured and discarded us like husks of corn. "You know, we *are* like crops."

She gave me a baffled look. "If you say so."

I spotted my friend Emma. "And here comes corn-fed right now." Her hair was slicked down, looking a deep russet color. Split lip or no, I realized I was happy to have spent the morning waltzing if it meant not getting thrashed in the surf. "Looks like Tracer Otto had them in the water."

But then my eyes went to the person coming in behind her. *Ronan.* Emma went to the lunch line, but he headed straight for us. I sat up straight, the bread a doughy lump in my belly. Ronan had taught my gym class for a whole semester—hell, he'd taught me how to swim—so why did I feel more exposed than ever in my gritty gym uniform?

"Amanda," he said in greeting. "Annelise."

My mouth went dry. He was the only person on this island who dared to call me by my first name, and the sound of it never failed to rattle me.

His eyes lingered on me. I tried to read them, but he kept them a careful blank. But they sharpened when he saw my lip. "What—"

I cut him off with a quick "Hi." Suddenly the last thing I wanted was to get into what had happened, or where I'd been, and with whom. His green eyes were just too intense. At the moment they were flat, with an expression that I swore might've been mistaken for sad. And I just didn't want to deal with sad.

He nodded as though he understood my mind's silent machinations, and dammit, he probably did.

Amanda shoved her tray aside, making room for him at the end of the table. "Where've *you* been?" She glanced at the dwindling lunch line. "You might want to get some food. It's slim pickings today."

But Ronan didn't grab lunch. Instead, he just sat, holding his steepled fingers in front of him as if considering something. His eyes cut to me for the merest fraction of a second, and then he reached into his pocket, pulling out a folded bit of paper that he slipped to Amanda.

Her face paled, if such a thing could be said of someone with skin the color and sheen of a dark, burnished stone. She swept a quick glance across the room, checking if anyone had seen. "Thanks, luv," she said, her voice oddly tight.

I looked from Amanda, to Ronan, and back again, and my stomach lurched.

Oh. Just, *oh*.

Seemed like Amanda and Ronan had a little something-something going on.

# CHAPTER FIVE

———

Between the nasty salad greens and my revelation about Ronan and Amanda, by the time Emma got to the table, my stomach was too knotted to eat.

"Hey." She methodically put her bag down, pulled her chair out, sat down, placed her napkin on her lap, adjusted her plate and cutlery in a way that appealed to her, and silently set to eating her meat pie.

Emma was acting her typical mute self, when for once I wished she were the sort to go for some good, vapid chitchat.

I stared at my hands. I could've used my butter knife to cut the tension between Amanda and Ronan. I cleared my throat. "Hey yourself."

And then nobody spoke. Four of us sitting at the table and yet . . . *silence*.

Unaware of it all, Emma chewed, and I was able to hear every gulp of her drink, every crunch of her bread. She swallowed and peered at my bowl of cold soup and plate of limp greens. "Not hungry?"

"You need more than bread and blood," Amanda snapped. She was shifting in her seat as if that note were burning a hole in her pocket.

I stole a glance at Ronan, sitting stiffly and silently. What was this? Middle school?

"Nah." I gave the soup a quick stir. It was shiny, looking congealed already, and I let go of my spoon. It made a dull plop, and orange liquid splattered the edges of the white bowl. "I'm all right."

I reminded myself that *never* had I *ever* suspected there was or could ever be anything between me and any Tracer on this island. Especially not Ronan, especially with that whole I-could-hypnotize-you thing he had going on.

In fact, I doubted there could ever be anything between me and *anybody* on this island. I was destined to die a virgin.

Check that. I was destined to die an as-yet-unkissed virgin. How lame was that? With my wide eyes, I'd always feared I resembled a frog, and now it seemed I'd never get a chance to see if a first kiss could turn me into a princess.

As if.

My mood took a nosedive. It didn't help that a handful of Initiates and their more advanced Guidon counterparts hovered near the table, all leggy, catsuited menace.

I cut my eyes to Emma. To the naked eye, she appeared clueless, sitting there chomping on her shepherd's pie. But I knew my friend well. Her face was drawn, her mouth tight. Like me, she feared these girls.

And with good reason. Emma was my peer, and therefore

my competitor, but so far we'd managed to avoid conflict. And it was all because she'd pulled out of the Directorate Challenge when she saw her name pitted against mine on last semester's fight bracket.

The vampires had been so *kind* about it all, assuring us the challenge was voluntary, and so when the girls realized each fight was to the death, several had bowed out. But vampires were never kind, not truly, and I'd known in my heart that it'd been a test. Making the challenge optional was a way to cull the most cutthroat of us from our less savage—our *weaker*—peers.

When Emma bowed out of the competition, she'd called attention to herself.

In some ways, it was the Initiates who were the most pissed. They believed *every* girl needed to pay her dues. Those who hadn't were already beginning to disappear.

And these girls, hovering near us, were angry. I could feel their wrath, and I could see by the way my friend sat rigidly in her chair, she could, too. Emma wasn't exactly in trouble. But she was under scrutiny.

"Acari Drew," Ronan demanded, and the sound of my official name on his tongue startled me back into the present. I realized he and Amanda had been trying to get my attention.

"Yeah . . . I mean, *yes*," I corrected. If we were under scrutiny, it was best to remain formal at all times. It wouldn't do anyone any good if people thought I had allies on this island. "Yes, Tracer Ronan?"

"Now that I've returned, I expect we will resume our regular lessons?"

*Swim.* My face fell. I hated swimming. Granted, it felt good that I'd conquered my fears and learned and yadda yadda yadda, but that was good enough for me. I might not sink like a rock anymore, but I still didn't *enjoy* swimming, like, as a pastime or anything. I'd been hoping I could move on. "But isn't it time to expand my horizons? I know how to swim now."

"Not well enough. Not yet."

What did *that* mean, and why had it sounded as if he was implying something else? When *would* I be done?

But before I could ask, Ronan stood and nodded an abrupt good-bye to the table. And then he simply turned and left.

I said, "Well that's that, then." If the Initiates hadn't been nearby, I'd have stuck my tongue out at his back.

"He's right." Amanda plucked her messenger bag from the floor and slung it over her shoulder. "You can swim, and bully for you. But it's not good enough to keep you alive, and you know it. You have to go the farthest. Hold your breath the longest. Be the strongest and the most fearless." She scooted her chair back and stood. "Now you have other pressing matters." She gave Emma a weighty look, apparently as aware as we were of the vultures hovering behind us, and I thought I saw sympathy flicker in her eyes. "Later then, dollies."

I scooted back my chair and grabbed my bag, too. Maybe we could make a quick escape before the Initiates attacked. Maybe if we pretended to make idle—and unaware—chatter, we could get back to the safety of our dorm rooms. I made my voice calm, playful even. "They're always on me about the swim thing, but never you. How is it *you* learned how, farm girl, out there in the middle of the country?"

No movement from behind me. *Still safe.* As I stood, I

clenched my arms at my side, willing the tray not to tremble in my hands. I tossed off a giggle and hoped it didn't sound too nervous. "Wait, don't tell me. I'll bet you had a swimming hole, right?"

Emma nodded. She had just opened her mouth to speak, when Masha plopped down where Ronan had been sitting a moment before. "Going so soon?"

Her Russian accent was a pert lilt, in contrast to the ginormous bullwhip found on her person at all times. In fact, it was only due to the restorative properties of vampire blood that I no longer bore a razor-thin scar where she'd once cracked that whip across my cheek.

*Crap.* I'd been in Masha's sights from the beginning, and it'd only gotten worse since the tournament. Maybe it was because Alcántara acted as if he favored me—I was still learning how it worked around here, but I didn't think vampires generally cared about Acari above and beyond how they might taste.

Whatever the reason, Masha took every opportunity to harass me—tripping me in the hallway or other equally mature exploits—and, at the moment, I really wasn't in the mood. Hoping to defuse the situation, I lowered my chin to indicate respect, while forcing my eyes to meet hers. Masha was one of the more advanced Guidons, and Guidons didn't like being ignored. "I . . ."

Hands clenched my shoulders from behind and shoved me back in my seat. "Yes, little Acari. Don't leave. We're not done with you yet."

# CHAPTER SIX

———— ∞ ————

The new set of hands clawed into my shoulders before releasing me. "You haven't even finished your lunch. Waste not want not, isn't that right, Masha?"

I recognized Guidon Trinity's voice as the one attached to the talons.

*Double crap.*

I snuck a glance. Trinity was the last person my friend would want to see. Ever since Emma had backed out of the challenge, Trinity had been harboring a real hard-on for her. And the funny thing was, they were two of the only redheads on the island. It was bizarre, like some sort of ginger fight club.

Other than the hair, they were opposites. Unlike North Dakotan slow-talking Emma, Trinity had a crisp, northeastern accent and stank of East Coast privilege. I'd bet that, like Lilac, she'd traded boarding school for juvie before finding herself in this place.

"That is exactly right." Masha toyed with the thin tip of her whip and shook her head, making a *tsk* sound. "People go hungry, and yet this Acari thinks to leave food on her plate."

Trinity sat down, and her eyes glinted as they settled on Emma. "But not Emma. *Acari Emma* is still eating."

I felt other Initiates come and hover around the table, not about to miss the spectacle. They didn't sit down, though. Apparently, this was to be Masha's and Trinity's show.

"Chewing like a cow," said Masha.

Trinity leaned in. "Did you have cows on your farm, Acari Emma? Because I think you still stink like shit."

Emma was pretty stoic, her face often void of expression, and it was no different now. Unfortunately, this had the effect of riling the Guidons. Trinity especially looked like she wanted to get a rise out of her.

"Look at her," said Trinity, and as her voice grew louder, the other kids in the dining hall got quieter. "Shoveling that food down like a hick. Are you *extra* hungry? Or is that just how hicks eat where you're from?"

There was the barest flash of emotion in Emma's eyes. I had no idea how she was going to handle this, and she didn't seem to, either. The hall was silent now—everyone would enjoy the show, nobody lifting a finger to intervene.

"Acari Drew." Trinity's eyes hardened on me, and I felt the attention like a slap. "Give me your tray."

I stared blankly.

Masha mimicked my stunned, open-mouthed expression. "And they say she's smart."

"She sure looks like a retard to me," Trinity said, then

continued, enunciating each word clearly and slowly. "I said, *give me your tray.*"

I kicked myself that I hadn't eaten every last crumb on my plate. I shot a worried glance at Emma and knew that was a mistake. She'd be the one to suffer for my moment of solidarity.

Trinity snatched the lip of my tray and slid it to my friend. "Pick up the bread."

Emma stretched a hand out, tentatively holding it over the heel of bread I'd left uneaten. It'd been too crusty for me to chew—stupid me and my stupid childish tastes.

Trinity slapped her hand onto Emma's, slamming it onto the bread. "Now."

She curled her fingers around Emma's hand, and I saw by Trinity's white knuckles how her nails clawed into my friend's flesh. "Pick it up."

Trinity pulled their hands up and smashed them into Emma's face, using fingers to poke every last bit of crust into her mouth. "And eat."

Emma chewed the oversized mouthful, her cheeks stretched out like a squirrel's. I forced myself to watch—I could do that for my friend, at least. She swallowed and swallowed again, and I saw by the red in her eyes how it'd scraped her throat going down.

"That's the way," Trinity said.

Masha began to snap her whip between both hands, holding it taut, then loose, then taut, then loose. "I think she's still hungry."

The eyes of the two Guidons met. "Soup?" they asked in unison.

Trinity flashed Emma an overbright smile. "You heard us. Time for soup."

Emma picked up the spoon and began to ladle the carrot soup into her mouth. It was cold by now and smelled foul. Her hands were shaking, and some sloshed onto the tray.

Trinity snatched her spoon. "Steady. Maybe you need to get a little closer." She snarled her fingers through Emma's hair and shoved my friend's face into the bowl.

My feet instinctively shuffled under my chair, as if I might pop up to help, and Masha shot me a deadly glare. "Do you have a problem, Acari Drew?"

Emma gripped the table, her spine stiffening as she held her breath. Her face was *in* the soup.

I opened my mouth, paused long enough to curse what a coward I was, then said a subdued, "No."

Emma's knees began to knock under the table, her hands a death grip on the table. I held my own breath, imagining what it might feel like for her, wondering how long she could keep it up.

Trinity ground Emma's face a little harder into the bowl, and a little whimper escaped my friend.

Maybe it was my mood; maybe I'd let myself wallow too deeply in thoughts of my own lonely loserdom; maybe imagining Ronan and Amanda together had made me surly. Who knew what inspired me? But I found my feet under me and realized I'd stood. Then I heard my voice sharp in my own ears. "Stop."

Trinity was so shocked, she let go of Emma's head, and my friend sprang from the table, coughing and gasping. In my peripheral vision, I saw her wiping orange muck from her face.

The Guidons went still.

"Stop?" Trinity slowly turned her head to look at me. "Did you just tell me to *stop*?"

"I think she did." Masha's voice had taken on an exaggeratedly marveling sort of tone.

I thought of Ronan and Amanda. Would they have helped me as I was helping Emma now? It was childish—I'd felt a part of their inner circle, and with the realization that they were a couple, it hit me—I wasn't their friend at all. Not really. I was the lame, outcast Acari. Just as I'd been the lame, outcast Annelise Drew before arriving on the island.

But I had a friend now, and that friend was Emma, and I would stand by her. I wasn't going to be the outcast any longer. "Yes. I said stop."

"Fine, Trinity," Masha told the redheaded Guidon, "you may stop now." But then she rose from her chair, unfurling her whip. "I'll take over from here."

*That whip again.* I should've known I hadn't seen the last of it. Trinity might've hated Emma, but Masha just *hated*. If she had it her way, I'm sure she'd see every last one of us thrashed to a pulp. All the times I'd felt that whip kiss the backs of my legs, my face . . .

My eyes swept the dining hall, taking in the other students. Everyone watched avidly and silently, visibly relieved they weren't me. It was everyone for herself in this place, and I was sure nobody would step in to help.

I looked back at Masha, meeting her vengeful stare. I decided to lead with my brain, trying to talk my way out. "Do vampires encourage such *public* hazing? Seems a little crass to me. Don't you think they prefer a good show instead—a little pomp, a little circumstance? I mean, where would we be if we all let loose and started killing one another at the drop of a hat?"

Seriously, it was a miracle any of us was alive with these girls eager to run shivs between our ribs at the first opportunity. And we were expected to take it. *Thank you, ma'am; may I have another?*

"Vampires encourage the natural order," she said. "In any form."

"Yeah, yeah. Kill or be killed. Very Darwinian of you. Like our own little Galápagos Island here, right?"

But then I considered the times the Guidons had tried to kill me—and *failed.* They'd locked me outside to run half-naked in the snow. They had dropped me in the middle of the island, in the middle of the night, surrounded by demonic creatures and my even more demonic fellow Acari. They'd tried to take me down, but I was still in the game.

Masha's ragged voice brought me back to myself. "You think to challenge the way we do things, Acari?"

"No, I think you're just pissy because you haven't been able to take me down. But look at me." Pulling my shoulders back, I stretched my five-foot-two-inch frame as tall as it would go. "I'm still standing."

"Not for long," she said, her Russian accent grown thick in her fury. "You go down now."

"I don't think so, *comrade.*" I tensed for the contact I knew was coming.

She gave a casual flick to her wrist, and her whip rippled elegantly to the ground, like a ribbon, or a cascade of black water. A smile cocked the corner of her mouth as she raised her hand, looking excited to flay the skin from my body in teensy tiny strips.

Maybe it *was* because of Ronan, and *just* Ronan. Maybe because I had a better chance of getting killed than getting kissed. But this time, when Masha came at me, I fought back.

She cracked that whip, and this time, instead of standing there to take it, I did the impossible. I caught it.

See, I'd been whipped by Masha before. She favored a girl's right cheek. And when her whip flowed toward me, this time it moved in slow motion. This time, I turned my head to guard my face with my open hands.

The leather sliced into me, and the pain was hot and immediate, like a knife carving my flesh. But that didn't stop me from clenching my hands, and snatching that whip, and wrapping it around and around my fists. I gave a sharp tug, and the handle flew from Masha's grip.

In that instant, I learned that vampire blood had done more than help me heal—it had made me stronger and my reflexes faster.

My second lesson? Guidons didn't take kindly to girls who fought back.

The dining hall erupted into chaos. I was surrounded by Initiates. There were no Tracers to be seen, or vampires, either, although *they* rarely entered the dining hall, anyway. A handful of Acari were smart enough to flee, while others stood, gathering close to watch the show, joined by vampire Trainees who were looking pretty gleeful at the prospect of a catfight.

Was Yasuo there, or had he left before the fight started? And if he *was* in the crowd, would he come to my aid? In a single, depressing flash, it struck me that he might not.

I needed to delay. The moment this fight began in earnest, the crowd would turn into a mob—and turn on *me*.

Swallowing hard, I shifted the whip from hand to hand so I could wipe the blood from my palms. My shorts were salty and sandy, and distantly I registered the sharp sting in my open wounds. "Isn't this a little excessive? I mean, shoving me down stairs is one thing, but a public execution is quite another."

"The vampires will thank me," Masha said, and I heard Trinity giggle.

My eyes hardened as I thought of the perfect excuse. "Even Alcántara?"

Something sharp flickered across Masha's face. I'd been wondering why she'd targeted me for her punching bag, but a possibility struck me. Maybe she resented that a vampire had taken a young upstart like me under his protection.

I scrambled for more excuses even though I knew that this train had not only left the station, but was careening down the tracks with me tied and bound to them. I backed up a step. "They'll be here soon. The vamps. They'll scent the blood."

"And each will be thirsty," Masha purred. "And your body will be carried from here, and you'll be theirs to feed on."

"Doesn't this need to be approved or something?"

She strolled to the head of the table, moving casually, as if she had all the time in the world. "On the contrary, they will thank me when I finish what Lilac started. But *I'll* do more than burn your pretty hair. I will hit you, and shame you, and whip you until you bleed. And then I will take your broken body, and I will hand it to the vampires myself."

"There you go with the body thing again." I almost laughed

at the surreal and gleeful barbarity of it all. *Almost.* "You've really thought this through."

"I've dreamt of it."

A bolt of savage pleasure ripped through me as I realized I had nothing to lose. If I was going to go down, I could go down fighting. I could exact every revenge I'd dreamt of since arriving. I gripped the handle of her whip, lifting it ever so slightly. "Time for a wake-up call, I think."

"*You* think to fight back? And with *my* weapon?" She'd spoken through clenched teeth—that whip identified her; it was an extension of her. She was *furious.*

"I think I can try." Taking a deep breath, I reeled my arm back and whipped with all my strength.

But instead of snapping, the leather only flopped, catching on the table and hitting the floor with a limp *thwok.* I might as well have attacked the girl with a fistful of overcooked pasta.

The bravado I'd known a moment ago plummeted. Girls began to titter, and some closed in—I could sense them at my back.

I was dead meat.

Masha gave me a slow smile. But rather than lean down for her whip, she selected an empty glass from one of our trays. "Harder than it looks, Acari. Shame you won't live long enough to master the skill." She raised her hand and smashed the glass against the edge of the table. There had been a bit of blood left in the glass, and it trickled into her sleeve as she admired the jagged rim. She beamed at the other girls. "Where shall I carve first, ladies?"

The crowd pulsed around me, and I knew in my marrow all they wanted was to gang up on me, to destroy me. To watch me be annihilated. My Proctor, Amanda, had warned me once: The girls were wolves, blinded by bloodlust at the scent of weakness. And there was nothing weaker than one girl against several.

My right leg flexed as I instinctively felt for the throwing stars I normally kept holstered in my boot—holstered in my *uniform* boot. But I was wearing only my gym clothes and sneakers.

A shaky, freaked-out feeling jittered through my body, and I took a deep breath to squelch it.

Masha's eyes narrowed. "Poor baby. Don't have your pretty stars?"

The crowd practically throbbed now. All they required was a spark to their tinder, one tiny inducement before they were *all* grabbing and smashing glasses into weapons. And then they would attack, and nobody would stand by me.

Rather, Emma would. Good old stoic, prairie girl Emma. I reached my senses outward and felt her standing at my back. I smelled her, too, all gross and carroty. I fought the absurd smile that threatened my composure.

*She'd* stand by me, just as when we'd been attacked by that Draug, months ago, before she'd even known me. She'd stand by me again, and we'd both be slaughtered, and the others would watch with glee, jubilant that it was us, not them, taken out on stretchers for somebody's midnight snack.

*Screw that.* I refused to give up any more of my blood than was necessary—I'd spill every last drop if it meant denying some creepy vampire.

"Screw this." I snatched a glass and smashed it, enjoying the shock that flickered in Masha's eyes.

But I'd struck the table too hard, and the glass shattered, leaving nothing but the base and a few ragged shards slicing into my fingers.

One of the Initiates sprang into action, reaching for some cutlery, but Masha spun on her. "Back off. Acari Drew is mine." She paced around the table, quickly now, her eyes not leaving mine. The crowd gave her space, ebbing back in a single wave.

Warmth seeped between my fingers. I was really bleeding now—I imagined even *I* could smell it—and it was in that moment I sensed the first vampires arrive.

Thoughts whirled through my head. *Chow time, boys.*

Masha sprang toward me, slashing her glass. "I've dreamt of this."

I hopped back a step, dodging her. "Oh, me, too."

*Killed, not kissed.* The thought fueled me. I decided I might as well give them a show.

Smiling my brightest, I dove in, slashing with the glass in my right hand. But it was a feint. As Masha defended one side of her head, I landed a massive hit on the other, pounding my slightly curved hand over her ear.

She shrieked, and the crowd sucked in a breath.

*Blaze of glory.*

She peeled back her lips in a snarl—she would *not* have liked the feline sound she'd made when I hit her—and her accent came thick, making her sound like a murderous inmate escaped from the Gulag. "You. Dead."

I heard the heavy dining hall door open and shut again, and then again. The vampires, gathering. Just in time to see me torn limb from limb by an outraged Guidon and her pals.

Masha sprang again, and I grabbed a chair, swinging it up and at her. The blood made my hands sticky and slippery, and my move was clumsy, but it was enough to stop her momentum.

A blast of cold air swirled in as the door opened again. But this time it brought a voice. "Enough."

Headmaster Claude Fournier.

Everyone froze.

Our headmaster was gorgeous, and suave, and French—and more carelessly lethal than any other vampire on this rock.

Fear twined through me like cold smoke in my veins. I didn't need Masha to flay me when *Headmaster* would do it for her. I'd seen him do it my first day here, gutting an Acari up the middle with as much emotion as I might show while cracking open a can of Coke.

His eyes swept over the lot of us. I couldn't imagine what went through his head as he noted every last detail—who held what, who stood where, and next to whom. His flat gaze settled on Masha. "What is happening here, Guidon?"

"I am attending to a"—she cast a beady eye at me—"discipline problem." Damned if she wasn't biting back a smile.

But that smile faded at Headmaster's tone. "You have a peculiar way of enforcing our laws. Unless your intention was to create this . . . carnival atmosphere." He surveyed the room once more, disgust playing on those handsome features. "*Assez regrettable.* Tell me, Guidon Masha, was this carnival your intention?"

"No, Headmaster," Masha said meekly.

"I will take it from here. Guidon Masha, we will discuss this later." He stared down the crowd. "All of you, *go*."

Acari, Trainees, and Initiates scattered like mice from the hall.

I bent to scoop up my bag with pretty much the only parts of my hands that weren't bleeding—the fingertips of my left hand.

"Stop," said Headmaster.

I dropped the bag, bolting to a rigidly upright position. I knew that would've been too easy. Emma and I were the only ones left in the hall, and I wished I could've seen her face.

"You and your peer must suffer some penalty. What say you, Acari? Should your punishment be corporal or custodial? Or perhaps a touch of each?" He seemed almost bored now, his gaze skipping between us as if we were a couple of tiresome adolescents. But his eyes hardened as he came to a decision. "Acari Emma, you will come with me."

My heart clenched for my friend. Would this be their opportunity to get Emma back for bowing out of last semester's Directorate Challenge? Would I ever even see her again?

"And *you*." Headmaster's eyes pinned me, and I flinched, my heart exploding into double time. "Acari Drew, you will report to Master Alcántara for your punishment."

# CHAPTER SEVEN

*Scared shitless* just about summed it up.

Crass, yes, but it was the only way to describe how I felt as I walked across the quad to Alcántara's office. I imagined the experience was not unlike, say, heading to the gallows. Or walking the plank.

Actually, no. It was *worse* than those things.

I slowed as the sciences building came into view. It was a squat stone structure, and if the teachers inside hadn't been vampires, it could've been mistaken for any academic building on any campus in the Northeast. All that was missing was some ivy crawling along the outside.

I chafed my arms, wishing I'd worn my thick parka instead of the lighter navy trench. Summertime, my ass. It hadn't been above fifty degrees in a week. Stupid Isle of Night . . . more like Isle of Crap Weather.

I was happy I'd dared the quick detour to my dorm to

change. I may not have had time to shower, but I did feel a little less vulnerable having traded gym shorts for my gray uniform tunic and leggings.

I slowed my pace even more, trudging up the stairs.

At least it was heated inside, the radiators pinging and knocking as though it were fall term already. The lights were dim, though—not many kids had independent studies in science or math. The remedial topics all seemed to be physical in nature, whatever *that* implied.

Alcántara kept his office on the second floor, and I headed to the stairwell at the end of the corridor, passing a row of darkened offices and my phenomena classroom on the right, and a library on the left.

"You have found me." Alcántara emerged from the shadows.

I jumped, putting a hand to my pounding heart. "Jeez. *You* found *me*."

It'd been a nervous statement made without thought, but he responded with a low, husky laugh as if I'd said something witty, maybe even suggestive.

"So it seems," he said with a smile on his face, and his demeanor threw me. As I took in his shaggy dark hair, the form-fitting black sweater over his taut body, his casual pose leaning in the dimness of the library doorway, I became acutely aware of the true and total sexiness of Master Hugo Alcántara.

A shiver rippled over my skin. I might have been a virgin, but I knew sexiness led to sex, and sex was something I'd never have with a vampire. I mean, technically they were dead—did all their boy parts even still work?

I cleared my throat, trying to clear the thought from my

head. Unfortunately, it was replaced by an even creepier thought. "How did you know I'd arrived?"

"I caught your scent. Only this time, it held something fresh . . . anticipation perhaps? It told me you were coming." A slow grin spread across his face. "To me."

He let the statement hang, and that shivery sensation of a moment ago became infused with an alarming warmth. I held my breath, fighting a woozy, must-fall-into-his-arms-like-a-limp-rag-doll feeling. Even as my body was susceptible to him, my mind shrilled, *No, no, no.*

*Alrighty, then.* It appeared Ronan wasn't the only one on this island with the power to control the impulses of others.

Except likening Ronan to Alcántara would've been ridiculous—talk about comparing apples to oranges. Ronan was *Ronan*, and I'd come to feel a sort of odd affection for him that I mostly tried not to think about.

Whereas *Alcántara . . .*

Hugo Alcántara was a centuries-old, undead, bloodthirsty creature of the night that I'd do best to fear above all things—to put it mildly.

The disturbing moment ended when he spied my split lip. His eyes narrowed in speculation. "I heard something had come to pass. A skirmish with an older Guidon."

My belly went queasy. He'd sure gotten *that* news quickly. I braced for the punishment that'd come at any moment.

But he read the panic in my eyes as something else, and he clarified. "There is no concealing such news. All who are Vampire know when, and why, blood has been spilled." His gaze drifted to my bloody palms and he stiffened. "But I see this skirmish was not . . . insignificant."

I fisted my mangled hands. There was enough vampire blood in my system that the healing had begun already, and by that point the stickiness was annoying me more than the pain. "I've had worse."

Actually, if I had a problem, it was where Dagursson had split my lip—it was only a tiny gash, but bothersome, like a paper cut. I pressed my lips together, but it drew Alcántara's eyes to my mouth in a way that made me intensely uncomfortable.

"Regardless, I beg you to come." He took several steps backward, retreating into the library. Naturally, he didn't trip or stumble. Instead, he was all regal grace, sweeping his arm in welcome as if he were the man of the house and I'd come calling. "I will tend to you."

I went on high alert. Why was he being so gracious? I'd come because I was in trouble, and here he was, looking ready to offer me a spot of tea. I followed him inside, and wariness made my movements stiff and hesitant.

He reached past me to shut the door, his body very nearly brushing mine. I locked my knees to keep from trembling. What kind of punishments would I endure behind a *closed door*?

"Are you nervous, Acari Drew? Or are you merely in pain?" Alcántara stepped back and scanned my body, lingering overlong on the bloody bits. There were just a few—and really, I'd had much worse—so why did it feel as if I were standing there in a string bikini?

*Nerves or pain?* How to answer that one? With the truth, I thought. Alcántara was too smart for anything but some version of it. I confessed, "I'm not certain how to answer that."

He startled me by laughing. "A lovely reply. As usual, I find your verve refreshing." His grin faded as he studied me. "Nerves," he said. "Nerves, not pain, have you suffering so. I remember enough of what it was to be human to imagine that, if you were in pain, your jaw would be tighter. Speaking through gritted teeth, yes?"

"Yes, I suppose."

"You are nervous that you're in trouble?"

I gave the merest nod, hoping desperately that I wasn't making any missteps on this very strange conversational mine-field. Then again, maybe this *was* my punishment. I'd get the crap scared out of me until my heart failed from the stress.

"Come then, and I will take your mind from these nerves." The overstuffed sofa creaked as he sat. The leather was the color of burgundy . . . *or blood.* He casually perched an arm up along the back edge. "I was reading when you arrived."

I assessed the scene, which didn't take long, seeing as I spent as much free time as possible in this very room. There was dark furniture, a fire blazing in the hearth, and towering book-shelves all around.

My choices were to remain standing, to sit on one of the armchairs facing him, or, the most unsettling option of all, to simply sit *next* to Alcántara on the couch.

He patted the cushion beside him. "Come, come. We have much to discuss."

I swallowed hard. Next to him on the couch, then.

"I must examine you. But first, something to take your mind from your troubles." The glint in his eyes sent chills up my spine.

I had no idea what he could possibly bust out that'd take

my mind off *this* freaky scenario, because I sure seemed to be facing some pretty deep *troubles*.

The leather creaked as I sat, sounding overloud in the room. I wondered what my punishment was going to be, and when it would begin. By that point, I just wanted to get it over with—all my speculation was shaping up to be quite its own torture. I was stiff and chilled, my body in a state of panicked readiness.

But I'd learned that vampires adored their theatrics, and so I forced myself to roll with it. I tried to get comfortable and feel normal, adjusting my tunic and leggings, and willed the fireplace to warm me.

Alcántara surprised me then. Instead of probing my wounds, or beheading me, or whatever creative gruesomeness he had scheduled, he simply ignored me and reached for a book.

Or rather, it was something that *had* been a book once. Now it was ancient and fragile, kept cushioned on white flannel and cradled in a tray. It looked as if it'd been buried in dirt for the past several hundred years. And who knew? Maybe it had.

"This is what I was reading when I sensed your arrival."

*Okayyy.* Was it a handbook of arcane tortures for unruly girls? Because surely the disciplining would begin at any moment.

He lovingly turned a page, and it crackled like the peel of an onion. "I think perhaps this is something you will appreciate."

*Here it comes.* I couldn't fight the curiosity—I had to glimpse what was in store. Adrenaline dumped into my veins, making me jittery and chilled, but still I managed to inch ever so slightly closer to him on the couch. *Must know.* "What is it?"

"It is a rare text, written by one of my favorite mathematicians."

*Huh?* Total disconnect. I gaped, trying to adjust what I'd thought would happen with the reality. "Mathematician?"

He paused for a subtle dramatic flourish. "Archimedes."

"Wait, what?" Archimedes was born in something-crazy BC—the book would've been as *old* as dirt, not buried in it. I sucked in a breath, the inconceivable truth blotting all other thoughts from my head. "Holy cr . . . crow. That's older than Christ."

His black eyes pinned me in my seat. When he spoke, his voice was gravelly and confiding. "I knew that, of all the others, *you* would most understand."

*Ru-roh.* I inched back to my original spot on the couch, chilled again to my bones. That had sounded really personal, and it seemed to me *personal* was a thing one did not get with vampires. "Y-yes." I did a quick scan of my memory banks. "The text must be twenty-two hundred years old."

Was *that* why he'd taken an interest in me? Because I could chat math facts with him?

"Older than that," he said triumphantly. "I have discerned other writings on these pages that are more ancient still."

I *almost* scooted closer on the couch—the nerd in me couldn't help but be fascinated. My mind raced with the possibilities—what else might be written on pages more ancient than the Bible?

But then my heart skipped a beat as I remembered why I was there.

I was in trouble, and I had no clue when the repercussions would begin.

He placed the tray down with a *clack*, startling me from my reverie. "Enough of my interests." Adjusting his body, he faced me on the couch and reached his arms toward me. I could only stare dumbly. "Your hands, Acari Drew. I told you I would attend to your hands."

*Oh crap.*

I held my right hand out, chagrined to watch it tremble ever so slightly. I could hope he wouldn't notice my fear, but I knew vampires didn't miss a thing.

He edged closer and took my hand in his.

*Here we go.*

# CHAPTER EIGHT

I forced myself to focus on what Alcántara was saying—
something about ancient Greece—rather than on the fact
that he held a part of my body cradled in his cool palms.

It took a conscious effort not to ball my hand into a fist.
Hand injuries were tough—the wounds were trying to clot,
but they kept splitting back open, and even though I'd washed
them at the dorm, they still oozed dark red. All that smeared
blood made me feel exposed.

He traced his finger along my palm—*in* the path of the
deepest cut. A creepy feeling wiggled up my spine, both
prickly and warm at the same time.

If Alcántara could tell how terrified I was, he didn't let on.
Instead, he just kept talking, his voice a soothing, Spanish-
accented lull. ". . . And Archimedes was the greatest of them,"
he was saying.

*Greatest of . . . mathematicians, Greeks, what?* I tried to tune in, holding on to his words as a way to normalize the situation—to stop that disturbing cold-hot that was spreading its way deep into my belly. I forced a stiff nod. "Yes, Archimedes. Ahead of his time."

"Would that I could have known him."

*Ohmygod.* Alcántara was leaning in. Dipping his head closer to my hand, like a dog about to sniff. Or lick. *Oh God.*

His lips parted.

*Oh please no,* a little girl voice keened deep inside me. He wouldn't *lick* my palm, would he? I wanted to pull away, but the vampire's cool grip tensed ever so slightly.

"Are you familiar with his work?" His breath was hot on my broken skin. His eyes, focused on my bloody cuts. Was he going to *feed* from me? My belly roiled with terror and revulsion.

*No he won't. No he won't. No he won't.* I tried to will him to keep his mouth away from my open skin. My heart was pounding so hard now, I felt the pulse throbbing in my head.

He'd said something—I needed to reply. My mind raced, desperate to remember some ancient Greek fun fact. Because that mouth was closing in.

"Yes," I blurted, more loudly than I'd intended. "Archimedes. He said he could lift the earth. If he had a long enough pole. Or a lever, I mean. If he had a place to stand and a *lever,* he could move it. The earth."

Though Alcántara's head was tilted down, I could read how my comment had pleased him, despite—or maybe because of—my nervous babbling. He chuckled, and I felt the puffs of breath on my skin. "So he did."

"But he was killed," I said, dredging everything I could

from memory. At the word *killed*, I gave an instinctive tug to my hand, but the vampire held on tight.

"So he was." Alcántara traced the lines on my hand, smearing faint trails of blood across my palm. He brightened, remembering the story. "They say Archimedes spoke his last words to an attacking Roman soldier. *'Do not disturb my circles!'*" He laughed, and gooseflesh crept along my arms. "Human creatures are so delightfully banal."

I tried to imagine what else he might've thought about us humans. Delightfully banal . . . *but loads of fun to kill.* Banal . . . *but for the musky aftertaste.* Because the other shoe was going to drop, and soon. This punishment was shaping up to be a doozy.

But still, the vampire didn't release my hand. Instead, he swept his cool finger along my palm again, harder this time, splitting the cut back open until I flinched from the pain. He held his finger up to catch the firelight. His skin was stained a pale pink.

I watched, horrified, as he brought it to his lips. And then his eyes caught and held mine as he sucked his finger slowly into his mouth.

*Crapcrapcrap.* There was *licking* happening. He pulled his finger from his mouth with a dull suck.

What else would he want to taste? Frantic, I did a quick mental inventory of all my other bloody parts. It was *not* good. I needed something, *anything*, to talk about.

"And the book?" The words exploded from me, sounding high-strung even to my own ears.

*Calm.* I needed to calm the hell down. I didn't want to rile him any more than he already was—I mean, did vampires get blinded by bloodlust? Who knew what happened once they got a taste of it. And I definitely wasn't feeling equipped to find out.

*Keep him chatting.* I glanced back at the book. "I mean, what is it? You didn't tell me. Which text is it? Is it original?" I tried to act avid and interested, but I was afraid I probably just sounded feverish.

"Ah, yes. My book." Momentarily diverted, he dropped my hand, and relief prickled through me, sending a rush of blood to my head. "It was a very exciting development in the world of mathematics. This particular text was discovered only decades ago." He smiled coyly. "It was later purchased at auction by an anonymous bidder."

"Which was you," I said baldly. If I hadn't been so panicked, maybe I'd have spoken with more deference, but I was too freaked to think straight, particularly since Alcántara's disciplinary techniques appeared to involve finger sucking. It gave my words a thoughtlessly casual edge. "You guys seem to have a lot of money. I mean you've had years to save up, right?"

But he didn't seem to mind my informality—I guess licking on a girl really loosened a fellow up. He considered it for a moment, answering thoughtfully, "We have resources at our disposal, yes."

I stalled then. I had nothing to say to that. My childhood had been a series of apartments in central Florida—luxury was when we'd made the leap to a two-bedroom.

He tilted his head, seeing the truth of it. "Little Acari. I dare say *resources* isn't part of your parlance, is it?"

*Oh no.* Getting personal again. "We didn't have much, no," I said tentatively.

"It is true, this axiom men have on the importance of living well. And yet the old adage isn't completely correct. You see, it's living forever that is the *best* revenge."

He smiled then, full-on, bearing two dagger-sharp teeth, which reminded me that, although *he* was undead, *I* could find *my*self very, very dead at the slightest provocation.

The image silenced me.

"But we were discussing my book." His tone was almost jovial, as if he hadn't just bared a pair of freaking *fangs*. "I've not yet told you the best part." He picked up the tray and tipped it so the pages could catch the light. "Look at the writing. Can you guess what it is?"

Guess? I could barely read it. Archimedes had been an inventor—Alcántara was probably reading instructions on how to build an ancient Greek torture device. *Position Acari's thumbs between screws; tighten.* "N-no."

"Do you know what a palimpsest is?"

Where the hell was *this* going? I gave the barest nod. "I . . . Yeah. . . . It's when they scraped the writing off a manuscript so they could reuse the pages. They'd just write over the old stuff."

He gave me a courtly nod. "Clever girl. But of course you knew." He turned a few pages, and the smell of mildew gave my nose a twinge. "It was once a common practice, when materials like parchment or vellum were too valuable to be squandered."

I nodded, even though I was familiar with everything he was telling me. And what was with the minilecture, anyway? Because I knew he had a point—I saw it coming in the satisfied gleam in his eyes.

"Acari Drew, you are like that palimpsest. Scraped clean of who you were. Altered, yes?"

*I'll say.* But was that a bad thing? I couldn't figure out where he was going, so I just nodded warily.

"We are reinventing you. Writing over the former you, as it were." He touched me then. It was the merest contact, outlining my shoulder, down my arm, but I felt the impact like a cannon shot.

I clenched my teeth, my knees, my elbows at my sides. Anything to keep my mind in control of my body. Because I made no mistake—Alcántara was trying hard to seize that control.

"Yet you still bear traces of your former self. All the best Watchers do."

He told me these things, and I was baffled, unsure whether there was a compliment or a reprimand in his words. But then his eyes raked my body, and again that naked feeling seized me, and I thought there might be something else in his words, too.

"Your body is the same—stronger, yes, but the same height." He brought his hand to rest heavily on my shoulder, his other hand on my head.

I had the absurd—and frightening—urge to cry.

"You, like those old sheets of parchment, are still recognizable. Your hair is shorter perhaps—a regrettable consequence of the Challenge." He sounded disappointed as he stroked his hand along my head. But rather than comfort me, the gesture made me feel like a pet whose pedigree he was considering. "And yet your hair still holds the same texture, the same brightness."

Moving from my hair, he extended a finger and touched it over my heart, pressing gently into the soft flesh above my left breast. I held my breath, my world reduced only to his touch and the shrilling alarm bells in my head.

"The essence of your heart remains unchanged. . . . I hear it speak when you are with your peers, and yet its beat is steadier since the *Eyja næturinnar*. You have killed, and it has made you stronger." He pressed more firmly, dragging his finger the barest fraction down my breast.

As if he might *really* touch me.

"Your father could not batter your heart from you. Nor could the other girls." He retracted his hand, and though his eyes were narrowed, the slightest smile curved his lips. "Nor perhaps any vampire."

The words sank into me, and I inhaled sharply, breathing again.

"Not just your heart remains unchanged," he said, continuing his litany as though he hadn't just been about to fondle me. "Your eyes are the same. The nose and brow. Your mouth . . ." He tsked, and leaning in for a closer look, said, "But I see we haven't finished tending your wounds."

"We haven't?" My voice crackled high and tight.

He raised his hand to hover just over my split lip, then paused, asking, "May I?"

He wanted to touch me again. And I was supposed to stop him?

"Yes." I cleared my throat of its warble. "You may."

His thumb was cold as it swept beneath my lower lip. "Open your mouth, please."

In my panic, I opened wide like at the dentist.

He chuckled, and the sound was pretty much the most terrifying thing ever. "Not that wide, *querida*. Simply part your lips."

I did as I was told. And somehow, sitting before him with softly parted lips horrified me more than my jaw-crackingly wide-open mouth had. I'd wanted someone to kiss me, but not now, not like this. Not with Alcántara.

"It is simply on the lip, and lips heal." His voice pitched low and husky, that chuckle long gone. "You see, I have much experience with broken skin." He parted his own lips, gently baring his fangs.

I got a good look this time, utterly mesmerized. They were long and sharp—far sharper than any canines I'd ever seen. They were sharper than a wolf's fangs, or even sharks' teeth. I thought of Yasuo's wiggly teeth, and how long he'd have to wait for beauties like these—Alcántara had been working on them for generations.

And, of course, he probably accidentally nicked himself all the time. My mind went to a really disturbing place, wondering what it would be like to *kiss* a vampire. Because surely a girl would get nicked then, too.

Why did I keep thinking about kissing? Alcántara was sitting so close, saying such strangely flattering things. My eyes returned to his mouth. It was full, with two sexy little indents below the bottom lip. I looked up and met his eyes. He was smiling. *Damn.* Had he put these thoughts in my head? I'd imagined myself immune to mind control. But surely I didn't deep down want to kiss *Alcántara.* Did I?

"The skin is pierced," he said, "but it always heals."

To prove his point, he bit lightly on his bottom lip, and a

tiny pinprick of blood appeared almost instantly. But then he licked it, and almost as quickly the pinprick disappeared. He gave me a slow, dirty smile, letting me see the end of his tongue. Red blood tinged the tip.

*No.* Definitely no kissing for me today.

"Would you like my assistance, Acari?"

"Assistance?" I could barely speak.

He stared only at my mouth now.

I was intensely aware of my body. How my skin had grown hot. How my split lip was a little swollen. It'd stopped bleeding, but the cut was open and raw. Did he mean assist, as in heal my lip? I didn't think I was nearly ready for anything of the sort.

I must've had a nutty, panicked look on my face, because he laughed outright. "My dear innocent, I think I've frightened you. I mean simply this: Your next mealtime, when you take the blood, you must rub it into your cuts, and they will heal quickly. Run your tongue, like so, along the wound." He licked his lower lip in a way that made me feel intensely uncomfortable.

He gave me a wicked smile. "Shall I ensure you're doing it correctly? Perhaps I will come to the dining hall to watch."

"I . . ." He'd made it sound so . . . *naughty*, and I *definitely* did not want Alcántara to show up at the dining hall to watch me do naughty-sounding things with my tongue.

So how did one answer such a question? I figured guys were guys, no matter the century, and it never hurt to be coy. "I wouldn't want to trouble you," I said hesitantly. "I think I understand. Thank you, though. Very much."

I held my breath, waiting to make sure I'd given the correct sort of reply. His answer was an amused grin, and relief washed through me. I automatically returned the smile, and our eyes locked for a strange, frozen moment.

"Now." All business again, Alcántara pulled away, sitting in that graceful, erect posture that vampires seem to have perfected. "We must administer your punishment."

"My . . . oh." *That* hadn't been my punishment? I felt the blood leach from my head.

He laughed. "How you pale. You perhaps expect to be given some menial task? A beating maybe?" His eyes lasered into me, reading my reaction, which of course was pure fear.

*Tasks and beatings.* Yup, that about summed it up. "A little more 'wisdom hammering'?" I tried to look blasé, but I feared my expression faltered.

He relaxed into the couch, smiling broadly. "I fear your headmaster expects something of the sort, yes. Claude is so very old-fashioned in some ways; yet he strives to be so modern in others. He thinks my habits are very medieval."

"Well, you are *actually* medieval." I bit my lip, making it sting. The thought had spilled from me before I considered it, and I hoped he wouldn't take offense.

But Alcántara laughed, delighted. "Indeed," he said, nodding and considering, "I am the Dark Ages become flesh." He grew serious. "Call it what you like, but my philosophy is that a warrior should be rewarded for his—*or her*—blood thirst. And so *brava*, Acari, for almost getting the better of Guidon Masha. I assure you, it is *she* who will face the severest of my punishments."

I was baffled. Then relieved.

"So . . . I did well? And it's Masha . . . I mean, *Guidon* Masha who's in trouble?"

"That is one way to express it."

"Can the same go for Emma?" I'd been so desperately afraid of losing my friend, her situation was the first thing to pop into my head. But I regretted the words the moment they'd passed my lips.

His features hardened. "Do not try my patience. I have told you before, there is no such thing as a *friend* on this island. *You* are your only friend. And Acari Emma needs to learn to fight her own battles."

That silenced me. I didn't want to bring any unwanted attention on anyone—especially on Emma; more scrutiny was the last thing she needed.

I dipped my chin, discovering it wasn't difficult to speak with deference when I was scared out of my wits. "Yes, Master Alcántara."

He crossed an ankle onto his knee, casual once more. "Although I do have something I think might be some punishment for you. Or you will perceive it as such."

I stiffened. *Here it comes.* The other shoe, dropping.

"You will be tutored. In German."

But I was fluent. I'd read *Faust* and the complete works of Kafka in their original German. "You mean *I'll* have to tutor it." I'd put it as a statement, not a question.

*"No,"* he said with exaggerated patience. "We have an important task ahead of us, and your current knowledge will do you no good where we are going."

*That* gave me pause. He was referring to our mission, off the island. I was dying to know about it.

"I need you to become conversant in modern business German and etiquette. When to say *Du*, to say *Sie*. How to bid farewell, or to moderate conflict. These are the things that will preserve you from the dangers of our mission."

"I understand." And I guess I did. I mean, *danger* was involved, and that was kind of exciting.

But then dread churned my belly. Because I knew who on this island spoke perfect German: *Tracer Otto.* "Who will tutor me?" I asked, while in my head I was devising ways I might respectfully protest the answer.

Only he didn't say Tracer Otto. It was worse.

"One of the vampire Trainees will assist you. The Australian. Joshua."

# CHAPTER NINE

*J*osh? Former Lilac-flirt-buddy Josh? As in the guy who looked like a blond Aussie surfer boy but really was a Harvard smarty-pants and winner of my Most Likely to Be an Evil Supergenius Award? *That* Josh? Tutoring me, in German? What was with the boys' club?

The news made me peevish and testy. Not in the mood to talk to anyone, I ended up avoiding the dining hall that night. Besides, after my lunchtime brawl, I wasn't exactly eager to bump into any of the Initiates. I didn't know if Alcántara had disciplined Masha yet or not, but I wasn't about to be anywhere nearby when it went down. Put simply, unlike the intrepid Watcher I hoped one day to be, I chickened out and hid in my room for the rest of the day.

And so I went to bed feeling hungry. And angry. And vulnerable. And with a lot on my mind.

A lethal cocktail.

By the time I ran into the boys the next day, I'd worked myself into a lather, with a thing or two to get off my chest.

Alcántara had told me to meet Josh in the languages building, which, ironically, was the one building I hadn't spent much time in. Seeing as I was already *fluent*. In several languages. *Including German*.

Scowling, I heaved open the door. I wanted to slam it, but the stupid, heavy wood didn't cooperate.

I heard them from all the way down the hall. *Predictable*. I stormed toward the sound of goofball boys, goofing in the lounge area.

I glowered at the lot of them, and it just made me surlier. I estimated they ranged in age from seventeen to nineteen, each good-looking in a clean-faced, strong-boned sort of way. It was as if I'd stumbled into the varsity soccer team on their break.

I'd come rehearsing the piece of my mind I was going to foist on Josh, but it was Yasuo I saw first. And I was angrier with him, anyway—I had a feeling he'd been there to witness yesterday's dining hall debacle yet hadn't come to my aid. It'd nagged me all night.

He glanced at me, and I could tell by the hesitant look in his eye that my suspicions were correct.

I crossed my arms at my chest. "You saw it all, didn't you?"

His deer-in-headlights expression told me his mind was racing for a reply.

"Dude," I said, not giving him a chance, "what is your problem?"

Yasuo flinched. "Yo, D. And hello to you, too."

"Don't *Yo D*. me. You left me hanging yesterday."

A couple of the Trainees laughed and backed off in an exaggeratedly I'm-outta-here sort of way.

"What was I supposed to do?" Yasuo ignored his departing friends and focused only on me. It mollified me—*a little.*

I exhaled heavily, realizing it wasn't so much that I was angry; it was that I'd felt betrayed. "I don't know. You could've done more than just stand there, maybe."

He stood and came closer, pleading his case. "You have no idea. It was killing me, watching those girls go after you and Em."

*Emma.* I'd thought for sure he had a crush on her, but he hadn't spoken up for her, either. I was ready to throw that bomb in his face, but a quick glance told me too many Trainees had hung around to watch our spat. And although I'd have thought nothing of embarrassing Yasuo, I wasn't about to throw Emma under the bus.

My stomach dropped just thinking of her. "She could've used your help, too. For all we know, she's out there right now, becoming the main ingredient in some vampire cocktail."

"Emma's fine," Yas said. "I just saw her. They had her clean toilets and do push-ups and stuff. But that's all. Seriously."

He knew how Emma was. My shoulders sagged—from relief but from some other thing, too. Something that should've known my friend was okay before Yas did. It took the wind out of my sails, and my tone was petering out when I said, "I just . . . I'd have liked being able to—I don't know—*see* you in the crowd at least."

But then I wondered, what would I have done if our roles had been reversed? Would I have risked everything to stand by his side? The way that question gave me pause bummed me out even more.

"Little D." His eyes skittered around the room, and when he spoke again, it was in a whisper. "There are *rules*. I *can't* challenge the Guidons."

He seemed nervous, and it threw me. I'd seen him concerned-nervous—as when I went into the ring to fight—but I'd never seen him like this, scared-nervous. A few more Trainees up and left us, and it struck me as significant.

"They're priming us to be vampires, D." He stressed the words as though trying to impart some message.

I heard it loud and clear. "Yeah," I admitted, "I get it. And you'll be one of the ones in charge someday—unlike us lowly *girls*. Best to keep your place above the rest of us."

"Not like that." His shoulders slumped, as if he really wanted me to understand. "You think you get it, but you don't. If I stand up to an Initiate? Hell, if I stand out *at all*, I'm as dead meat as you are. No. *Deader.*"

"That's not a word," I grumbled. Boys could be such . . . *boys.*

Sighing, I broke down and shook my head. He was right. Kids like me and Yas didn't make the rules—we lived and died by them.

I gave him a rueful smile. "I get that I have no idea what it's like for you. I just . . . I wish you could tell me . . ." I gave him an opening even though I knew I could cajole all I wanted, yet never would he divulge the Trainees' secrets.

Yas was quick to return my smile. "So we're okay?"

"Yeah, we're okay." Yet I couldn't help but wonder what the implications were for our future friendship. There seemed to be a line drawn in the sand, carving a deep divide between guys and girls. Trainees and Acari.

*Vampires and Watchers.*

If Yasuo and I survived this, someday I'd be taking orders from him. He'd be the one able to take my life on a whim, the one telling me where to go and what to do. I wasn't ready to think about how *that* dynamic might play out.

It was all the more reason for me to hightail it out of there. Escaping from an island tightly guarded by a bunch of vampires and located in the middle of a freezing sea seemed eminently easier to navigate than the new-to-me waters of friendship.

"Later, then. Off to class." He thumped his chest and gave me a fist salute. "Peace out, Blondie."

"Yeah, you're such a gangsta." I'd tried to be playful but was feeling a little too out of sorts to sound it.

That left just me and Josh.

I'd burst in there on the warpath, but then my interaction with Yas ended up less showdown and more Dr. Phil. Honestly, it'd just made me kind of *depressed.* I turned on Josh, eager to make him my next target. *"You."*

He was cute and scruffy and blond. We were on a place called the Isle of Night—so how the hell did he still seem to be sporting a tan?

I cut him off before he could open his mouth. "You say *gidday* and you're a dead man."

He raised his hands. "I'd not deign to greet you, oh rampaging Acari."

Damned if his stupid comment didn't startle a laugh out of me. I blamed the accent. But my flash of good humor gave him an opening I hadn't wanted to surrender.

"Go easy on Yas, eh?" he urged in a chummy tone, his accent making Yasuo's name sound something like *Yaehz.*

"He's got a lot on his mind, and you know he can't tell you the lot of it."

"Well, aren't you two cozy," I said, feeling defeated.

But Josh remained calm, refusing to rise to the bait. "We're roommates. We talk."

Well, *that* was news. There was a lot the girls didn't know about the creepy castle on the hill that was the guys' housing, but someone's *roommate* situation seemed like pretty basic information. "How did I not know that?"

Josh paused. "We aren't supposed to talk much about things. But . . ." He met my eyes, thought for a moment, and decided to continue. "Don't be mad, mate. It was new this summer. Our last roommates were . . . They died. So they put us together to make room for more. They *just* did—I swear. I'm sure Yas would've told you himself if you hadn't come in here ready to tear him a new one."

His Australian accent had loped along, rough and lazy, making his words sound more offhand than they really were—because he was talking about boys dying, and it chilled me. As did all the mystery—I knew Acari dropped like flies, but I had yet to find out what killed the Trainees, or who.

I realized he hadn't spoken, and I looked up to catch him ogling my mouth. "Goddammit, *mate*." I lunged closer and gave him a shove in the chest. Though the gesture was playful, I let my hand push a little harder than was strictly necessary. But then I fisted my hands at my sides, assuring myself those were definitely *not* rock-hard surfer abs beneath his uniform sweater. "Not you, too. What is with you guys?" I licked my lip, feeling the scab there. "It's almost healed up. Learn a little control, would you?"

"Control is difficult, where you're concerned." He winked, and I didn't know if he was flirting with me or just making fun.

"Do *not* go there. Seriously, this"—I waved my hands between us—"this tutoring thing is unpalatable enough."

He clapped a hand to his chest. "I'm not to be palated? Harsh."

"*Palated?* Not a word, Harvard boy." I put my hands on my hips, fighting a smile. "I swear, you are asking for it. If you can't even speak English, what could possibly be this arcane German knowledge you possess that I don't?"

"Easy, easy." He reached down to grab his messenger bag and slung it over his shoulder. "Look, my father worked for one of the big pharmaceuticals, and we were based in Germany for a while. I know you speak the language, but some of the business etiquette is . . . different. When to be formal, when not—stuff like that."

My stomach growled, and I put a fist to it. "Jeez, will *nothing* cooperate?"

Josh gave me a funny look, trying not to laugh. "Does that mean Acari Drew is actually human? Because I'd been under the impression you were some rare breed of supergenius wunderkind."

"Shut up. I haven't been to the dining hall."

"Since dinner?"

I paused a moment, then confessed, "Since lunch yesterday."

A look of understanding dawned on his face. "Oh, *that*."

"Were you there?" I lost my appetite just thinking about it. Masha wasn't done with me yet. And I needed to eat sometime.

"No, just heard about it." He chucked my chin. "But *I'd* have come to your aid."

I laughed, more cynical than amused. "Sure you would have. Real knight in shining armor, right?"

"I might be." He waggled his eyebrows. "How would you know when you never try me?"

"I tried last semester, but Lilac blocked the view."

He barked out a laugh, then said in a teasingly somber tone, "All is not what it seems. Maybe I was actually secretly pining for you."

I felt my cheeks flush red—I was so not used to guys talking to me this way. "Flirty banter is not what I signed up for."

He leaned down to whisper in my ear, "You think I'm flirty?"

I flinched away. "Is this part of the German instruction?"

"No, but lunch is." He put his hands on my shoulders, turning me down the hall. "You can't learn if you're hungry."

Grudgingly, I fell into step with him. "Yeah, like you actually have something to teach me."

"Look, don't take this out on me. You're hungry, and you've got to go back to the dining hall sometime. Come on. I'll walk with you."

Willing to stand by my side in public? It was more than Yasuo had done yesterday.

I began to waffle. My traitorous stomach growled again as if it wanted a vote.

He steered me toward the exit. "We'll talk on the way—no vampires, no Lilac. And if we walk, and we talk, and we get there, and if you don't hate me by the end of it, I'll tell you some things to read. You can give it a go, and if you want, we'll meet next week to talk more. Easy, right?"

I stopped at the door. I really *was* starving. "Okay. I don't know. Maybe."

"Maybe yes, or maybe no?"

"Maybe yeah." I nodded reluctantly. "I guess so."

"You don't have to look so happy about it." He held the door open for me. "I promise I won't bite. *Yet.*" He flashed a wide grin, and I realized what I'd thought were a couple of regular teeth were actually halfway-grown-in fangs.

I looked away quickly, as if I'd accidentally walked in on him in the bathroom or something. "You've got . . . teeth."

His fangs were more developed than Yasuo's, but I guessed my friend's teeth couldn't have been far behind. He snapped them playfully. "The better to nip you with."

I swatted him a little harder than necessary as I stormed out the door.

He caught up to me, rubbing his arm where I'd hit him. "Crikey, Drew. They said you were strong, and they weren't lying."

His unexpected comment made me self-conscious. "They who? Who says I'm strong?"

He shrugged, refusing to buy into the drama. "Some of the other Acari. It's cool, though. You are strong, right?"

"I guess so." I'd never given it much thought. But he was changing the subject—I didn't want to talk about me; I wanted to talk vampire teeth. "I thought you arrived when Yasuo did."

He nodded.

"So, why do you have fangs and he doesn't?"

He grew wary but kept talking. "Some of the changes happen fast. Yas will get his soon, I imagine."

What the hell other changes happened? I shuddered to think.

I decided I'd gotten enough information out of Josh, and this time I was the one who changed the subject. And anyway, I wanted to get this business German nonsense over with as quickly as possible.

As we headed across the quad, he actually did have some stuff to teach me.

*Some* stuff.

We arrived at the dining hall, and the specter of those heavy oak doors had my chest clenching tight. "Look. Maybe this was a bad idea."

"The indomitable champion, Acari Drew, nervous?"

I looked up to glare at him. Stupid boy was unexpectedly tall.

He gave a little tug on the strap of my bag. "Come on, it's early yet." He glanced at his watch, a larger version of the girls' standard LED digital. When he spoke again, his voice was kind. "Really, Drew. It's just eleven forty-five. We'll be in and out before the Initiates even get there. I promise."

"Okay." I let him drag me in.

The sight that met me didn't strike fear in my belly, but it sure did make my heart sink. Ronan was there. And his wet suit was slung over the chair beside him.

I guess I knew what *I* was doing after lunch.

# CHAPTER TEN

—⁓⁓—

As I headed to the table, I caught Amanda and Ronan sharing a secret glance, their eyes glinting with some private joke. I tamped down a spurt of jealousy.

So there *was* something going on between them—it made perfect sense. Because . . . what? I'd thought he'd been hanging around at mealtimes because of *me*?

I slung my bag down where they sat with Emma and a few girls from our floor. It was common for Acari to sit with their dorm Proctors—in our case, Amanda—and now it was obvious why Ronan came with the territory.

"We good?" Josh gave me a nudge, pulling me from my thoughts. He glanced at a table of Trainees, and I could tell he wanted to go sit with them.

I nodded. "You're released."

"Wait. I've got something for you." He pulled a book from his bag.

"Something for me?" I read the title: *Etikette und Protokoll für Machengeschäft in Deutschland.* "Gee, thanks. And to think some girls like flowers."

"Business etiquette and protocol. Riveting stuff for a little ripper like you." He gave a gentle punch on my arm. "We'll meet next week, then?"

"Yeah." I shrugged. "Why not."

I would've agreed to anything, just to get one step closer to the lunch line. Now that I was inside, I was practically weak with hunger. Snagging a tray, I filled my lungs with the rich smell of curry and chips, and my stomach grumbled with joy.

But then I heard a deeper call and made a beeline to the fridge first. I'd skipped last night's dose of the blood and was feeling as jittery as an addict with D.T.'s. It was unnerving. I'd become more dependent on the stuff than I'd realized, and I tried not to think what it might mean for me if I ever did find my way free from this rock.

Balancing a full tray, I rejoined the others. As I approached, I spied as Ronan slipped Amanda something under the table. A chill prickled up the back of my neck. Surely a relationship on this isle was forbidden. I willed them to be careful—I might have been green with envy, but it didn't mean they weren't my friends. I wanted them to be safe.

I pushed the prickly feeling away, donning temper as my armor, and cast a beady eye at Ronan's wet suit as I plopped down. "Don't tell me. We're swimming later. And me having such a banner week already."

He held back a smile. "Aye, I've heard it's been a difficult couple days."

"That's one way to describe having Initiates out to get us," I said, catching Emma's eye.

She gave me a nod, looking her usual stoic self, though I knew she'd be feeling as nervous and vulnerable as I'd been back in the dining hall.

Amanda tossed her dreads over her shoulder. There was such calm self-possession in her movements, it added a shade of despondency to the jealousy I'd been feeling. "Don't forget you'll soon have a mission to survive," she said. "These birdies are a walk in the park compared to that."

I gave her a flat look. That was *so* not the point. "Getting whipped at lunchtime hardly qualifies as a walk in the park."

"Forget the other girls. *Focus.*" My Proctor scooted her chair closer, and it made a big scraping sound on the floor. "The only thing you should be thinking about is your little field trip off-island."

"I'm trying, Amanda." I pushed big lumps of curried chicken around on my plate. "It's not that simple."

"Trinity hates me," Emma said matter-of-factly.

I added, "Masha's had it out for me since day one." I debated cutting a chunk of meat in half, then just speared the whole thing on my fork and shoved it into my mouth. I chewed and swallowed too quickly, eager to add the snarky comment that'd just occurred to me. "You'd think she had a thing for Alcántara, and I was fronting on her territory."

Ronan and Amanda exchanged a look. It was a quick one, but something about it turned the chicken in my belly to a cold lump.

I leaned forward on my elbows. "I saw that."

"Saw what?" Ronan was the picture of innocence.

"That look." Though, considering their relationship, they probably gave each other looks all the time, and I just hadn't noticed before. The notion put an edge to my voice. "You looked at each other."

This time they really did look at each other.

I put my fork down, my belly gone sour. "What did *that* mean?"

Amanda stacked the dishes on her tray in a neat pile, considering. "It means you should mind your words, dolly."

"And mind your own business," Ronan added.

Emma wiped her mouth with her napkin and pushed away from the table.

I gave her a pleading look. "Where are you going? I just got here."

She glanced around as though there might even now be Initiates hiding under the tables waiting to get us. "I'm taking their advice. And . . . I don't know, Drew. Maybe you should, too."

What was up with my friend? Brave Emma, who'd helped me survive a night in the wilderness, eating roadkill and killing the evil demon Draug? But then I watched as her gaze rested on Yasuo for a moment before skittering away again.

Maybe what was up with my friend was that she had a reason to keep a low profile. Maybe she was suddenly open to advice because of a certain Japanese American Trainee with baby fangs. I vowed to grill her the next chance I got.

My shoulders slumped; I was feeling just a little bit more alone than before. "I'll be careful. See you back at the dorm."

The moment Emma left, I leaned in close, using my no-nonsense voice. "Now will you tell me?"

Ronan and Amanda were the picture of ignorance.

"Please," I pressed. "I can practically see your thoughts churning. What aren't you telling me?"

Amanda sat back in her chair. "All right. Seeing as you won't let it go." She sucked in a deep breath, a look of patient wisdom on her face as if she was about to relay the story of the birds and the bees. "You see, some girls form . . . *bonds*. With certain vampires. These girls tend to get jealous. Protective."

She'd tossed it off as though it were no big deal, but I knew she was implying something that was a Very Big Deal. Were they saying that Initiates had *affairs* with vampires? "You make it sound like girls . . . *go there*."

"Oh, they go there," she said with a naughtily cocked eyebrow. "I've not bonded myself, so I don't know what it's like. But I think their bitchiness is one-part chemical—you know, some exchange that happens with the blood—and then I think one part is just plain-old jealous girl drama."

I looked to Ronan for a rebuttal, but his face was a blank mask. This was no news to him.

A million questions popped into my mind—most along the lines of *Can vampires* . . . ? *How do they* . . . ? *Do their bodies—you know?*—and I asked the least embarrassing one. "Did Masha have something with Alcántara? Does she still?"

Ronan looked to Amanda, then shrugged. "We don't know."

"And I'd not ask," added Amanda. "They'd bite your head off."

*Holy crap.* I shuddered. "The vampires?"

"The *girls*, dolly. The girls would have your head."

"See, not all the Initiates are like Amanda here," Ronan said playfully, patting her hand.

Not all Initiates had illicit affairs with Tracers, he meant? Was anybody here to learn, or was I the only naive loser celibate nerd? "Jeez, this is just like high school."

"Wipe that look from your face, Drew." Amanda was looking at me sternly.

"It was only a matter of time before you found out," Ronan said. "But still, this shouldn't have come from us, here."

I schooled my features. "Yeah, yeah, I'm cool." Though not *that* cool, apparently.

"Now finish your lunch," Ronan told me, "and we'll go for a swim like usual."

Discovering that he and Amanda had a little something-something going on made me feel vulnerable. I needed to learn how to conceal these pangs until I could figure out how to tamp them down permanently. For now, the last thing I wanted was to put on my wet suit and flounder around at his command. "With all this on my mind, do you think we could skip swimming today? You know—so I can recover and all?"

Ronan was back to normal, dunking fries in his curry sauce and chowing down as though he discussed vampire affairs every day, which I guess he did. "What do you think?"

With a sigh, I tossed back my little shooter of blood. A shiver rippled across my skin, the feeling like rain soaking parched land. "I think no."

"There's a good Acari," said Amanda.

"I'll swim," I said with a frown, "but I don't think I need the lessons anymore." My protest was weak, and mostly out of habit.

He pushed his tray away and met my eye. "Do it for me." His voice was gravelly and firm. I reminded myself that Amanda was right there and that his irresistible accent was *her* territory.

But his gaze didn't waver, and at the command in those deep green eyes, I felt myself waffling. Maybe swimming wasn't such a bad idea. I squinted hard at him, not trusting the notion. "You're not doing your trick, are you?"

His brows furrowed. "My trick?"

"You know, the persuasion thing. I hate swimming, but you told me to do it, and now, all of a sudden, I'm thinking it might not be that bad."

He laughed, and I think it startled us both. "That's you just wanting to swim." Lowering his voice, he added, "I've explained it before—*you* I need to touch for my 'trick' to work."

He was able to persuade people to do his bidding using his voice alone. Everyone, that is, except for me. Apparently a high IQ was good for something. It made my brain like Teflon.

"Lucky girl." Amanda gave me a playful scowl, and I felt suddenly annoyed with the both of them. I didn't want to contemplate how his persuasion might work in a relationship. *Ick.*

He pressed the issue. "Why? Did you want me to persuade you?" He reached a hand out as if he might give it a try, and I flinched away. He was being reckless, and I didn't understand.

Rubbing my hand where he'd almost touched me, I brought the conversation back on track. "You can't mean I actually *want* to go swimming."

Though I supposed it did make a sort of sense. Swimming gave me the alone time with Ronan that I'd begun to crave.

Not even knowing he had a thing with Amanda could staunch that.

It'd snuck up on me, but Ronan was one of the few people on this island I trusted. That he was letting me glimpse these stolen moments with Amanda only solidified it—he may not have liked me in *that* way, but it seemed at least he trusted me.

"Is it so surprising you might actually fancy a swim?"

"Not so much surprising as miraculous."

Amanda reached over and patted his shoulder. "He's just a good teacher."

*Ugh.* This time I almost said it out loud. Glimpsing their stolen moments was one thing; having my face rubbed in it was quite another.

Her words and that cloying expression echoed in my mind until, later that afternoon, I spat them back at him. "*Good teachers* don't lure students to their untimely death."

Ronan was rowing us beyond the breakers in nothing more than a little dory. It was going to be my first deep-water swim lesson. My knuckles were white as I gripped the lip of the boat. Its paint was old and peeling, and I used my thumbnail to scrape brown flakes into the water, contemplating when and how I might go about vomiting over the side.

"Comfort in deep water is crucial for every swimmer." Every pull of the oars tightened his already-snug sweater around his biceps.

I forced myself to look away from his flexing muscles. Unfortunately, that left me staring into black water. I estimated there was one-foot visibility, max. "Isn't deep-water training for more advanced swimmers?"

"You're thinking of breath-holding exercises."

Panic pulled my skin into goose bumps that even the thick neoprene of my wet suit couldn't prevent. "You're going to make me hold my breath, too?"

"You're an advanced swimmer, so you are ready for both."

I opened my mouth to protest but clacked my teeth shut again as a thought hit me. The island was receding in the distance. If I had skills like Ronan claimed I did, why couldn't I just escape? As in, skip out even before Alcántara and I went on our mission?

It silenced me. The only sound was the *slap-slap* of his oars in the water as my mind raced. How big was the island? I'd seen the middle of it during my midnight punishment, but why had we never been to the other side? What was there? Somewhere there'd be larger boats to be found—was that where they were docked?

I craned my neck, studying the jagged coast. There were gray rocky beaches, towering cliffs, misshapen chimney stacks carved of million-year-old granite. But what was on the far side?

"Why don't we ever go the other side of the island to swim?"

"It's just cliffs over there."

"Well, don't I need to learn how to cliff dive or something?"

My mentioning cliff diving would understandably put him on his guard. Pinning his eyes on me, he warned, "You'll want to stay away from the far side of the island."

We'd gotten far enough away that I could begin to trace the curve of coastline with my eyes. It seemed to be just more rocks and cliffs, disappearing into gray mist in the distance.

But what if I stole a boat? Would there be someplace to row to? And why was he warning me away from the other side?

He dipped his oars in the water, dragging the boat to a stop. "I think *this* is far enough," he said, implying so much more.

I squinted harder, and my heart kicked up a notch. Small white dots had wavered into view. Was I imagining it? *Houses?* "Do people live here?"

"You're here, aren't you?"

I shot him an exasperated look. "Seriously, Ronan, it's me you're talking to. You can trust *me*." I gave an exaggerated look around. "Nobody can hear us. Now please, do people live here? I thought I saw houses."

His answer, when it came, was careful. "There are some people on this island, aye."

"You're shitting me."

He glowered at my language.

"Sorry, sorry. It's just . . ." I peered into the distance, seeing them clearly now. Tiny cottages dotted the coast, like a little fishing settlement visible in that spot just before the island curved out of sight. "Who would live *here*?"

"People who were born here."

"People have *babies* here?" I remembered the day, so long ago now, when an old man with questionable dental hygiene had picked us up at the airstrip. Did he have grandkids running around? Did that mean there were things like schools and gas stations and grocery stores?

He paused for a moment. "I was born here."

"You *what*?"

"Leave it, Annelise."

But how could I? He might as well have just told me he was

from Mars. I held his gaze, trying to read the truth in his eyes. He'd mentioned once before that he was from here and that his sister had died here, but I'd just assumed he'd meant they'd come later. Not that he had *relatives* here.

Did *Amanda* know that about him? But of course she did. Maybe he'd even snuck her home to meet the folks.

I couldn't wrap my mind around it all. "Your family is here? Do you . . . Do you, like, go home for Christmas and Sunday dinner and stuff?"

Pain flickered in his eyes.

I'd hit a nerve, and I regretted it. "I'm sorry." A sizable swell rolled under us, and I had to grip the edge to steady myself. "But . . ." I knew I shouldn't press the issue, but I had to know. Questions hurtled scattershot into my brain. "If you and your sister are from here, and she was an Acari and you're a Tracer, then are there vampires from here, too?"

"Naturally," he said, his voice clipped.

*Naturally.* There was nothing natural about it. He'd expressed wariness about the vampires before. But if there were some he'd known growing up, some with his same accent, who'd had the same friends, the same neighbors . . . "Do you trust them more than the others? I mean, if you're all from here . . ."

"Those I knew did not survive the change. Although folk have talked of one . . . an elder, of clan McCloud . . ." His expression shuttered, as if only then did he realize he was telling me these things. "No more questions," he told me in a flat voice. "We're here for a purpose. If I'm to get you back in time for your next meal, we'd best get to it."

Ronan set about giving me deep-water instruction as

though he hadn't just dropped a bomb on me. I mean, *people* lived here. Like a community. Among the vampires and Draug and whatever other beasties that lay in wait. How did they stay safe . . . or did they?

I shivered.

"Dive in before you get too cold," he ordered.

"Huh?"

"You're not getting out of this. So get in and get it over with." He'd stowed the oars and sat there, looking all business, arms folded across his chest. "Remember what I told you about treading and rhythmic breathing techniques. It's different in deep water."

I glanced over the side of the boat. "Yeah, there's, like, one-inch visibility."

"Just because you're not seeing the stripe at the bottom of the pool doesn't mean you can't do it."

He'd sounded so stern, I had to laugh. "Jeez, it's as though you're mad you told me about your childhood."

"You're unbelievable." He shook his head, softening. "I haven't even begun to tell you about my childhood. And I never will."

"Unless I get in the water?"

He narrowed his eyes at me, but it didn't hide the humor I saw there. "Are you afraid you can't do it?"

I looked over the edge again. Was it possible for water to *look* cold? "I didn't say I *can't* do it. I said I don't want to."

"I'm not giving you a choice."

I talked all brave, but secretly I did worry I couldn't do it. As I remembered our earlier conversation, an idea struck me. "Maybe you could, you know, use your trick on me.

Make it easier for the both of us." I gave him my best winning smile.

"My trick." His flat tone matched his irritated look. "This again?"

"Yeah, do the trick. Please? Convince me to get in the water." I was actually excited now. Maybe *hypnosis* would make me want to dive into a black, fathomless, frigid sea. "Do it. Give me the googly eyes."

I'd expected him to laugh, but instead his smile disappeared, his whole expression shutting down. "I will not. And I am certain the vampires would not look kindly upon your speaking so freely of my gift."

I peered hard at him, trying to detect a conscience at the bottom of those deep green eyes. "You don't like doing the trick, do you?"

"I don't. And stop calling it that."

"Can the vampires do it?" I recalled Alcántara, and how my thoughts had gone to such unsettling places the last time we were together.

"The vampires can do many things."

And how, or so I'd learned at lunch. "Yeah. Who knew *girls* were also on their can-do list?"

"Annelise." He spat out my name in a scathing, chastising tone, and it made me feel like a disobedient child.

I swung my arm, gesturing to the wide-open sea. "It's not as if anyone's around to overhear us. Anyway, don't act so innocent. I can tell you and Amanda have a thing."

A dozen expressions crossed his face, but the clearest were shock, then discomfort, and finally anger. "That's complicated."

"Sorry." I felt stupid for pushing as I had. I hated when we argued. I hated that I was having these feelings of inferiority when I'd known from day one there could never be anything between Ronan and me. And, at the moment, I mostly hated that he might take his mood out on me while in deep, freezing seawater.

He nodded curtly toward the water. "You've postponed long enough. Get in."

"Okay, okay." I rose to a squat and sat on the edge of the boat. It wobbled and bobbed with my shifting weight. "I'll get in without the trick."

Before he could scold me one last time, I rolled backward into the water.

The cold was a fist seizing me, tightening across my chest, and stealing my breath. A sharp ache shot from the soles of my feet up my calves. I began treading water at once. Ronan was right—deep water was very different from any pool.

Swells that'd seemed small from the boat felt huge to me now, splashing water in my face and whisking me away from him. The sea was so totally vast around me. And—*oh God*— beneath me. Panic kicked in my chest at the thought of the terrifying things lurking below the surface, eager to take a bite out of me. I was dangerously close to hysterical, and it came through in my voice. "Are there sharks?"

Ronan, however, was as maddeningly calm as ever. If this was his way of getting back at me, he was doing a bang-up job. "You're on an island with a bunch of vampires, and you're worried about sharks?"

"You betcha." I scissor kicked wildly, operating on pure instinct.

"Quiet yourself. Slowly now."

I didn't listen. My body apparently had the notion that if I kept moving, I'd be safe. And currently, I was only too happy to cede control to my animal instincts.

He leaned his elbows on the edge of the boat, considering me. "Truly, Annelise. I promise you. No sharks will be attacking today. You'll tire out far too quickly moving like you are."

His words registered. He was right—I was feeling winded already. I tried to lengthen my strokes. To slow my breaths to match.

"That's it," he said. "You can move more slowly than you think. You're lucky it's not windy today. Not much chop on the water."

The swells had seemed alarmingly huge, but I saw how really they were gentle rolls. It calmed me a little.

"Imagine yourself a part of the sea. Imagine it's not your enemy, but an extension of yourself. That swimming is a return to your true nature. You're a creature made mostly of water, after all."

His words became a dull hum in my head, soothing me. I pictured a globe of the earth, and all that blue. I imagined myself as an impossibly tiny speck somewhere in the North Sea—alive and vital, not yet defeated, not drowned. My heart rate began to normalize.

"On your back now," he said.

I relaxed, and I felt my belly slowly float to the surface. Floating on my back, I longed for those swells now, for the feeling of bobbing up and dropping down. I spread my arms out from my sides, imagining myself like a starfish.

"Slow your breath. Exhale slowly and hold. Inhale from your belly."

I did as he told me, not opening my eyes. My stomach rose with each inhale, and that part of my wet suit grew cool. I became calmer still. Distantly I wondered if it was my own doing, or if he'd somehow used his powers to lull me into this state. But really, it didn't matter. I was languorous now, a creature of the sea floating without care. Perhaps this was how I'd escape—I'd simply drift away.

A hand wrapped around my ankle. I felt a tug. My relaxed arms whooshed over my head as I was pulled closer to the boat. I'd been floating away.

Ronan's hand lingered on my calf, cupping it from below. Was he reluctant to let go, or had my perception of time simply slowed?

Or maybe he was just using his trick—I was so tranquil now, so composed. My breathing was so slow, I thought I might fall asleep. I knew then I could hold my breath for a very long time.

He let go, and there was a clattering and a splash. He'd set the oars.

I blinked the water out of my eyes. The gray sky was a fraction darker than before. How long had I been floating there? With a shake of my head, I righted myself and grabbed onto the side of the dory.

He gave me a knowing smile. Once again, he'd known I could do something, and once again he'd been right.

I glared, reluctant to give him another victory.

"What's wrong?" he asked.

"You're smiling."

His eyes wrinkled, making him look perplexed. "And that's bad?"

"It makes you look like a pirate."

He laughed. "Just get in the boat."

I wanted to coax one more laugh from him. I wanted to erase the discomfort of our earlier conversations. I wanted to make it all okay. "Does that mean you forgive me?"

His eyes rested on me for a long moment. "It means I knew you could do it."

I took that as a yes.

# CHAPTER ELEVEN

I slowed to a halt. Yasuo and Josh were sitting on the low stone wall in front of the Arts Pavilion. Chatting and lounging with legs swinging, they looked more like a couple of college dudes than what they really were: two recruits in a deadly vampire-training program.

My eyes zeroed in on Josh. The sight of my so-called tutor put up my defenses. It was time for dance class, which was bad enough. I wouldn't put it past the vamps to force me to practice my business German while performing a traditional Bavarian folk dance.

"What are you doing here?" I asked warily. "We're not meeting again till next week."

"*Gidday* to you, too."

The clichéd Aussie greeting rankled me, and he knew it.

"Do you practice being so maddening, or did you study it at Harvard?"

"A guy's got to have a major," he said, not missing a beat, and then he actually winked.

Like that, the stupid boy brought a grudging smile to my face—again.

"Easy, little D." Yasuo hopped down and brushed off his pants. "He's just keeping me company. Though"—he slugged Josh on the arm—"*you* could've warned me that your mere appearance would get my dance partner's panties in a twist. I need Blondie in a good mood if I'm gonna pass summer school. I am so not taking *this* class again."

So Josh wasn't joining us for dance class—that was something. But still, I couldn't help my eyes from sweeping up and down the length of him. He was a little shorter than Yas, with broader shoulders. Great looking, great surfer, great student, great personality—knowing Josh, he was probably a great dancer, too. And I didn't trust such general greatness one little bit.

"Shoo." I waved my hands at him. "Before Master Dagursson gets any ideas."

"I'm gone, I'm gone." Josh slid from the wall and had the gall to whisper in my ear as he walked past. "Don't forget your etiquette homework, *meine kleine Gummibärchen.*"

I growled at his back, feeling my cheeks flame red to the roots of my hair.

"Sorry, Drew. I'll talk to him." Yas put his arm around me and guided me toward the stairs. "Did he say something?"

I grimaced. *Worse.*

I remained silent as we walked into the dance studio, with Yasuo looking more solemn by the minute. "Seriously," he said finally, "did he just totally curse you out?"

I gave a sharp shake of my head. "He called me his . . ."

"His *what*?" Yas was worked up now, and he flung his bag on the floor against the back wall. "I'll rip the bastard's lungs out. I'll smite him. I'll superglue something in his sleep."

That got a chuckle out of me. "I won't allow any paste-related crimes to be laid on my head."

"Come on, little D.—then tell me."

Hands on hips, I stood, my fierce expression daring him to laugh. "Fine. He called me his—his little gummy bear."

He made an obnoxious guffawing sound, but just then Master Dagursson strode in, and his appearance cut off Yasuo's snort, making it sound as if he were choking on something instead of having a laugh at my expense.

I gave Yas a smug look.

"Oh no," he whispered suddenly, looking over my shoulder, jokes about gummy bears long forgotten.

I followed his line of sight and had to agree. "Oh cr— crud." I quickly corrected myself, having learned the hard way not to curse in Dagursson's presence.

"Good day, class." The thin skin of Dagursson's face crackled into a thousand wrinkles as he gave us an evil grin that told us we were in for it. Sticking his head back out the door, he called impatiently, "Come in, come in."

A couple Trainees I didn't recognize skittered in, keeping their heads down and wheeling the sort of cart a hotel bellman might use. But instead of suitcases, there were stacks of boxes. *Shoe boxes.*

I wriggled in my boots, apologizing to my toes in advance for whatever indignity those shoe boxes represented. "What the . . . ?"

Our teacher clapped us to attention, and the Trainees scampered out. "Today you have a rare treat in store."

Rare treat for *him* maybe. Yas and I shared a quick, apprehensive glance.

"Because today you will learn to dance the Paso Doble." He beamed as though he expected us to explode with gratitude. Strolling before us, he looked like a peacock—a nasty, wrinkly, gratified peacock. "I confess, it was not my idea, but rather the suggestion of one of my colleagues."

My chest tightened. *Paso Doble* sounded suspiciously Spanish. And I happened to know a suspicious vampire, also Spanish. Alcántara's hands were all over this.

"But before we dance, there is a critical element that has been missing from your ensemble." He gestured to the boxes, and I braced for what I knew was coming. "Footwear."

We all stood there frozen, and he began clapping maniacally. The guy was always clapping—maybe that was how his hands had gotten so long and bony. "Hurry now, hurry. You will find a shoe awaiting you in your size. And I should hope the difference between boys' and girls' footwear is self-evident."

I shuffled to that cart, scanning the stack for my size five. I worked the box out from the bottom of the stack and opened it. I wasn't sure whether I wanted to laugh or cry. Inside was a typical pair of women's ballroom dance shoes, which meant, they resembled objects of torture. High, black, and strappy, and in my petite size, they seemed suitable for Minnie Mouse.

They were going to be the death of me—if the lack of dignity didn't kill me first. I glanced down at my Acari uniform. Gray tunic and leggings, with *these* things? I'd look ready for a Bollywood dance number.

"Is there a problem, Acari Drew?"

*Crap.* I'd caught Dag's attention. "No, Master Dagursson. Simply ensuring I've selected the appropriate size." Ever since he'd slashed my lip in our first class, I'd taken to speaking as politely and articulately as possible.

"Very good." His face split into another grin, this one meant for my consumption. "Because I'd like you to be my partner as I teach today's class."

I kept my mouth stretched into a tight grin. "That would be an honor, sir."

He looked up to address the whole class. "Your clumsy boots simply won't do. You need to learn how to dance in the proper footwear, and now is the time."

He rambled some more, but I only half listened as I sat down, kicking off my beloved, broken-in boots. My feet were sweaty in that been-wearing-shoes-all-day way, and I had to jam them sockless and sticky into the shoes. The straps cut into the bones of my feet and across my ankles. I'd have blisters by the end of the session.

Yasuo leaned close. "Mine are worse."

One look, and I knew he was right. His *were* worse. Laughably so. They were shiny black oxfords that looked like formal menswear except for the bizarrely feminine chunky heel. Three inches high, it was shorter than mine, but still it was a *heel.* I swallowed a giggle. "You'll look like Prince."

"Or Tom Cruise, maybe." He wiggled his ankle. "You know, for height?"

"Don't talk to me about height," I grumbled. Mine had spiky heels, and it was only a matter of time before I bit the dust.

Yasuo studied them, a look of male wonder on his face. "I dunno, Blondie, I think they're kind of hot. You might break an ankle, but at least you'll look smokin' doing it."

"Up, up." Mr. Clapper clapped again. "You must pay special attention. For you will be using these skills at an end-of-summer dance."

We all looked at one another, uncertain we'd heard correctly. Did he mean dance, as in the verb *to* dance, as in we'll have to dance at the end of term for a final test or showcase or something? Or was he saying dance, as in *a* dance—the noun—as in homecoming, hoedown, ball, fete, prom . . . *dance*.

"We shall," he continued, "all of us, be gathering to celebrate the end of the Dimming and the blessed return to darkness. Trainees, Acari, Initiates, Watchers, Vampires, too. And in preparation, Acari Drew has generously volunteered to partner with me for today's instruction."

I gulped.

Yas muttered under his breath, "Get back, sister."

I glared. My friend was lucky I didn't impale him with one of my newly acquired heels.

Master Dagursson held his hand out, beckoning me closer. "She will obviously have a different partner at our dance. But, for now, hopefully I will suffice."

I went cold. *A different partner.* Dagursson had said it as though he knew something I didn't, and I got the feeling he wasn't referring to Yasuo. The implications made my skin prickle with foreboding.

"The word is Spanish, for 'double time,'" Dag said, droning on about the Glories of the Paso Doble.

My belly knotted. *Spanish.* I knew just who'd ordered this, and I had a feeling it was a special request going out just for me.

"It is to be performed with drama, with strength of feeling and movement, full of spectacle. It is a man's dance, like a bullfight, with the leader acting the part of the matador."

*What?* Yasuo mouthed at me.

*Bullfighter,* I mouthed back. A man's dance. Surprise surprise.

"And the female . . ." Dagursson paused for dramatic effect.

I raised a brow. Girls danced the part of *the bull*?

"Dances the part of the *cape*," pronounced Dagursson with a grin. "Though some say she enacts the role of the matador's shadow."

My shoulders slumped. I couldn't even play a bull? We might be fearsome kick-ass killers, but girls seemed to be the submissive ones on this island. Apparently we didn't even get to enact the role of an animate object—instead, we were expected to dance around like some guy's cape, or shadow.

Dagursson strolled to his iPod. There was an overloud clicking as he zipped to the correct track. And then Spanish trumpets blared and ostentatious classical guitar thrummed off the studio walls.

The ancient Viking began prowling his way toward me, and I had to swallow a laugh. It was just too surreal. With one hand over his pelvis and one in the air, he was sashaying those hips as if there were no tomorrow.

He came to stand beside me, speaking in his grand dance instructor voice. "The Paso Doble is a dance of passion." He did a little step-step grapevine move, and it was a wonder he didn't dislocate something. If only his ancestors could see him now—I didn't imagine he was winning his ticket to Valhalla with these *Dancing with the Stars* moves.

"You must loosen your joints," he said, slinking behind me. "Free your hips. It is a dance of sensuality, of sexuality. But it is also a dance of power." He grabbed me from behind, and I startled. "A contact dance."

I hoped my disgust wasn't apparent on my face. I stifled a shudder as he pulled me back into his stomach.

"Take my hand," he ordered. "Spread your other arm."

The moment I did, he startled me again, spinning me in, then out again. So much for sexy . . . Mostly I just felt dizzy.

He reeled me back in, slamming me into his chest, belly to belly this time, and my breath escaped with an *oof.* I didn't know jack about the Paso Doble, but I didn't think it was supposed to feel this erratic.

He hugged me closer. "Grab me."

I did not. I would not.

He snatched my hips and ground me close, shouting, "Grab me, Acari. From behind."

I had no choice. I put my hands on his bony ass, and it made my skin crawl.

"Passion, Acari Drew. Passion, children. It is about passion." He shoved me from him, and I stumbled back a few steps. He prowled right back to me, not taking his eyes from mine.

The whole thing creeped me out. He slunk around like a tango master after a few too many sangrias, and the way he held my gaze made me intensely self-conscious. Even worse was the dreadful suspicion that I was going to have to dance this with Alcántara someday.

I waited for his next move, unsure what to do with myself. I knew I shouldn't, but finally I had to ask, "What do I do?"

He addressed the class at large. "Acari Drew stands there. Watch as I walk around her." He high-stepped another circle around me, prancing in time to the music.

"I go to her." He grabbed me and slung me into position, chest to chest. He put an arm around me and grabbed my hand, as if we were ready to tango.

And maybe we did—from that point, the class was a whirling, nauseating, horrifying blur.

To think I'd dissed German folk dancing—doing the Paso Doble with Dagursson made a rousing Bavarian jig seem pretty ideal. I'd have been grateful to dance anything else, with anyone else—even with stupid Josh.

Little did I know just how grateful to Josh I was going to be.

# CHAPTER TWELVE

That night, in the dead of darkness, the sheets were torn from me. My eyes flew open, and even in my sleepy state, my instincts took over. I curled into a ball, covering my head with my arms. But it didn't help.

I stole a peek over my clenched elbow. I saw that trademark sleek black bob and bangs, framing the face that had it in for me.

I could say I was startled, or shocked, but honestly I was neither. I'd been expecting this.

Masha's revenge.

It'd been several days since our dining hall run-in, and she and her fellow Guidons had been mysteriously quiet. I'd known it was only a matter of time.

Hands grabbed roughly under my arms, dragging me to the floor. The dorm was never fully dark now, and my room was an eerie, colorless gray. I blinked rapidly, making out a handful of girls, menacing in their dark Initiate uniforms. Most kept their mouths shut, and all I heard was their heavy breathing, the sound in the calm of my room disturbing.

One voice spoke, a Russian accent, crisp and husky. "Time to take out the trash."

*Masha.* Large and in charge. This would've been her brain-child.

They pulled me down the hall, and my feet stumbled to keep up. I was pissed and wanted to piss them off, too, and even though it was stupid, I let my body go limp.

I fell forward into someone's back and heard a brittle curse. I hoped I'd clipped a kidney.

But they didn't stop; they just kept dragging me toward the stairs, my legs trailing limply behind me.

I felt sharp tugging around my arms—girls' hands like claws—and then a kick on my butt. "Move, fatty."

"She weighs a thousand pounds."

"Push her." More hands, lifting me, then shoving me.

"Your vampire can't help you now." It was Guidon Trinity's voice.

I'd receded deep into myself, but when I heard Trinity's voice, awareness burst through me. *Emma.* Where was she? Did they have her, too? I tried to look behind me, but a hand grabbed my hair and shoved my head back into place. I'd seen enough to know I was alone—no Emma. This treat was reserved just for me.

"Blindfold her." A ragged strip of cloth was bound tightly around my head, cutting into my skin. The unnerving feel of something pressing on my eyes, crushing them, was worse than any humiliation.

They reached the end of the hall, and I sensed open space gaping before me. *Staircase.* They were going to throw me down the stairs.

I swung my feet under me, catching myself in time. They ran down the steps, pulling me with them, and I stumbled along, my feet galloping awkwardly.

I'd experienced middle-of-the-night hazing before. At least now it was summer—the temp would be a bitter high forties, but no snow on the ground. That was something.

The front door opened. A gust of wind swirled around my legs. My nightgown was flannel, but it wouldn't do anything to protect me. I chuff-chuffed rapid breaths, bracing.

"Is little Acari chilly?"

"It's going to be a long night for you, little Acari."

They dragged me outside, and I went limp again, but the path scraped my bare skin, and I flinched, pulling my feet back under me.

"Poor Acari. Do you miss your shoes?"

A shove, and I stumbled, then caught myself. A shove from the other side. Another from behind. I lurched drunkenly, but I stayed on my feet. It was a tiny victory, but in that moment it was everything. I clenched my jaw, girded. This Acari would fight back.

One more push, and I staggered as the terrain changed beneath me. Rocks bit into my bare feet, and cold dampness squished between my toes. I swung my hands blindly in front of me. We'd left the path—one of the vampires' cardinal rules, broken.

"Strip her." Rough hands were all over me, everyone wanting to be the one to rip my clothes off. Girls yanked and jostled me, trying to rip fabric. The flannel pulled tight at my neck, jerking me back. I heard a short tear, then another, followed by a long, crisp ripping sound as my nightgown was rent from top to bottom. Bitter air gusted in, billowing it like a tent behind me.

I regularly slept in a jogging bra and panties to save time dressing in the morning. I'd worn them to bed last night, and how I loved myself for it now.

"Look at the fat ass. Too ashamed to sleep naked."

Girls kicked me and laughed. "Look at her jiggle."

Another kick sent me stumbling forward, but I caught myself on a tree. I clung for balance, and bark jammed under my nails.

My arms were wrenched behind me as my shredded nightgown was torn off. "Pull it off. Strip the fat ass."

I'd been trying to keep cool, to keep my mouth shut and minimize the damage. But I'd had enough.

A foot pressed onto my butt. My skin wobbled, and of course it did, seeing as someone's *foot* was grinding into it, but still the girls crowed over and over, "Fat slut."

"As if I care," I mumbled. I should've shut up, but I couldn't. Did these ridiculous adolescent taunts work on some girls? "Am I supposed to cry?"

"I'll make you cry." It was Masha.

*Crap.* I should've kept my mouth shut.

Another girl's voice sounded, nasty and screechy. "Make her jiggle some more."

More Initiates kicked me. A few kicks were clumsy, grazing off my calves. But some landed hard. I'd be bruised and scraped.

"Tie her up." A final push propelled me forward, and my face slammed into the tree.

"Turn her around." They spun me and pinned my arms at my sides. Bark scraped my back. "Get the plastic wrap."

There was a crackling sound, and cool plastic touched my belly. Sheets of it wound around me. Panic dumped adrenaline into my veins. I was being Saran Wrapped to a tree.

"What the fuck are you doing?" I wriggled, but hands held me fast. "You think Headmaster is going to put up with *this*?"

The plastic wrap got tighter and tighter, and they wound it higher and higher, and some animal instinct flared to life, my heart pounding *Fight, run, fight, run.* I was going to suffocate. I'd wanted to be cool, but I struggled wildly now, and still they wrapped higher, and lower, and tighter, down to my ankles and up above my shoulders.

"I think by the time Headmaster finds out, you'll be ground beef. He'll be so psyched we packed him a little snack, he won't care who did this. Wrap her up tight, girls. Gotta keep her fresh."

This wasn't hazing. This was murder.

"Alcántara is preparing me for a mission." The words burst from me, and I didn't know if it'd pour oil or water onto the fire. "He'll have your heads."

I was bound in a cocoon now. My face was free, but plastic covered my body, and my skin felt smothered. The cold made my feet numb and my nose run, but beneath the plastic, sweat soaked me, running between my breasts, under my arms, and down my spine to the crack of my butt.

Hot breath whispered in my ear, "Caught like a fly, Acari, and we're going to eat you alive."

I wriggled my shoulders but couldn't budge. "Alcántara will find you. He'll get you for this." Panic fueled my words—I wasn't quite sure what I'd meant by them, or where they'd come from.

Masha's voice closed in. "So you think you're Hugo's favorite? So sure, are you?"

*Hugo?* She and Alcántara were on a first-name basis. It silenced me.

"That's right. Don't speak about what you don't know." She jammed fingers under my blindfold and ripped it off, tearing hair from my scalp with it.

I blinked, my eyes adjusting. The sky was steel gray, and it was impossible to tell what time it was. Half a dozen Initiates surrounded me. Most were older Guidons, like Masha and Trinity.

The Russian girl was in my face, smiling wickedly. Even in the dimness, her black bob gleamed. "I want to watch your eyes as you suffer."

Blood oozed down my cheekbone where her nails had raked my skin. It focused me.

Alcántara had said *she* was the one who'd be in trouble. That girls who fought were rewarded . . . and I wasn't going down without a fight. "This isn't about me. This is about you, *Guidon Masha.* You couldn't best me in the dining hall, and Alcántara scolded you for it."

She stepped back, disgust shriveling her features. She brushed off her hands, and blond hair fluttered to the ground—my hair. She pulled a Sharpie from her boot and thrust it at an Initiate. "Decorate her."

Girls took turns writing on my belly, my forehead, over my

pelvis. Childish crap like *Eat me* and *fat slut*, and some chilling things, too, like *lunch*.

Trinity grabbed a fistful of my hair to color strands of it with her Sharpie. She pulled hard, and I forced my head to remain upright even though the pain made tears run down my face. "You gonna cry, Acari? Boohoo. Can't call you Blondie anymore."

I heard boys' voices from across the quad. So it'd been dawn, not midnight, when Masha's crew pulled me from bed.

They grew louder, approaching on the path. I'd thought I couldn't care less what a bunch of Trainees thought of me, but still, I cringed. It seemed shame was a thing hardwired in my brain.

Trinity backed up to admire her handiwork. Girls began to laugh, catching her attention. "Here come the boys," someone said.

She turned and saw them when I did—three Trainees stopped on the path before us. She gave a little *squee* of delight. "Just in time for the fun."

I forced myself to face the guys straight on. I recognized them from Yasuo's group. Kevin, Rob . . . and Josh. Something about seeing a familiar face made me want to cry. Even if it was just stupid Josh. I stiffened my lips—I wouldn't get emotional. I wouldn't tremble in front of the guys.

Masha strolled toward them. "Come join us, boys."

Rob spoke up. He was tall and a little gangly, still filling into his length. He gave a rueful shake of his head. "Shouldn't leave the path."

"Oh, but you can make an exception." Trinity was excited now. "We say so."

"Gotta follow the rules," Kevin said, "and the rule is, *Stay on the path*."

"We order it." Trinity's atonal northeastern accent had lowered to a threatening growl.

Masha rubbed her hip where she normally holstered her whip, now notably absent—had Alcántara taken it from her as part of her punishment? The notion cheered me for about a millisecond, until she spoke again.

"Come on," she beckoned. "It's okay for you boys. Come and take a piss on our Acari." *Piss* has a distinctive sound when pronounced with an impassioned Russian accent.

"Mark her like the dog she is," a brown-haired Initiate said.

Trinity smiled wide. "Now's your chance."

Rob's face split into a grin. He stepped off the path. Kevin was right behind him, his hands on his zipper.

I swallowed convulsively. My throat ached with shame, but I refused to cry. Not in front of these apes.

Josh stepped from the path.

*Not him, too.* I swallowed and swallowed again. It was almost too hard to make my throat work around the ache.

But then he reached out, grabbed Kevin's shoulder, grabbed Rob's shoulder. "Really, mates?"

Rob leered at me. "Why the hell not?"

I stared at the young Trainee, memorizing him. Someday he would be a vampire. And someday I would stake him. The thought was errant and vivid and shocking. And, I realized, so very true.

I still dreamt of escape. But if that didn't pan out, my revised list of personal goals wouldn't be a short one. First, I'd find and obliterate *this* jackass. Hell, I'd obliterate the whole vampire race, if necessary.

The thought so startled me, my eyes widened. It felt dangerous, reckless, maybe even treasonous, to let such a thing dance along the edges of my mind.

Josh looked at me and must've misread my expression, because his voice hardened. "Why not?" His grip became so tight his fingertips disappeared into the boy's sweater. "Because I say so."

The two Trainees looked uncertain then.

Josh flung their shoulders from his hands. "Now, stop being such douche bags and go to class."

He approached me, not waiting to see if his friends had left. Wasn't he afraid they'd stab him in the back? Given the looks on their faces, some caution might've been advisable.

"Ladies, ladies." He tsked at the girls. "Isn't this quite enough?"

I watched in disbelief, amazed at the sheer insanity of what I was witnessing. Dude had a pair of cojones the size of Kentucky.

"We were just getting started," Masha said, sounding seriously peeved at his gall.

Josh matter-of-factly slid a switchblade from his pocket and sliced the plastic along the length of the tree. "Show's over now."

The Initiates didn't move. "But we own her."

"She owns herself, I think." He straightened, leaning against the tree, and his hand moved slowly, as though he were bored, clicking his blade into place. Flicking it out. Clicking it into place. "Truly, girls. This has been great fun. But I think it's time to call it. Wouldn't want to be caught by Headmaster. This sheila ain't worth it, I think."

"He's right," Trinity said in a monotone, and I gaped at her, stunned at what I was hearing.

Then Josh looked at each one, catching and holding their gazes. He spoke slowly, telling them, "Now catch up to the boys."

I wondered if I was witnessing some nascent vampire mojo going on, because damned if they didn't disperse and catch up to the boys.

All except for Masha.

He turned his back to her, and for the second time, I mentally accused him of being stupid. The guy was going to get a knife in his back one of these days.

I watched her, not even letting myself blink. But she only stood there, glaring at Josh with astonishment, the rage rolling off her in waves.

He casually set about peeling the plastic from my body. When he spoke again, his casual surfer-boy voice was back. I realized he was addressing Masha. "There's been one incident already, eh? Call it a morning, Guidon. The dining hall will open soon. Don't want to miss Thursday's omelet bar."

Finally she left, and I supposed it was wise. Without backup, I didn't know if she could beat a Trainee in a fight. But the lasers coming out of her eyes told me it wasn't over.

At the moment, I didn't care. I was freezing to death. I tried to pull the plastic from my body, but my fingers were too cold and clumsy.

Josh stopped me. "Stand still. I've almost got it."

I could've thanked him, but I had another pressing thought on my mind. "I kn-kn-knew you were dumb." The words were barely discernible through my chattering teeth.

He laughed. "How's that?"

"T-t-turning your back on those people." Never again would I turn my back on Masha.

"Maybe I'm not stupid." He waggled his eyebrows. "Maybe I'm just stronger than they are."

The concept gave me pause. Had he risked that theory just to save me from getting peed on? I refused to believe it.

"Either way, they couldn't sneak up on me if they tried. I'm too fast." He stood and pulled off his sweater. His T-shirt tugged up his back, giving me a glimpse of carved abs. It stopped all thought in my brain.

My eyes shot up, but he'd caught me checking him out.

He smiled, and my mortification warmed me right up. And then he obviously checked out my own state of undress. *Oh God.* My hands fumbled to cover myself.

He laughed and tossed me his sweater. "As much as I appreciate the view, you should put this on before you catch a chill."

"Th-that something you learned in med school?" I eagerly pulled on the sweater. It hung down to the middle of my thighs and was still warm from his body. I thought I just might be eternally grateful.

"No," he replied. "That's where I learned about *shock*."

I was shivering violently now, and he put his arm around me, chafing my arm. "You're chattering because you're shocky. You need a hot shower and strong coffee. Come on. I'll walk you back."

He led me in the direction of the Acari dorm. Gradually, my shivering subsided from violent to merely intense.

"Why'd you help me?"

"Yas asked me to look out for you."

"Oh yeah. Of course." My spirits sank, just a little bit. Every girl wanted to think a guy would come to her rescue, you know, *just because.*

"You nutter." He chucked me on the chin. "I helped because I wanted to help."

I nodded shyly, not completely believing him, but liking the sentiment all the same. I risked a quick glance up at him.

He was watching me, smiling his crooked grin. "And you're welcome."

I let myself smile back, slumping my shoulders dramatically. "Aw, hell."

He pushed away, looking genuinely distressed. "Why the hell?"

I gave him a playfully angry stare. "Because *eternally indebted* is a long time to be thankful to a vampire."

With a laugh, Josh gave me a quick half hug.

But the smile soon faded from my face, because there were only two ways to view what just happened. Either Yasuo was wrong and Trainees *could* stand up to Guidons, or, thanks to me, Josh was going to have some serious hell to pay.

# CHAPTER THIRTEEN

I t was a gray, blustery Saturday morning, but I was achy, moody, and way behind on my reading, and somehow crappy weather felt like just the thing.

I hobbled across the quad as fast as I could with a sore hip, my butt still bruised from stupid Tracer Otto's stupid stick-fighting lesson in gym class. Blinking against the mist, I pinned my hood over my head with one hand and used the other to hold my messenger bag at my side—anything to stop that damned German etiquette book from thumping against me.

My sole goal was the overstuffed armchair in front of the science library fireplace, and with a relieved sigh, I reached my destination, stretching my legs toward the hearth and digging out the onion bagel I'd snagged from the dining hall. Someone had already built a decent fire, and a good thing, too, since my leggings were soaked through.

This was my favorite reading spot on campus, even though

Alcántara's office was just upstairs and I was tempting fate by just being there. I felt a little dread at the prospect of running into him, but a part of me had come on purpose. Dance, German . . . This bizarre curriculum had a million questions rattling through my brain—questions I hoped I'd finally mustered the courage to ask.

I fished out Josh's silly book. *Etikette und Protokoll . . . Shudder.* I'd never been tutored in my life, and it was a real ego buster. I was going to spend the day with it—I told myself it was so I could cram and be done with it, but honestly, I also kind of wanted to impress him, too. Josh *and* Alcántara.

The content was simple, though I had to admit there were some crazy details. Alcántara was right—I was fluent in modern and Old High German, and none of it would've helped me a bit with this stuff. I could do declensions in my sleep, but who knew German businessmen knocked on the table after a good meeting?

One thing was for sure: I had no clue why I needed to learn all this. Was our mission to take place somewhere in *Germany*? How far off-island were Alcántara and I headed?

Plus, he'd mentioned danger. Summer-term gym classes were running heavy on combat. Were those skills I'd need for the mission? Would I be forced to open up a can of whoop-ass in the middle of a formal business meeting?

The vampire with the answers appeared as though bidden. One minute Alcántara wasn't there, and *boom*, the next he was, leaning against the back wall with his arms crossed over his chest while looking all blasé, as if he'd been kicking it there for the last half hour instead of materializing as though from thin air.

I knew a swell of satisfaction—he'd sensed me here, and he'd come. Then dread came, quick on its heels. It would be dangerous to forget just whom I was dealing with. Seeking out vampires was a dangerous game . . . a deadly one.

"Acari Drew." That voice, a sultry rasp. That hair and those eyes, black and gleaming like a panther's.

I sat upright. My hands trembled with the adrenaline dump I experienced whenever he appeared like this, and I folded them primly in my lap. "Master Alcántara."

"Why have you come?"

Good question. He'd know that, with his office just upstairs, I'd pretty much thrown myself in his path simply by being there. I'd wanted to find out more about our mission, but did I have other questions, too? That he might have a flirtation with Masha was just too intriguing. That *many* girls had special relationships with vampires, too compelling.

So why seek him out privately, instead of in a classroom setting? Was it that I wanted to bring *our* relationship to some sort of a head? And if so, was it *really* because I wanted it, or did I just want to best Masha?

There was no way in hell I was sharing any of *that* wacko stream of consciousness, so I went with a half-truth instead. I flashed the spine of my book. "I came to study. Brushing up on my business protocol, just like you asked."

"But so near me." He was unwilling to drop it; yet he still managed to look bored, unconcerned, and vaguely put out as he glided across the room to sprawl in the chair opposite me. Alcántara might have been a fourteenth-century royal mathematician, but his hot indie rocker impression was spot-on. "Was encountering me your intention?"

I neither agreed nor denied. "This is my favorite place on campus."

"Surely you knew you'd run into me." He stretched, and his black boots came to rest perilously close to mine.

He was bringing his A-game, and what else had I thought would happen? I was just a stupid, stupid girl, playing with fire.

I laughed nervously. "That's pretty direct."

"Do I have reason not to be?" A teasing smile spread across his face. "Is there something you'd have me avoid?"

I was squirming, and clearly the guy was enjoying it. "No, direct is good. . . ." Scrambling to change the subject, I began riffling through my book and practically felt a cartoon light-bulb flash over my head. I pointed with authority at one of the passages. "Just like they say in this manual here. See, Germans value directness. To the point of discomfort."

That bored demeanor of his shattered with an explosive laugh. "You have done your homework."

"Always." I couldn't help but feel pleased at his praise. But—*crap*—did that prove I *had* sought him out? Was I seeking his approval?

"Truly, you are as quick-witted and as versatile as we'd hoped." He concentrated on my face, and it made me nervous. What was he looking for . . . or finding? "Tell me, young Acari—what else have you learned?"

That to have flirty banter with a vampire was to be out-matched?

Obviously, I gave a different reply, rattling off some of what I'd gathered from my reading. "German businessmen value structure. Hierarchy, formality, and titles are important. Oh, and punctuality, above all things."

A slow smile spread across his face—it was the same smile that always kicked my heart rate into panic gear. "It sounds as if you describe those of us who are Vampire."

I paused, needing to get this *just right*. I imagined the first time I inadvertently insulted a vampire might be my last. "Yes, you're right. It's reminiscent of life on this island. All the best aspects of traditional culture." I gave myself a ginormous pat on the back for that little gem.

He leaned forward, elbows on knees. "As with vampires, traditional German businessmen have many rules. Is that not so?"

Hella rules. Though obviously I phrased it differently. "Yes, in a typical meeting, there are many conventions to be followed."

"Such as?"

"You must already know."

"Amuse me."

I rattled them out rapid-fire, figuring it was an easier topic than why I'd chosen the sciences building as a hangout. "Men enter a room before women." I was sure the vamps must've loved that one. "Use a formal greeting and a quick, firm handshake. Stand until you're asked to sit. Confrontation, exaggeration, and emotion are to be avoided."

He stopped me with a raised hand. "That will suffice."

"Why do I need to know all this, anyway? Are we going to Germany for our mission?"

He laughed, and it was a little on the patronizing side. "No, *querida*. We are not going to Germany for our mission. In time, you will learn all you need to know. For now, you have sufficiently grasped this aspect of your preparations. Trainee Joshua did well."

Actually *I* did well—all Josh did was give me a book. But credit where credit was due and all, so I said, "Yes, he gave me a good book to read."

"I heard that's not all he did."

I bristled. Of course he'd have heard about the latest hazing. Using reasoning that might appeal to a vampire, I tread carefully, answering slowly. "I found myself in a compromising situation, and Trainee Joshua proved himself a gentleman."

Alcántara didn't look too happy about it, and it freaked me out.

I was dying to ask if Josh was in trouble now. If Trainees couldn't stand up to Guidons without consequences. Josh and I weren't exactly buddies, but it didn't mean I wanted to see him eviscerated or anything. Plus, it was hard to avoid the fact that, if he was in trouble, it was because of me. *I* was accountable.

I had to change the subject, take the attention off Josh. I could think of only one way, and it was the moral equivalent of batting my eyelashes. Normally I wouldn't know a feminine wile from a hole in the ground, but I decided to go for it.

And okay, maybe I could've thought of *other* ways, but for some reason, something deep down inside me wanted to go there. Maybe it was discovering that all these girls were enjoying private intrigues with vampires. But in the wake of discovering the whole Ronan/Amanda thing, I wondered at my own appeal—doubted it, really. Either way, I felt ready to push the whole fate-tempting thing.

How did girls do this? I kicked my legs in front of me, trying to mimic Alcántara's sexy sprawl. But his eyes remained flat on me.

*Alrighty, then.* On to step two. Cue the lazy smile.

I busted out my most languorous smile, but Alcántara remained a granite statue across from me—an unreadable, unemotional but very attractive slab of granite. Yet I *knew* that'd been an obvious softball I'd lobbed his way—wouldn't he have had *some* reaction? Maybe all this nonsense about vampires having affairs was just that . . . nonsense.

Fine. Step three. I'd bring out the big guns: my hair. Shiny and blond, it'd always gotten a big reaction. I casually twirled a bit around my finger, because that was what flirty girls did, right? They toyed with their hair?

But only when I lifted it from my cheek did Alcántara's eyes flare to life. He knelt before me in an instant. And it wasn't my hair he was interested in. It was the huge bruise my hair had concealed.

He studied my cheekbone intently. When he spoke, his voice came out in a strange whisper. "What has come to pass?"

"Stick training." I eased away from him, self-conscious and a little embarrassed, too. "Tracer Otto faked left but went right."

He closed the distance I'd put between us. He lifted his hand, then gently traced a finger along the line of the bruise. "All that blood, just beneath the surface."

*Of course.* Of course he didn't go for sexy smiles or flowing hair. It was the blood that floated his boat.

"It's not a big deal," I demurred, making my voice steadier than I felt, when really all I wanted to do was flee. I'd taken his mind from Josh, that was for sure.

He inhaled deeply. "Black, blue, green, purple, yellow . . . every color but red. And yet just below the surface, all those burst vessels, pooled a rich crimson."

I wriggled deeper into my seat, totally creeped out. "Happens all the time."

"So brave you are. Did you know they once treated bruises with leeches? The leech would suck, ingesting the excess blood." His eyes grazed from my cheekbone to my mouth. "We have other ways now."

Alarm bells shrilled in my head. *Run run run.* But I couldn't. It wasn't just because of Josh, or me, or any of that other stuff. The specter of Masha kept me glued to my seat. I needed Alcántara on my side if I wanted to stop Masha from coming and slaughtering me in my sleep.

He dragged his fingertip down the side of my face, to the tip of my chin. He pinched it, then tilted my face to look at him eye to eye. "*Mi Acarita*, I wonder if you'd be brave about all things."

I knew he meant kisses. Would I be brave about kisses? I'd thought I might. But I realized now, the answer was a resounding *no.* Not about kisses from him, at least.

This was my own fault. I'd been a kid with a box of matches; I'd played with fire; I'd tempted fate—all the clichés in the book.

How quickly this had gone from blood to kisses. Inside, I recoiled. But I kept my face a placid mask on the outside. I stayed still, my gaze locked with his.

Something happened—a shift in the world around me, and my skin grew cold. The air whooshed from my ears and the room grew dim—as though I might faint. And then I fell into his eyes. They were black, and deep, and bottomless, like gleaming shards of obsidian.

I trembled, fighting the sensation. I didn't want to kiss him. So why was I leaning closer?

I was wrong to have been this bold. This wasn't what I wanted. I blinked hard, fisting the heat back into my hands. I curled my toes in my boots till my feet cramped.

The world snapped back into clarity, and I sucked in a great breath.

Alcántara's low laugh came to me as though from a great distance. "Touché. For now, *querida*."

A vampire wouldn't be my first kiss. *Yet.*

I'd won the battle. But I still worried how I might fare in the war.

# CHAPTER FOURTEEN

"Finally." A cramp seized me, and I shook out my calf as I hobbled to keep up with Emma. My bruises were almost healed, but I still stiffened up at odd moments. One more drink of the blood should get me back to full strength.

"Finally *what*?" Emma stopped and, noticing my limp, let me catch up.

"Finally we get a moment together. You and Yas have been attached at the hip." I rubbed my lower back as we walked.

"Are you okay?"

"My ass hurts," I grumbled. "Tracer Otto kicked it for me."

She held the dorm door open and slowed her pace for me. She studied me as we made our way up the stairs to our rooms on the second floor. Pulling the hair from my face, she said, "That's some bruise."

I flinched away. "Unfortunately, you're not the first to notice."

She shot me a questioning look as she came to a stop in front of her bedroom door, rifling in her bag for her key.

I leaned against the wall with a sigh. "Alcántara. Apparently all that blood under the skin is tantalizing."

"Ugh." She grimaced. "Did not. Need. To know." She pushed open her door, assuming I'd follow.

I didn't. The Initiates hadn't yet targeted her for a special hazing treat, and it'd been on my mind since my whole Saran Wrap ordeal.

"Get in here," she said, her *get* sounding more like *git*, "before anyone sees us."

"Actually"—I snagged her arm, pulling her back out and down the hallway—"come on. Let's hang in the common area instead."

She hesitated. "But . . ."

"But the Guidons? We can't hide, Em. *You* can't hide. Your turn is coming. This situation is going to come to a head, and the sooner we face it, the better." I plopped onto one of the couches, a cozy beast of a thing upholstered in dark red wide-wale corduroy. "We need to show them we're not afraid."

"We?" She gave me a tremulous smile.

"Naturally, *we*." I chose to ignore my instincts and all Alcántara had warned about friends—these tentative relationships had come to mean too much. "We're in it together, right?"

"Right," she agreed, and I had to give her credit, because, though her expression was uncertain, her voice was her usual solid, calm, farm girl self. She settled next to me on the couch. "So . . . Alcántara?"

"Yeah. He's got a thing for bruises."

Even though we were alone, she looked around. Seeing the coast was clear, she hissed, "That's disgusting."

"Tell me about it." I leaned in. "It gets weirder."

She gave me a flat look. "Of course it does." After a pause, she prompted, "Well?"

I hedged, uncomfortable with how I'd handled it. "I was scared he was going to be angry about Josh and the hazing thing. So I tried to change the subject. In a dramatic way."

Her eyes narrowed ever so slightly. "Dramatic, how?"

"Okay, okay. I panicked," I said, on the defensive already. "Dramatic, as in I—I think I was flirting with him."

"You *think*?"

I flopped back, idly picking at the plush corduroy. Her stoic farm girl expressions really could feel accusatory sometimes. "Well, I don't exactly have loads of practice."

"Did he flirt back?"

"Yeah." I gave a rueful laugh. "I was in over my head in, like, three seconds." I glanced away, weighing my words, then confessed, "I think he was going to kiss me."

That woke her up. Her face came alive. "Did you *want* him to kiss you?"

"No way. At least . . . I don't think so." I waffled, not really sure *how* I felt about any of it. For the first time in my life, a guy wanted me—my luck it was a dead one. "I don't want a vampire to be my first kiss."

She marveled at the concept. "I wonder if it'd be cold."

"Gross. You mean, like his tongue, too?" We both shuddered. "I guess it might be."

She nodded gravely. "They are dead, aren't they?"

"Technically speaking."

That silenced us for a moment, until Emma quivered, stifling an unexpected giggle.

I stared at her, amazed. "What?"

"There's always the dance," she said, with an uncharacteristic smirk. "Maybe he'll ask you to be his date."

I glared. "The *dance*. Don't remind me. I wonder if they'll issue uniform prom dresses."

"Black, floor-length."

"Yeah, like Morticia." I joined her giggling. "And black capes with super-high, velvety collars. We can hobble around like the brides of Frankenstein."

"I hear you even learned some *smooth moves* for the dance floor."

"You sound like—" I froze, gaping, then elbowed her. "*Yasuo* told you that." I scrunched lower into my seat, frowning. "I can't believe he told you about dance class. I'm sure he's out there right now trying to devise ways to blackmail me."

A bunch of Initiates came into the lounge, buzzing with conversation and bursting our bubble. Emma darted a nervous glance my way.

I sat up and put a steadying hand on her arm, whispering, "Not afraid, remember? We're just hanging out. We have as much right to be here as they do."

They were across the room, studiously ignoring us and draping their taut, catsuited bodies across couches, over armrests, on the edges of coffee tables. Their yammering drowned out our voices.

Emma's face turned pleading. "Can't we just go to your room to hang out? What if Masha comes?"

"I'll face Masha any day of the week." I sounded braver

than I felt, but I knew I spoke the truth. "Listen, Em. We can't act scared. These girls can smell fear. We go into hiding, and I swear it'll trip some sort of animal-instinct urge to hunt or something."

I felt someone staring; I turned. Trinity loomed at the end of the hall, arms crossed over her chest and her gaze zeroed in on us. She curled her lip in disgust before joining her friends.

Her eyes didn't leave us, though. She sat on an armchair, staring, legs crossed severely and hands clawed on the armrests. Slowly, she pulled a weapon from her boot. It was a long, thin, steel thing, like a cross between a file and a dagger. With a pretty tilt to her head, she began to stab robotically at the arm of the chair, over and over. She made it look like an idle gesture, but we knew better.

I felt Emma freaking, and I tried to ease the tension, murmuring from the corner of my mouth, "Guess she doesn't like the furniture."

She began to gather her stuff. "Seriously. Let's just go."

I squeezed my hand where I'd rested it on her arm, then gave her an encouraging look. "If we leave now, we'll just look weak. We need to stay. Now, take out your knife."

"My what?"

"Your knife. You know, that big-ass Buck knife you have. I know you carry it around." It was thick and serrated, and the last time I saw it, she'd been stabbing a Draug in the back, saving me. "Come on, farm girl." I gave her a small smile. "You've faced worse than this."

She furrowed her brows but, with a sharp nod, obeyed.

"Now do something with it."

"What?"

"Do something with it," I repeated.

She looked around as if she might find the answer inscribed on the worn upholstery of the student lounge couch. "Like what?"

"I don't know. Clean your nails or something."

The room had quieted a bit. Chatter still came from across the room, but I felt how a handful of Initiates had begun to watch us.

Emma mouthed the words, *My nails?*

I had to hand it to my friend—she really trusted me, and I loved her for it. I gave her an encouraging nod, and she began picking at her nails. I don't know how she did it without drawing blood. It really was an ugly blade, looking more suitable for boar skinning than an impromptu manicure.

Trinity's voice rang clear across the lounge. She was outraged. "Have you forgotten your place?"

I adopted an innocent tone. "So, cleaning your nails is forbidden now?"

One of the Initiates began to stand, and Trinity shot a brief look to stop her. She brought her attention back to me, stabbing her weapon deep into the arm of the chair. "Watch out, Acari. Because soon we're going to finish what we started."

Other weapons appeared in the Guidons' hands—mostly blades, but some weird stuff, too. A needle-thin stiletto. Brass knuckles. One girl slid some arrow-tube-looking thing from her sleeve, and I made a mental note not to cross *her*.

I didn't know where my guts—or stupidity—came from. All I knew was, I'd stood up to Guidons before and had been all but rewarded. Vampires appeared to be big fans of the whole survival-of-the-fittest thing.

"Promises, promises." I eased my hand closer to the throwing stars I kept tucked in my boot.

Trinity didn't like my bravado—I could tell by the way her porcelain cheeks flushed red. But her voice remained cold and even. "Maybe next time we'll strip you completely naked. Unless the sight of you in your training bra scared the boys off for good."

The other girls tittered.

"You're seriously going that route again?" I pulled my shoulders back, sitting tall. I was *not* flat-chested. Not entirely. "At least *I'm* not a clench-jawed Connecticut poor little rich girl with the intellect of a Happy Meal and the heart of a virago." I glanced at Emma. "It's like if John Cheever had written horror."

"The fuck?" Trinity was on her feet. "What *the fuck* does that mean?"

I bit my lips not to laugh. I'd known Trinity wasn't the brightest bulb, and now more important, I'd just learned how much she hated it.

I sensed someone plop onto the arm of the couch. "Language, dollies."

Amanda had appeared, but Trinity's glower didn't budge from me. "Whatever."

Our Proctor scanned the room, taking in all the weaponry. The line between her brows told me she'd grokked what was going down. "Toys away."

Emma complied, but the older girls only glared in challenge.

Amanda stiffened. "I said *weapons down*."

One by one, all the sharp things were stowed away—however reluctantly.

"Brilliant." She turned her attention to the Guidons, her attitude a sort of forced business casual. "I came for you third-years. Priti says class isn't at the gym today. She wants us to meet her at the cove. Something about medium-range combatives. In the surf."

There was grumbling as the girls dispersed. I was glad I was sitting, because I was sure a few of them would've shouldered me on their way out.

Amanda remained, standing over me and regarding me with a sort of stern appreciation. "Acari Drew, you have *got* to learn when to stand down."

I nodded, but in my heart, I completely disagreed. All of this—the hazing, the posturing, even the flirting—was a part of some greater test. I was almost certain now.

Because there was only one group on this island who could demand total submission. And it wasn't us girls.

# CHAPTER FIFTEEN

"Walk with me," Amanda said, shooing us off the couch. It didn't sound like a request, and I hopped up, relieved to be dealing with an Initiate who wasn't such a raging bitch.

Emma was more hesitant. "Not me. I have to catch up on reading." She hefted her bag up as evidence.

I hoped she was right—that she did have work to do and wasn't just making excuses to hide in her room.

Amanda gave her a weighty look. "Fine, dolly. I'll talk to *you* later."

I dropped my bag off in my room, and Amanda and I headed toward the small cove where many of our training exercises were held. The winding trail was gorgeous in a bleak, miserable sort of way, all craggy and rocky, the faraway water shimmering an eerie silver in the Dimming's half-light.

I caught my toe on a rock, cursing under my breath as I stumbled. "Why don't they just give us cars or bikes or something?" The cove lay about a mile down the coast, and, aside from the few SUVs the Tracers were allowed to drive, the sole mode of transportation was our feet.

"They're an old-fashioned bunch, our vampires." Amanda smiled, and it struck me how pretty she was, all angular lines, flawless dark skin, and shoulder-length dreads. Lately, her expression had been tight, but now that we were away from everyone else, she was relaxed enough to let a little of her true self glimmer through. I wondered how much of her tension stemmed from her relationship with Ronan.

We rounded a bend, spotting Masha and her crew about a quarter mile down the path in the distance. "Oh, fabulous," I said, slowing down. "Maybe I should join you at the cove. Masha and her crew can waterboard me in the surf."

"Don't give them any ideas." But then her smirking expression grew serious. "Look," she said, slowing her pace to match mine, "you have a knack for trouble. And now you've caught the fancy of some real aggros."

"I'd hoped my relationship with Alcántara would protect me."

She stopped in her tracks. "That right there. That'll get you killed."

"But he's shown me attention."

"We're discussing *Alcántara*." She enunciated each word slowly and clearly.

I bristled. "I know whom we're discussing. I might be younger than you, but I'm not a total imbecile."

"I see." But the tone of her voice indicated otherwise.

"Dammit, Drew. I saw this coming. You have got to mind yourself."

I had the nagging feeling that, despite her years on the island, Amanda still didn't quite *get* it. "Don't you think his attentions might, I don't know, protect me?"

*"Attentions?"* She grabbed my arm, hard. "What attentions? Has something happened?"

"No," I hedged, but she heard the hesitation in my voice.

"No, nothing happened, or no, you're not going to tell me?"

Her fingers were cutting into my arm, and I flinched away. "Fine," I admitted, rubbing my arm. "I think he almost kissed me."

She glared, so I rambled on in my defense. "Seriously, Amanda, I think the fact that he likes me might protect me."

"Bollocks."

"Bollocks nothing," I said, my tone as sharp as hers. "I'm serious. I think it's worthwhile to operate within the system."

"You can succeed here without kissing any vampires."

We'd reached a fork in the trail. A smaller, rocky path unfurled below, leading to a thin stretch of beach. A half dozen Guidons were already there, doing wind sprints on the sand and push-ups in the surf, looking generally badass.

Movement in the water caught my eye. It was Ronan, surfing. I felt Amanda notice him at the same time, and we watched silently for a pregnant moment. The waves were big today, not foamy and choppy, but crisp swells colored a deep gunmetal gray in the sunless daylight. He'd caught a big one and was riding it into shore. It was like witnessing grace and power combined.

Amanda marveled. "Bloody fantastic, isn't he?"

As he reached the breakers, he dove off his board into the surf. He emerged from the waves, carrying his huge longboard as though it were merely a bit of driftwood he'd snatched up.

"Yeah. He's something." I tore my eyes away. He belonged to Amanda, whereas all I had was a vampire with a bruise fetish.

Childish, sure, but it annoyed me. Also annoying was how she was treating me like a silly schoolgirl who didn't know better. I spoke without thinking. "Maybe *you* should be careful of *your* relationships. Maybe *you* should operate within the system a little more."

She glared at me. "You presumptuous little slag. Where the hell did that come from?" She took a step back, as if she couldn't stand to be near me. "I'm not sure what you *think* you know, but Trinity was right. You forget yourself. Just because I've been friendly doesn't mean that I'll put up with your nonsense, or go out on a limb for you, or really, that *anyone* will. There are no teams here. No alliances. You are alone. So time to start guarding your tongue and minding your business."

Ronan had spotted us and was headed up the path. "Ladies." His tentative greeting matched the question in his expression.

"Ladies yourself. This one's all yours." Amanda brushed past him, storming down to the beach.

"Wait," he called to her.

After a beat, Amanda did, but with a huff. She held her shoulders tight and hands fisted. She seemed super pissed. I must've really hit a nerve.

Ronan reached behind his back and pulled the toggle of his zipper, unpeeling the top of his wet suit. The muted light cast charcoal shadows along muscular arms and broad shoulders. Not knowing where to look, I decided simply to pay extremely close attention to his fingers digging in a hidden pocket, because watching his hand was an entirely different thing from checking him out, right?

But my mind blanked when I saw what he'd pulled out. It was a tarnished brass key—one of those old-fashioned skeleton keys—long and thin with an elaborate loop at one end and jagged, misshapen teeth at the other. It was like something you might use to unlock a haunted house.

He held it out to her, *offering* it. The whole thing made me desperately curious. What on earth was it to? A dungeon? The city? His heart?

She glared at it, shot me an icy look, then glared back at Ronan. Finally, she snatched it from his hand and slid it into her coat pocket. She gave him a brisk nod of thanks, tossing another sneer my way for good measure. "Do me a favor and tell this nutter she shouldn't be kissing any vampires." She stormed off to join the others down on the beach.

"What was that about?" he demanded, his face suddenly shuttered of emotion. His green eyes, unexpectedly vibrant in the steely light, were focused hard on me. His hair, jet-black when wet, jutted in messy spikes along his head.

As I caught the boyish sight of it, an errant pang of affection twinged my chest. Was he angry? Or was this him giving a damn?

I didn't let myself think twice—I just dove in. "Alcántara almost kissed me."

Those green eyes froze into a hard stare. "Walk with me." He set off briskly down the other fork in the trail, not looking to see if I followed, toward the small dirt lot where he'd parked the Range Rover.

I followed in silence. Suddenly, it felt too much to bear. Maybe it was the fault of the Dimming—I was desperate to feel the sun on my face, or to see the blackness of night around me—but this constant twilight was making me crazy. It was making me emotional.

I was learning some hard lessons about myself, among them that I was a hormonal teenager who liked to flirt with danger. But I wasn't proud, and this profound burst of self-knowledge didn't stop me from trying to get a rise out of Ronan. "He's been friendly. Alcántara, I mean. Just chatting and stuff."

"It's the *and stuff* that worries me," he said through a clenched jaw. "I've warned you about getting close to the vampires."

He stood at the back of the SUV, and I stayed at the front, leaning against the hood to give him privacy. I heard the splash of fresh water he kept in a jug for rinsing, followed by the rustle of clothing. I waited till it grew quiet, then said, "Alcántara and I aren't close."

"You have no notion what you're toying with."

I crossed my arms tightly at my chest. "Please give me a little credit. Contrary to popular opinion, I wasn't born yesterday."

"No. Not born yesterday. But you could die tomorrow. If you go on like this." He sounded angry. Maybe his relationship with Amanda clouded his judgment, or worse, was a sign of bad judgment to begin with. I wished I could challenge him on it, but I'd learned my lesson from my chat with Amanda: *Don't go there.*

He came around the front, towel drying his hair. His

T-shirt clung to his still-wet torso. "Are you attracted to him? Is that something you want?"

"No . . . I . . ." The tight T-shirt coinciding with a question about attraction threw me, and I cringed at my faltering reply. Not only was I a hormonal teenager; I was also an *awkward* hormonal teenager.

But I saw in his eyes that I'd taken too long to reply.

"Never mind," he snapped. "Don't answer that." He tossed his towel in the back, standoffish now, as though he'd made up his mind about something.

I wanted to tell him to wait, that we could talk it through. That it *was* something I wanted, just not with a vampire. I craved attraction and all the things that came with it—stupid stuff like sharing jokes and French fries and secrets. The feeling of someone caring if I lived or died. I wanted to tell him how I worried I might really die before I ever experienced it. That *he* was the closest thing to someone who'd ever cared about me—and how messed up was *that*? That I thought about relationships all the time, speculating about vague boys I'd never met, or him, or Josh, or vampires, too, but it was because I was young and healthy and normal, with normal, young, healthy urges. That I worried about him and Amanda, and speculated about Emma and Yas, and wondered how people even found themselves in relationships in the first place, since all *I* ever seemed to do was heal from bruises and sprains, and evade death as best I could.

But he didn't give me the chance to tell him any of that. He simply said, "I'll see you back on campus." Then he got in the truck and drove away.

And he didn't even offer me a ride.

# CHAPTER SIXTEEN

"You're a Gloomy Gus." Emma nudged my butt with her boot. She was seated a few steps above me, hanging out on the dorm stairs.

It was the first "sunny" afternoon in days—meaning the sky had gone from gray to a washed-out white—and I'd let her and Yasuo drag me outside. Guys weren't allowed in the girls' dorm, and we'd taken to hanging on the front stoop. Annoying as it was, when the Trainees were around, the Initiates tended to leave us alone.

I craned my neck to look up at her. "Only *you* would say something so corny as *Gloomy Gus*."

"And get away with it." Yasuo winked at Emma, and farm girl actually *giggled*.

I rolled my eyes. "It's only because she knows she could fillet us with that crazy Buck knife of hers."

She glowed from the compliment—as bizarre as it was. "We don't say *fillet*; we say *skin*."

"Okely-dokely, redneck." I leaned back to elbow her in the calves.

I was trying to cheer up for her sake, having spent the past couple weeks moping around. Since the thing at the beach, both Ronan and Amanda had been acting distant.

To cope, I dove one hundred percent into my studies. Forget German business etiquette—I was ready for the freaking United Nations.

Once Alcántara had seen I'd mastered the business stuff, he asked me to review my Old High German. Not only had I done that, but I had brushed up on my Latin, too. I'd even become halfway decent at the waltz. Nonetheless, I was desperate to know why he was forcing me to focus on such an odd hodge-podge of subjects. I mean, decorum *and* Althochdeutsch? Weird.

The irony was, all of my discipline had put me at the top of Alcántara's teacher's pet list. He was seeking me out more, reviewing my work himself, he'd even alluded to our upcoming mission once or twice. Which didn't do much for the Ronan/Amanda situation—more irony there.

Whatever. I was getting the hell *off* this rock. I was sure of it now. I'd travel off-island with Alcántara and make my escape at some point during our mission.

I'd escape the likes of *Kevin*, the jackass Trainee who'd almost urinated on me, whom I now spotted headed our way. "What's *this* meathead want?" I grumbled under my breath.

"Yo," Yas called to him.

I shot my friend a dirty look. "Do you have to be friendly with *everyone*?"

"That's just how I roll, Blondie." Yas had spoken the words to me but hadn't taken his eyes from Kevin, whom he greeted with a lazy nod of his head.

Kevin joined us, and to my surprise, he looked a tad nervous when he caught my eye. I gave him an evil smile.

"Whatcha got?" Yasuo asked, referring to the large rectangular box in Kevin's hands. "You bringing D. here a peace offering?" He guffawed in that dopey way boys have perfected through the ages.

"Actually, it *is* for Acari Drew." Kevin walked up the few stairs to hand it to me. If I was surprised before, I was floored now. I took it from him, but my blood froze when he added, "With regards from Master Alcántara."

Kevin and Yas proceeded to make lame chitchat, which I completely ignored, aware only of the box in my lap. It was long but not too heavy, like a coat box. Emma and I exchanged our WTF looks.

Kevin left—*finally*—and Yasuo asked, "Are you going to open it?"

Emma scooted down a few stairs to sit next to me. "I bet it's her dress."

Yas turned to me. "You haven't gotten yours yet?"

"What are you talking about?" I looked between them, settling my frown on Yasuo. "And what do *you* know about dresses?"

"Everyone's getting dresses," Emma said. "They're issuing them for the dance."

"Farm girl got hers this morning." Yas had an appreciative gleam in his eyes that irked me.

Emma was the closest thing to a bestie that I had on this

island—shouldn't *I* be the one she turned to for dress chat? I gave him an incredulous look. "How do *you* know?"

"I saw her on the quad after she got it."

He and Emma shared a look, and it made me feel even more alienated than before. I knew they had it for each other, so why didn't they just come out and tell me? I *was* their best friend after all. I could be trusted.

It felt like Noah's ark around here, everyone pairing two by two, while the only person who seemed to have the hots for me wasn't even a *person*. Scratch that. Alcántara didn't have the hots for me so much as he was jonesing for a taste of my blood.

I'd flirted with a vampire, and he'd flirted back. I was so screwed. It sucked to be me—pun intended.

I placed my hands flat on the top of the box. It felt like a thousand pounds on my lap.

Emma gave one of her stoic shrugs. "I don't think it means anything."

"Maybe it's because you're his favorite," Yas teased in a singsongy voice.

I gave him a look that could kill. "You shut up, or next time we're on the dance floor, I'm stomping on you with my fancy new stiletto heels."

"I'd like to see you try, shortie." He nodded at my package. "Well? You gonna open it or not?"

The box was a nice one, thick cardboard covered in shiny gold fabric, just as I imagined an old-fashioned hatbox might be. I slipped the lid off.

But I slammed it shut again. There was indeed a dress inside . . . with a rose on top.

"What?" Yas reached for it, and I held it out of his reach. "What's your problem? Can't hide nothing from us, girlie."

"There's . . ." I opened it again, just a peek. "There's a flower."

Emma nudged the lid farther. "A rose."

The petals were like lush suede, and a red so deep they looked almost black. Thorns covered it, like sharp, deep purple claws emerging from the long stem.

"Dude." Yas inched away from me.

"I didn't get a flower," Emma said, sitting more still than usual beside me.

I thought, *Yeah, I'll bet*, but my mouth was too dry to say it.

Careful not to snag its thorns on the fabric, I set it aside to study the dress. It was very red, like the rose.

"My dress is green," Emma said. I must've had *some* expression on my face, because she quickly added, "But the dress is the same. I think they all are. Like a uniform. Except we all have different colors."

"Oh goodie." I shook it out to get a better look. "Mine just happens to be the color of blood."

I had to admit, it *was* pretty, with a satin bodice and a frothy tulle skirt that looked about knee length. "I suppose there are worse things than looking like a slutty ballerina. But . . . crap. It's strapless." I held it up to my chest. "It's not as though I have anything to hold it up with." I shot a nod to Yas, realizing I'd gone to a place normally reserved only for girl talk. "Sorry."

Putting a brave look on his face, he said, "Fret not, little D. It stays up."

"Wait." My hands flopped back into the box, crumpling the dress. "You saw Emma's dress?"

They shared another look, and this time it was obvious. It was a *look* look.

"That's it." I crammed it *and* the rose in the box and stood abruptly. "I can't deal with this without food. I just need to drop *this thing* in my room."

There was an awkward moment of silence. A few students walked by, headed in the direction of the dining hall, and Yasuo suddenly looked eager to join them. "I'll just see you ladies there. Give you some girl time, you know?"

"Yeah, sure," I replied, but then I spun on Emma the moment we were inside. "How does *he* know how your dress fits?"

"I . . . tried it on. He wanted me to stand in the window so he could see."

"What is this—an eighties teen-angst movie? Since when is *Yasuo* standing under your window?" My reaction was selfish and irrational, but still, I couldn't help getting stormy. Yas and Emma were having secret interludes, and the realization stung. I unlocked my door, tossed in the detested dress, and shut it again. "Did you guys hook up? Why didn't you tell me?"

She turned that true beet red that only redheads managed. "Of course not."

"If you guys want to get together, you should get together already." I headed back down the stairs, feeling low and left out.

Emma caught up to me on the landing. Her face bore a horrible combination of agitated and anxious. I mean, she was *distraught*, as if I'd just told her there was a bomb in the building and she had two minutes to defuse it or a roomful of kittens would die in the blast, all because of her.

It stopped me in my tracks. I'd known there was a spark between her and Yasuo, but was it more than that? "Oh. My. God. You like Yasuo. Like, *like* like."

I think her face actually turned a shade of purple. "Yes . . . I . . . *really* like him."

"Wow. Prairie girl meets gangster's son."

It made sense. She was so reserved and introverted, whereas Yasuo was just the opposite. He was easy to the point of doofiness, but nice, too, and it'd drawn Emma out of her shell. Some guys would feel uncomfortable with such a strong, stoic girl, but Yasuo's big personality made her quirks seem like no big deal.

I considered how much *he'd* be interested in *her.* I'd noticed him watching Emma when she wasn't looking. He'd grown up with his mom and had managed to remain down-to-earth despite living in hiding in the belly of Los Angeles, which to me spoke volumes about his mother. He didn't talk about her a lot, but they must've been close. I imagined she might've been as pure and true as Emma.

I burst into a smile. "Just . . . wow. I can totally see it." I nudged her shoulder in mock anger. "But why didn't you tell me?"

She nearly crumpled with relief. "I was afraid. . . ."

"Of *Yas*?"

"No." She paused, mouth open, hesitating. "Of you."

That knocked the wind from me. "Me?"

"Yes. Of how you'd react. Since we're all friends." She was looking nervous again.

I felt like a heel. "Seriously?"

She nodded slowly.

"Aw, hell, Em, I am so sorry." I gave her a quick hug, then held on to her shoulders as I searched her face. "How could you think that? Are you kidding? I'd be totally thrilled if you and Yas hooked up."

A pair of blond Acari walked into the dorm—Margaret and Nance, an annoying couple of fitness hounds we'd nicknamed Mancy—and we shut up.

I nodded toward the door. "Come on."

Had Emma really been afraid of my reaction? Could she really think I'd begrudge her happiness? Once safely outside, I ranted, "Jeez, Emma. How could you think I wouldn't be supportive? If you can find someone on this rock? If you could be even a *little* happy? Oh my God, I'd be thrilled for you." I shook my head, marveling at my own flaws. "How could you think I wouldn't be? Clearly, I am the crappiest friend ever."

"You're a good friend," Emma said, which for her was downright effusive. "A wonderful friend."

"Apparently not." Then, seeing the tentative expression on her face, I added, "I can see you're still thinking. Spit it out."

"Well," she hedged, "you've been kind of . . . off. And then you kept looking at us funny. I didn't want to bother you with it."

She was right—I guess I had been giving them the stink eye. But it wasn't for the reasons she thought. "If something bothered me, it was feeling like I was the last to know." I stopped, looking around to make sure nobody was within earshot. "Please. You have to promise not to hold out on me. I know you're the strong, silent type, but seriously, Em, you can confide in me. How could you even doubt that?"

"Okay, I promise to tell you everything."

I pretended disgust. "Good God, not everything!"

She gave me a smile, and that heart-shaped face of hers lit up—she was so pretty when she smiled. "I'm just not used to the whole friend thing, I guess."

"That makes two of us." I linked my arm with hers, and I wasn't sure which amazed me more—her news or the fact that I was walking arm in arm with a friend. "Wow," I repeated after a moment. "You and Yas, huh?"

She halted, and alarm obliterated her smile. "Don't say anything to him. I don't think . . . I'm not sure he's interested."

"Oh, Em." I tugged her forward and had to laugh at her innocence. "He's a guy. He's interested. Duh."

I could see by her frown that she wasn't completely satisfied by that answer, but it was the best one I had. We slowly walked to lunch, and I did my best to help her replay old conversations, interpret comments, strategize interludes, all that. And though I wasn't exactly a genius when it came to matters of the heart, I was a good friend—really, I was.

And yet, all the while I couldn't help but think, so much for asking advice about *my* stuff. This was Emma's big crush moment—like a female rite of passage—and I didn't want to steal her thunder. Because bringing up ancient vampires sure would step on a girl's buzz.

See, I'd *wanted* to confide about Alcántara—how he was treating me like his favorite, and what the rose might mean, and what would happen when we left the island and were alone together, and what did it mean that I was feeling more comfortable with him and was that just a dangerous illusion. But how could I broach any of *that* when she was all starry-eyed for Yasuo? So I decided to put my problems off. For now.

We got to the dining hall, and Emma automatically went to where Yas was sitting. It happened to be with Ronan and Amanda.

Great.

I chose the lunch line instead, wondering how quickly I could shove the food down my throat and make a break for it.

Someone walked up behind me. *"Gidday"* was a whisper in my ear.

*Josh.*

I looked behind my shoulder at him. "You sure are friendly now that Lilac's out of the picture."

I'd thought my sarcastic tone would take the sting from my words, but—*wow*—he actually looked kind of hurt.

"I've always been friendly. It's you who's the ice queen."

Ice queen really hadn't been my intention—it was just how things came out of my mouth sometimes. Maybe *that* was the problem with my love life.

I put my tray down to give him my full attention, making an effort to be charming and *warm*. "Oh, I see. That you and Lilac were attached at the hip wasn't your fault. Because you can't help it that girls fall all over you."

He grinned at that. "Exactly. That's me—ever at ease with the ladies." With an encouraging look on his face, he spread his arms wide. "So?"

Josh was a guy. And he was flirting. A little. With me.

I wondered if he might be someone I could be interested in. Then I gave a shake to my head. I needed to get a hold of myself. Alcántara hadn't liked Josh's concern for me, and I definitely didn't want to be putting any boys in danger with any vampires. So even if I were remotely interested—and who wouldn't be? I mean, premed, scruffy, *and* an accent?—it was a nonstarter. I just couldn't do that to the guy.

I picked my tray back up. "No way, bucko. Jury's still out on you."

The words were harsh, but I'd said them with a wink. I was learning.

I joined the others at the table just as Tracer Judge did—now there was a guy. He'd been my phenomena teacher last term. Cute, with floppy hair and warm, puppy dog eyes. A what-you-see-is-what-you-get sort of guy.

"Acari Drew, I haven't seen you around." He sounded genuinely pleased to see me.

"She's been busy with Alcántara," Amanda said in a flat voice.

My smile faded a bit at the barb. "I'm still alive," I told him, ignoring her comment as best I could. "Despite Master Dagursson's best efforts at dancing me to death. I've been spending a lot of time with Alcántara, too. But I have to." I shot her a look. "Our mission is next month."

"No idea where you're going yet?" Yas asked over a mouthful of stew. Now *there* was someone who could do with some etiquette training.

"None." I took a swig of blood from my little crystal shooter, and a shiver rolled over me. The cold drink had grossed me out at first—all thick and viscous, the color of a red jewel—but now the taking of it was a deeply pleasant sensation.

The table had grown silent, and I couldn't figure out why. Well, I knew partly why. Yas and Emma were quietly in their own world, cutting their eyes at each other. Only now it no longer annoyed me—it was novel and exciting to be privy to their burgeoning relationship. I felt like an anthropologist. Or a friend.

It was really the Ronan/Amanda/Judge triumvirate that made the table hum with tension. It seemed to me they were making it uncomfortable for everyone. And to think it'd been so nice to see good old benign Tracer Judge.

Ronan blurted, "I have to go." He stood and exchanged a weighty nod with Amanda.

Then Amanda stood, too—*surprise, surprise.* "So do I."

I put my fork down, tired of all the secrets. Couldn't people just say what was going on in their lives? Lately it felt as if my friends wouldn't tell me anything if I didn't drag the information out of them.

As Ronan and Amanda left, I decided to spy on them. I shoveled stew into my mouth, crammed a hard roll into my pocket, and wasn't far behind them. Keeping a safe distance, I followed, certain I would catch them in the act.

Confronting Emma about her crush on Yasuo had taken a tremendous weight off my shoulders. It felt good to talk about things instead of being on the outside looking in. I'd find Ronan and Amanda and talk to them, too. They'd know that I knew about them, and maybe this tension would ease a little.

I trailed them as best I could, which was pretty well, if I said so myself. All that intense training was good for something—I was a regular James Bond.

But then something unexpected happened. I hid behind a hedge along the path, watching as they reached the Acari dorm. And then, without even a hug between them, they said good-bye, and Amanda went inside.

Had they fought? Were they just being discreet? They weren't acting as I imagined lovers normally acted.

I jogged to catch up to Ronan as he picked up the trail to the coast. But why there? He didn't have his surfboard or his wet suit, so he wasn't going for a swim.

And why didn't he just drive? He was one of the few people who had the use of the campus SUVs. Did it mean he went somewhere he didn't want people to know about?

He walked, and I followed, and just as I was beginning to think it a fool's errand—my luck he'd turn on me, shout, *Gotcha*, and make me do water drills—he walked right by the beach, taking a tiny path I'd never seen before.

And then he headed inland, toward the other side of the island.

I didn't think twice. I followed.

# CHAPTER SEVENTEEN

A nd then he left the trail, and I did think twice.

*Don't stray from the path*—it was one of the main-stays of the vampire rule book. Nerves tensed my muscles, tightening my stride. I'd become hardwired to follow the rules, because with them came survival.

Ronan had also warned me to stay away from the far side of the island. Could that be where he was headed? Was he going to see his family?

Maybe I was just desperately curious for a glimpse of the real Ronan. And maybe, somewhere in the back of my mind, I considered myself safe from trouble—that if it came down to it, I'd be protected by Alcántara. Whatever the reason, though it was stupid and reckless, I followed.

The farther inland we went, the trickier it got. I was able to see him from quite a distance—it was crazy, but this whole episode made me realize just how much my vision had improved since drinking the blood. Even so, there were few trees and fewer rocks, and I was intermittently forced to let Ronan slip out of sight lest he spot me.

Finally, I had to put more distance between us. The landscape had become too barren, all gravel and flat plateaus as opposed to the crags and cliffs of the shoreline.

But Tracer Judge had covered rudimentary fieldcraft in last term's phenomena class. I knew how to track, and how to avoid being tracked myself. Following Ronan thus far, I'd relied on some basic techniques. It was time to see just how much I'd learned.

I scanned the dirt for what Judge called a *track trap*—an area in the terrain that lent itself to marks. Marshy ground, mud—anything that held a footprint. In my case, it was gravel.

And there I saw it, up ahead, a particularly gritty spot. Ronan's footprints were easy to detect. There were faint depressions in the terrain with hints of damp—dark streaks among light gray—representing bits of gravel recently displaced.

I squatted to study the prints. The wind was up, and these tracks would fade by the end of the day. If it'd been sunny, the telltale dark patches wouldn't have lasted more than a couple hours.

I followed due northwest. Every once in a while I lost his trail but always managed to pick it up again. And then something changed. I squatted again, studying.

There was a new pattern, visible only in the deeper patches of grit. His toes were digging more sharply into the terrain, with halos of gravel exploding from the heel. Ronan had begun to jog.

I began to jog, too, tamping down a spurt of nerves. Why had he upped his pace? Did he sense someone was following him? Did he know it was me?

Or maybe he was just eager. He'd given Amanda a key. Maybe he was running to her, to their secret rendezvous.

The footprints changed again, deeper, cutting hard to the right. He'd changed direction, due northeast. Back to the water.

I dug my thumb in the soil to check the depth and dampness, to see if it was telling a true story. Because the tracks told me he was running now.

I ran eastward following him, and the landscape got hilly again, bringing more boulders and crags with it. Cold prickled the back of my neck. A sensation nagged me—I felt watched.

My imagination, I told myself. Refusing to bow to nerves, I looked around. Sure enough, I was alone. I felt silly that I'd even let my head go there.

And then I cursed myself. I'd lost his trail. I knew better than to let emotion or imagination overwhelm me. It'd been lesson number one: Don't lose control.

Had I lost Ronan for good? Suddenly, I felt so alone, and with the solitude came a burst of irrational panic. There were aspects to tracking I hadn't mastered, such as determining the age of a print. Maybe I'd been following a trail that was laid weeks ago. Maybe I'd never been following him in the first place.

The boulders were getting taller the closer I approached the northeastern edge of the island. It was a place I'd never seen before, far from campus, far from the southern edge where I'd spotted those houses from Ronan's boat.

The path had grown so jagged, I didn't know what lay around each bend. I was freaking and ran too recklessly, my eyes glued to the ground, scanning desperately for his trail. Before, I'd wanted to track him, but now I just didn't want to be alone. When I looked up, I spotted him. Too close.

"Oh crap." I skittered to a halt, dropping and rolling behind a low rock, my heart in my throat.

I peeked back around, but Ronan hadn't seen me. Patches of scrubby grass grew in the shadow of the rocks, and it looked foreign amidst all the gray. Beyond, the ground seemed simply to end, a straight drop to the sea, which was a steely haze on the horizon. He'd slowed to a brisk walk, no longer running. And who wouldn't, navigating along the edge of a cliff?

But then he disappeared over the ledge, and I gasped. I scuffled as close as I could, and I spotted him, picking his way down a hidden path, winding down the granite face.

My eyes were playing tricks on me. The skies of the Dimming lent an eerie sort of light, and I squinted to make sense of the ragged rocks, mud, and what tufts of greenery were tenacious enough to cling to the steep, windswept cliff face.

I couldn't get any closer without being discovered, but I stared until the white and gray haze burnt into my vision. And then he simply vanished.

It was the only reason I saw the cave.

I scrambled to the edge on hands and knees. Scrubbing my hand over my eyes, I peered again. His trail had narrowed—by the cave mouth, it was no more than a ledge. The cave itself was no more than a black smudge on the rock face. Its height was hard to judge from this distance, and although it was obviously large enough to fit Ronan, he'd had to bend to enter.

He stayed in there forever.

The sky was unchanging, but the wind picked up, and my belly quickly leached its warmth into the cold, gritty ground. I rubbed my hands together, trying to chafe warmth into them.

I debated returning to campus, but curiosity won in the end, and I stayed. Besides, I was a little scared of whatever might be lying in wait out there—I didn't want Ronan to discover me, but I didn't want to stray too far from him, either. I focused only on the cave mouth, forcing my mind to go blank—if I treated this as a meditative exercise, maybe the cold wouldn't be so numbing, my nerves so frayed, and my position so uncomfortable.

A lighter color emerged from the black. I thought my tired eyes might be playing tricks, so I blinked hard and squinted again. But it was Ronan, exiting the cave.

And he wasn't alone. It wasn't Amanda, either—I could tell by the height.

It was another man, hunched in the mouth of the cave. Wearing a long, hooded cloak, he looked like an apparition of death. A chill rippled my skin. That cloak whipped in the wind, the movement the only thing assuring me he wasn't just a figment of my imagination. But then the figure vanished back into the rock face, leaving me wondering if I'd ever really seen him.

I needed to get up and go, to conceal myself so Ronan wouldn't catch me. But I was frozen in place, deeply unsettled, and distracted.

It meant I didn't hear the thing breathing behind me.

# CHAPTER EIGHTEEN

Months of grueling combat training kicked in, and the moment I heard rustling, I rolled. Something landed beside me with a thump, and I skittered sideways, spinning onto my knees to face it.

A Draug.

Panic hammered in my chest. I'd kept my distance from Ronan, but now all I wanted was for him to find me. I didn't want to be alone.

I had been right. Something *had* been watching me. There were *things* hiding among the rocks—hungry things.

Like the Draug that'd attacked Emma and me, this creature had been human once, a man who hadn't survived the vampiric process. It'd have the superhuman strength and speed of the undead but also the primal nature of a rabid animal.

But instead of emaciated, this Draug was swollen, like a drowned corpse. I could make out features amidst the greens and blacks of rotted skin. There were tufts of matted red hair beneath layers of filth. It was the red hair that made me cry out, my tone sharp and keening. This had been a *person*.

It prowled toward me on all fours, and I inched away. The smell of it filled my head. It stank even worse than the last one. Fouler than the foulest primordial dung heap, it *stank*. My stomach convulsed, and I covered my mouth, choking back a gag.

I backed away some more, until I heard the distant clack of pebbles as my foot met open air. "No," I cried out, my voice sharp and manic. If I slipped from the ledge, my body would tumble and bounce, crashing onto the rocky seashore, one hundred feet below.

The creature stopped. Studied me with a tilted head. Sniffed the air.

"Shit shit shit," I whispered, watching as the thing sized me up.

I was trembling violently from the initial adrenaline dump, and I imagined my heart slowing, my breath elongating. I crept sideways, away from the edge and the creature.

But its eyes tracked me with a disturbingly human expression. Its face was bloated and its tongue swollen, but not so much that I couldn't see humanity there. I knew with chilling certainty that this Draug had died young.

"What do you want?" I demanded, though I knew the thing wouldn't answer me. It just kept prowling closer, while I kept edging away.

But it didn't strike. It simply studied me, as though I were just beyond recognition. The inaction was freaking me out more than the attack had.

"What are you?" My voice sounded hysterical, and I checked myself. *Calm.* This thing was staring at me—did it have rational thought, too? I measured my tone. "*Who* were you?"

It didn't like that. With a feral jerk of its body, it hopped to its feet. I shrieked.

The Draug walked just along the ledge, not caring about the drop—its eyes were only for me. I glanced from it, to the ledge, and back again, deciding there was no way to shove the thing over without falling myself.

It prowled closer, like a wildcat about to pounce. Whatever humanity I'd seen on its face was gone. The only thing in its eyes now was bloodlust.

It bounded for me, and I dodged it, jogging backward and reaching for my throwing stars. Thank God I'd worn my boots with my weapon of choice tucked in them. Last time I faced a Draug, I'd stupidly gone out unarmed. I rarely did *that* anymore, if I could help it.

Keeping my eyes glued to the monster, I slipped my fingers into the makeshift holster at my calf and touched them: four shuriken stars. I pulled them out, keeping my movements slow and smooth. I palmed them—my coldly perfect, reassuringly sharp, best-friend-forever steel.

The temptation was great to throw like a maniac. But I held still. Watcher Priti had taught me this. Cool deliberation. Monklike focus. *I am roots in the earth. I am water that flows. I am grounded. I am Watcher.*

I threw. My beautiful shuriken struck a perfect landing, sticking in the creature's cheek. But the thing continued to stalk toward me, my star doing a sickening wobble in its flesh.

I backed away. I threw again. My star lodged in its throat. And yet still the thing kept coming.

"I am grounded. I am Watcher." But I *wasn't* a Watcher, not yet. And I worried I was no longer quite so grounded, either.

I had two stars left, one in each hand. I tightened my grip, and the razor-sharp steel cut into my fingers, but they were a part of me, and I didn't care.

Where to target? Other words came to me. *A stake through the heart does them in.* There were no throwing stars in that sentence. I didn't have a weapon to impale it. Surely there was another way to destroy a Draug.

It bared its teeth ever so slightly, the upper lip curling, trembling, revealing a mouthful of disturbingly white teeth. And a pair of fangs—they were small.

*A Trainee.* Or what was left of one.

My stomach lurched. This had been a boy, a teenager like me. I forced the thought from my head. His young fangs were no less deadly.

I had to do something. I targeted the left side of its chest. Maybe if I threw hard enough, I could nick the heart. I raised my hand to throw.

It leapt then. So fast. Too fast.

Before I could act, the monster had its arms around me, squeezing. Nails like talons sliced into me. Impressions flooded me—the sound of fabric tearing, a blast of cold, and then the warmth of my own blood, pulsing from my body, streaming down my forearm and at the small of my back.

The Draug grunted, a throaty, squealing sound, like a stuck pig. It shoved me away and jerked its head down, clamping its mouth over the wound on my arm. Its jaws worked spasmodically, trying to get purchase. I pulled away, and its fangs tugged my flesh as I wrenched free, leaving my skin ragged and torn. But its claws were in me again, piercing my upper arms.

*My blood.* I saw my blood running down the Draug's face, watched that swollen tongue lick its lips clean, and I heard myself scream, the sound a hollow echo in my brain. The creature came at me again, hungry for my bloodied flesh.

*My stars.* I still had two stars. I wrestled one arm free and stabbed the monster. I'd aimed for the heart, but its face got in the way, and I slashed at the cheek instead, ripping it. The skin hung open, dangling from its jaw like something in a bad zombie movie. The thing let loose a terrifying sound, a growl as if it were the devil himself I'd angered.

The Draug swatted my hand, and the star flew from my grip. Tears stung my eyes, fear paralyzing me. The creature looked bloated and useless, but sheer, unfathomable strength drove its punch.

Was this how I'd die? I wished Emma were here by my side. I thought how Ronan would find my mangled body. I regretted that most of all.

We grappled, and the only thing that saved me from instant death was my size. I was tiny and wily in its bloated arms, but despite my desperate wriggling, I couldn't manage to slip completely free.

I felt its fingers in my hair, yanking hard, craning back my neck, immobilizing me.

The Draug let go, but sweet relief was cut short when it grabbed my ear instead. It pulled until the skin tore at the seam, and that catalyzed me. It was such an odd thing to focus me—so specific, so surreal. But I was *not* going to lose an ear.

I still held one star. I couldn't stake the Draug with it. But I could blind the thing.

I gripped the star hard, till I felt blood pool in my palm, and then I slashed at its eyes, and again, until there was a sickening pop, and blue drained from the Draug's eye, drizzling down its cheek, a revolting indigo in the twilight.

With a roar, it threw itself into me, raging and feral, all power and wild fury. We went flying. My back crashed onto the ground, and the thing slammed on top of me. It began to squeeze. I wiggled, but the Draug had me pinned tight. It was suffocating me, crushing me, stealing the air from my chest until my ribs creaked. And then there was a hideous snap, followed by a stabbing so sharp, so intense, it stole all thought from my brain. A rib.

I gasped for air, struggling, but there was no getting free. There was no fighting anymore. My vision started to dim. The thing wanted to kill me, and I couldn't stop it. I would die.

Was dying.

I heard myself call out nonsensical things, crying "No," over and over, until just the one word stretched into a single, pathetic wail.

But then the thing lifted up, stiffening. Its eyes shot open, and its body convulsed. Sludge like black tar spewed from its mouth. Screaming through my blinding pain, I skittered backward, free of the monster.

Only then did I see Ronan.

# CHAPTER NINETEEN

⸻

Ronan stood over me. Ronan had killed the beast.

Our eyes met and held for an eternity. I panted in staccato breaths, but my chest was so tight, I thought I might suffocate under the pressure. My breathing was shallow. I was certain I'd broken a rib, but had I punctured a lung, too? I wondered if I might drown in my own blood.

His expression was so grave. Would he yell? Surely he'd guessed I'd been spying on him. Would I die, knowing only this excruciating pain and Ronan's anger?

But he didn't scold; instead, he knelt before me. "Ann." He grabbed me to him, but his hold was gentle, and I felt the tug of his fingers in my hair as he cradled my head in his chest. His Scottish accent came out thick and guttural. "Ach, girl. You're a powerful wee thing." He stroked my hair, and I wondered if his tenderness was because I was dying. "You'll get yourself killed someday."

"Someday?" Did it mean I wasn't dying? My chest spasmed, trying to get enough air. Tears ran hot down my face, but it wasn't because I was crying. My body had taken over.

"Steady on now. You're going into shock." He put a hand at my back to support me and ran his other along my torso, his fingers moving over each rib, his touch gentle but firm. He didn't watch as he did it; rather, his eyes stared blindly into the distance in intense concentration. "I need to make certain you're in one piece."

He grazed a spot on my lower right side, and I flew about an inch off the ground. I yelped. "Hurts."

"Be still." His tone was stern, but I saw the concern clear on his brow. "If a rib has snapped in two, it could pierce an organ."

That stilled me, all right.

He used his thumb now, drawing along the edge of the rib. The pain was so unbearable, I wondered if I might faint from it. I bit my lips to not make a sound, but tears ran unbidden down my face.

He squeezed my shoulder. "Breathe."

Each breath was an agony, and now I was scared if I inhaled, I'd puncture a lung. I shivered uncontrollably, trying to shake my head but quivering too hard to do so.

He rubbed my arm. "Breathe," he ordered. "*Now*. In and out."

My chest was too tight. The gray sky grew dimmer, and distantly I registered how odd the light became as darkness closed around my vision. But still I took only tiny sips of air— the pressure across my ribs was too great. My ears began to buzz.

"Annelise." His tone was unforgiving. "Stay with me."

He gave me a quick shake, and I inhaled sharply then, crying out with the stab of pain. I hunched over, leaning into it. I made unintelligible sounds—it hurt so badly.

But I was breathing regularly again, and the world became clear again. My scalp and lips prickled with cold, like numbed parts returning to life.

"Now keep breathing," he said.

I did, and I found my voice, too, complaining between breaths, "But . . . it hurts."

"Hush. I need to make sure the lung wasn't punctured." He put his hand near my mouth. "Exhale. When a lung collapses, air goes in but doesn't come out."

I did as he told me, afraid to do otherwise. Biology was hideous enough; *my* biology was unthinkable.

"No," he said, "your lungs are good."

Simply hearing that my lungs were intact eased my chest until my sips of air slowly elongated into longer, steadier inhales.

His eyes went to my bloodied arm. "But this . . ." He gently took my arm, turning it this way and that. Then, scooting back, he peeled off his black sweater.

He kept a slim wooden stake strapped to his left forearm. I imagined the stake that currently protruded from the Draug's back had once been attached to Ronan's *right* arm.

But then my eyes went to his shirt, a plain white cotton tee. I could see the planes of his chest and the faint shadow and texture of hair running in a line down his chest.

"What—?" *What are you doing?* I wanted to ask, but I couldn't finish the thought, because Ronan had begun to strip off his undershirt, too.

My cheeks blazed hot, and I looked away, then back again. But he'd slipped his sweater back on and had begun to tear the white cotton T-shirt into strips. He worked silently, and I wondered if he was as self-conscious about all this as I was.

"We need to stop the bleeding," he explained.

"Of course," I stammered. "It's okay. Since drinking the blood, I've been clotting quickly."

"It's not your healing I worry about. It's your scent." He met my eyes, looking grave. "The blood will call the others."

"You mean I'd be bait?" I gave a nervous laugh. "Like chumming for sharks?"

But he answered in all seriousness, "Precisely like that."

He wound the strip around my arm. The fabric was still warm from his body, and ironically it gave me a shiver. He knotted it off and pulled me to standing, supporting me for a moment at the elbows.

His hands went to my face, cupping it. I held my breath again, but this time for an entirely different reason. His eyes were so green and so deeply locked with mine, but I didn't for a second think he was doing his hypnotic thing. I knew in my heart, in this moment there were just the two of us—no magic, no vampires, no compulsion—just Ronan and me. Not taking his eyes from mine, he tenderly smudged the tears from my cheeks. The gesture cracked my heart as surely as my rib had been.

But then he thumbed some foul sludge from my cheek and wiped it on his pants. I drooped. Of course. It *was* Ronan and me—Tracer and Acari. So much for our moment.

"Can you walk?" he asked.

I managed one step and then another. I hunched to the

right, curling into the pain, but I was mobile. "Yeah," I said, a little surprised at myself. "I can."

He nodded. "Lying down is more painful than walking."

I frowned at that.

"Don't worry," he added, with a sarcastic gleam in his eye. "The worst is always the second day."

Now I really frowned at him. "I think you're happy I got hurt."

He ignored that. For now. "You'll need to massage the muscles to keep them from hardening up."

He bent over the Draug's body, retrieving our weapons and calmly pulling them out as if he were carving the Thanksgiving turkey. Black sludge had puddled around the monster's head and oozed from the stake wound. "Others will come soon, drawn to the smell."

Ronan's jostling made more of that tarry crap seep from the body, and I held a hand over my nose and mouth. "The smell? They can probably smell this in Iceland."

"A Draug is rotting. It carries diseases. How do you think it'd smell?" He grabbed a clump of coarse grass and cleaned my stars and his stake, then offered my weapons back. "They'll need a more thorough cleaning when you get back."

"Gross," I murmured, although I was thrilled I wasn't the one who'd done the initial scrub. The gore really was thick like tar, looking all gummy and bubbly.

"Now," he said, "we've got to get out of here."

I spun on my heel, gritting my teeth through the pain. "You don't have to tell me twice." I wasn't eager to meet whatever creatures there were that'd actually be *drawn* to such a putrid thing.

With my injury to contend with, our progress was slow, but once we put some distance between us and the corpse, I began to talk. I had questions, yes. But mostly I was worried about whatever lecture Ronan was cooking up for me in his head. Wanting to distract him, I asked, "So there are other Draug on the island?"

He gave a tight nod.

*Okay.* Apparently, he wasn't going to be chatty. But then I began to wonder. . . . "Why do the Draug just roam around waiting to attack *us*? I mean, you'd think they'd just attack and eat *one another.*"

"They long to eat, yes. They need blood to survive. But there's another longing, too. To be near the living."

"I don't know if I needed to hear that." I shook off the creepy, goose bumpy feel *that* that thought had given me. I was glad Ronan had shown up when he had, or I wouldn't have been among the living for much longer. "What was that weapon you used to kill it?"

"I keep these"—he slid the stake from his sleeve—"at all times." He seemed to unclench at the topic of weaponry, and it was a relief.

My curiosity wasn't exactly a stretch, either—his stakes might've been compact, but they were clearly lethal. Did other people have secret weapons stashed away that I didn't know about? More important, did *I* need stakes?

"May I?" I held out a tentative hand and knew a thrilled shiver when, after a pause, he handed it to me. It was long and sharp, with a satisfying heft. I was surprised to realize it was carved of wood. "Cool."

"So it is."

"Did you make it yourself?"

He hesitated, then gave a sharp nod. "Aye. Though it's not something I generally discuss."

So they were *secret* stakes. And of course they would be. Vampires wouldn't want to think about non-vampires roaming around bearing anti-vampire weaponry. The secrecy lit a fuse inside, and I was desperate to know everything. "Is it a special kind of wood? And where did you get it on *this* island, anyway?" With the isle's scant, scrubby greenery, a stake chiseled from granite seemed a far easier thing to come by.

"There's material to be found," he said. "If you look."

Questions flooded my mind, and I knew my eyes must've burnt bright with them. "Does it *have* to be wood?" I thought of all the old myths. "Like *Dracula*—a wooden stake in the heart?"

Reluctantly, he shook his head. "You're right that only impaling and beheading destroy them for good. As for the material, anything works if the force behind it is great enough. Wood, steel, iron—whatever you have that can do the job."

I hefted the stake in my hand. It definitely didn't feel very substantial—it rather reminded me of an oversized pencil. "I'd think you'd have one in steel."

"And where would I get steel, Annelise? The vampires don't exactly *issue* such things." He snatched it back and returned it up the sleeve of his sweater. "Besides, wood isn't picked up by metal detectors."

That shut me up. Why would he need to travel with stakes if the monsters were *here*? What would happen if a vampire discovered them? And, seriously, why did he need them, *really*? Had *he* ever considered escaping?

But I could never ask that—knowing Ronan, he'd see right through me to guess at my own objective. Instead, I chose the most banal of my questions. "Why wouldn't the vamps want you to have it? Can't you just say it's to protect you from the Draug?"

"They believe the way for humans to stay safe is to remain under their purview."

I watched avidly as he settled them back at his forearms, thinking of all the homegrown weaponry *I* could make. If I were really going to escape, chances were good I'd need more than just throwing stars and my wits to survive.

I'd be on the lookout for the right kind of wood. When the time came, I could borrow Emma's Buck knife to shape and sharpen. "I'm totally going to whittle myself a stake."

"You'll *totally* do no such thing. And you won't be speaking of it to anyone, either. If the vampires were to discover you bore a weapon that *they* didn't give you, they'd turn and use it on you. You must promise me you'll forget we had this conversation."

I gave him a reluctant nod, though the seed had been planted.

His tone of voice had said he was done with *that* topic, but his frown told me he was working up to another. Not wanting the reprimand I knew he owed me, I shifted gears—fast.

"How do you know all that medical stuff?" I asked. "Like binding wounds. And checking breathing. And how you felt me . . . for broken ribs." I'd meant it innocently, but stupid, hormonally challenged me stammered after the *felt me* part of that sentence. *Idiot.*

But he didn't seem to notice. Instead, he answered in a flat tone, "You'll get that in combat first aid, next semester."

Ronan had grown tenser the closer we got to campus, his voice duller, and by the time we reached the quad, he was strung tight as a violin string. My lecture still hadn't come, which was odd.

Something felt wrong, and then it struck me. More vampires than usual were milling around the quad. They glided down stairs, drifted from buildings, materialized from the trees, their elegant gait making it look as though they floated rather than walked.

"The blood," Ronan murmured to me. "They scent your injury."

Master Dagursson emerged from the Arts Pavilion as we passed. "Acari Drew. What has happened?" His faux concern didn't fool me—I knew he'd slice and dice me for a midnight snack if but given the opportunity.

What I'd done struck me then, truly struck me. I'd gone off the path—way off the path. I'd followed a teacher without his knowledge. I'd traveled to a forbidden part of the island. I'd broken every rule in the book.

My stomach turned to ice as I realized maybe Master Dagursson might just get a chance at his midnight snack after all. Because surely I was in for some disciplining now.

How to begin to explain? My mind raced, trying to formulate my answer.

But Ronan spoke up before I had a chance to. "Sparring accident," he said, his voice flatter and colder than I'd ever heard it. "I took Acari Drew to do some extra credit work. We were practicing our throws, and she landed on a rock, hurting her back and slicing her arm."

I shut my mouth not to gape. Ronan had lied. For *me*.

Which meant we shared a secret. Two secrets, if you counted knowledge of his hidden stakes. Which meant he trusted me.

It was a shift that implied other, more dire and complicated things. But what those things might be, I couldn't fathom.

# CHAPTER TWENTY

I'd chosen the lawn in front of the gymnasium for shuriken practice. My run-in with the Draug had been a wake-up call—I needed to be as good and as prepared as I could be at all times. My rib had a hairline crack just to the right of my sternum, but this island was life or death, and injury was nothing more than an excuse. I had enemies, and apparently I had predators, too, and neither would be sympathetic, so despite the screaming pain, I kept at my workout.

The small, outdoor target area was best suited for my twofold purpose. Twofold because, yeah, I wanted to practice throwing my stars, but I also wanted to show off, just a little. I was known as the nerdy girl, and it never hurt to remind the Guidons I was as strong as I was smart.

Ronan emerged from the gym, toweling off his face and neck as he bounded down the stairs. Seeing me, he stopped short. He was still panting from his workout, his cheeks red and clothes sweaty.

Something about this overt display of male vigor set me off kilter, and I babbled in lieu of a greeting. "I don't know how you can bear wearing just a T-shirt in this weather. I mean, I know it's summer and all, and I guess if you were born here—"

"You seem to be healing," he said, cutting me off.

My babbling had sent a fresh spike of pain shooting through my chest, and I cradled my ribs, curling into my right side. "Actually, I feel like I'm dying. But thanks for asking."

He looked around, then stepped closer. "You've recovered well enough to hear what I have to say. Tell me, *Acari Drew*, what part of *Don't leave the path* is unclear?"

Here it came—my lecture. I'd thought I'd dodged that bullet. Silly me had expected the same tender, wound-binding, lie-telling Ronan, but I seemed to be about to enjoy furious-teacher Ronan, instead.

It put up my hackles. "I know the rules."

"You're forbidden from leaving the path."

I was sick of being treated like a naive schoolgirl. I'd won last semester's challenge—check that—I'd *kicked ass* in last se-mester's challenge. I was cool, I was smart, I kept my friends' secrets. Hadn't I earned his respect?

I couldn't help it. I looked around and said innocently, "I *am* on the path."

He looked as if his head might explode. "You know what I mean."

"Hey, I was just following *you*." I wasn't about to mention I'd spied him with the cloaked man—something told me I should keep that little nugget to myself. "You left the path. Surely the vampires wouldn't appreciate *you* wandering all over the place."

The muscles in his jaw clenched tight. I'd hit on something. When Ronan had lied to Master Dagursson about my whereabouts, I'd thought it was because he trusted and wanted to protect me. But now I realized, maybe he'd been protecting himself, too.

"You're a fool." He spoke through gritted teeth, seething with disdain. "I don't know why I expect more. You think you're a maverick, Annelise. That you're above it all. But it was just this sort of recklessness that killed my sister." At the mention of his sister, the fury leached from his voice. "Impetuous, juvenile behavior killed Charlotte, and it'll kill you, too."

"I'm not your sister." My voice was tight with exhaustion—physical *and* emotional. I was angry with him, and now I was sad, too, but it was the anger that won out. I limped to the target, retrieving my throwing stars. "I am *not* juvenile. I've taken care of myself my whole life. At least you had a family—I didn't. You have no idea."

"Is it that you have a death wish?" he asked at my back.

"Don't be ridiculous." I bent to stow my shuriken in my boot, and the movement stole my breath.

"Then you need to stop acting like such a child."

I stood straight at that, forgetting the stabbing pain and meeting his eyes with a glare. "Then stop treating me like one."

Ronan's face went suddenly, utterly blank. His posture stiffened as he looked over my shoulder.

A chill rippled my skin, and I felt a change in the atmospheric energy, as with a coming storm. In the air thickening around me, I felt the vampire's presence.

*Alcántara.* There was only one reason the vampire would show up here, and it was *me.* Ronan looked back at me, and I met his meaningful glare with a smile.

It was as childish as he'd accused, and I knew both feminine triumph as well as deep regret. A part of me knew he was right—I'd made some dumb, impulsive choices, and here I was, yet again stooping to some pretty immature depths.

He said, "Good day, Acari Drew," and there was no warmth in his voice, no old Ronan, no *Annelise.*

Ronan and Alcántara—the two were mutually exclusive. The closer I got to one, the more distant the other became.

My emotions were complicated and unsettling as I watched him walk away. I feared I'd lost a friend but gained a vampire.

But maybe I needed to harden my heart. Amanda had told me herself—there were no allies on this island. And the only judges with final say were the ones with fangs.

I braced myself, putting a poised smile on my face, and turned. "*Buenos días,* Master Alcántara."

*That* pleased him, and I was met by a smile, slow and full of promise. "When we are alone like this, *querida,* you may call me Hugo."

I opened my mouth to say something, but I was speechless. *Hugo?* I was floored. And suddenly very nervous.

He gave a sultry chuckle and put his hand on my shoulder. "Fret not, young one. Think of it as practice. For our upcoming mission. You must accustom yourself to subterfuge. The way of pretending to be someone you are not."

"Hugo, then." My voice was breathy. I was navigating some seriously treacherous terrain.

My ribs were killing me, too, his touch a burden on my shoulder. I forced myself to stand up straight, not to lean into the pain. A new path was one thing, but I wasn't ready to have him ask about my injury. I had a giant, purple bruise on my chest that I imagined would've really floated his boat.

He stepped closer. "Did you like your rose?"

I consciously stayed put, defying every instinct to step back. "I did. Thank you."

"You are like that hothouse flower." He shifted, and my body froze in place as he began to run his hand slowly down my arm. And then I forgot my pain completely, because he was lowering himself to kneel before me. He brushed his hand over my hip, grazing it lightly down my leg, until his fingers came to rest at the top of my boot. He pulled my remaining throwing stars from their holster and stood again before me, stroking the blades. "You, a rose, with these very sharp thorns."

It was too intense. But it was so amazing, too, and flattering, I couldn't help but glow at the attention. Particularly after the disastrous conversation I'd just had with Ronan. As creepy as it was, at least Alcántara didn't treat me like a child. He treated me like a *woman*.

"And your dress?" He held my gaze, and I couldn't look away. His eyes were black and bottomless, and their intensity made me feel as if I were the only person in the world. "Did you like that, too?"

"It was lovely." I let myself bask a moment in his attentions, even though I knew, holding his gaze, sharing his smile, it was reckless. But I let myself believe, just for an instant, that this was normal, that this was merely a guy who liked me and whom I could trust. It wasn't, though, and I couldn't. Alcántara's hypnotic eyes and voice made Ronan's powers of persuasion seem like child's play.

With a modest bow, he swept his arm toward the target, ending our moment. "But I have interrupted your training."

I blinked, gathering my thoughts. "No interruption. I was just finishing up."

He strolled to the tree, fingering the holes in the bull's-eye I'd hung there. "Might I watch you?"

"Certainly." *Not*. Performing under Alcántara's scrutiny was the last thing I wanted. This was my own damned fault, though—I'd been the one who wanted to show off, practicing in public for all and sundry to see.

He still held my stars and studied them. "Such lovely craftsmanship. Did you know shuriken are illegal in many countries? England, for example. They are so small and so lovely, and yet so lethal." He brought one to his face and kept it still as he looked through the points, meeting and holding my gaze. "Much like you, no? Small, lovely, lethal."

What on earth to say to that? "I . . . I try."

"Do not forget, I have seen you fight, *Acarita*. You do more than try. You succeed." He tilted the star, and despite the gray skies, the flawless steel glimmered. When he handed them back to me, our fingers touched, and his skin was nearly as cool as the steel.

"Watcher Priti tells me you have a proclivity for such things," he continued. "More than strength, more than talent, I believe you possess great focus. This is the hardest of all skills, I think."

He looked as if he expected me to say something, but should it be modest or confident? I said carefully, "I imagine it's a lot like meditation."

"Show me." He nodded toward the target. "Show me how focused you can be, practicing before me. Most humans become so discomposed in our presence."

Contrary to what Ronan thought, I wasn't a dumb bunny. I knew there was more going on here than Alcántara simply wanting to check out my skills.

I gathered every nerve I possessed. "Not discomposed at all, I assure you."

I breathed slowly. . . . *I am roots in the earth.* I breathed deeper, and a hot spike of pain impaled me. I gritted my teeth, keeping my expression blank, and made myself hold still as I tried again. I relaxed my diaphragm and exhaled, and it was a struggle not to lean into my cracked rib. I concentrated, using every meditative trick in the book, until finally my mind found a shimmering patch of clarity above the pain.

I connected mentally with the target. . . . *I am grounded.* My surroundings narrowed to the black and white of those concentric circles. I focused on the sound of my blood pumping in my ears, and my world constricted further, till there was nothing left but a fine, black point—the target's center, my only goal. I threw.

*Bull's-eye.*

The urge to laugh broke my concentration, and pain exploded back to the forefront. I gritted myself on the inside, but couldn't stop my hand from holding my right side. I pretended I was just catching my breath rather than cradling my agonized little rib cage.

When I faced him again I was serene and composed, even though what I really wanted to do was jump up and down, clapping giddily. "Shall I throw another?"

He laughed then, and I puffed at the sound. "No, that was quite sufficient, *Acarita*. Watcher Priti was right. You are grace under pressure."

He crossed his arms at his chest, studying me. "I understand certain aspects of the physical training have not been easy for you . . . swimming, calisthenics. And yet you have been dauntless. Bringing a discipline to your studies the other girls envy."

I was envied? The praise made my heart soar, and for a moment I forgot who he was, and that I should be nervous. I forgot, too, that I didn't want to be there. It was such a minor success, but for the flicker of a moment, I felt I'd found my place. That I'd slipped into my groove, discovered my life's meaning. "I enjoy working hard."

He gave me a gratified nod. "It pleases me how thoroughly you've prepared for our mission. And now there is one final subject in which I'd like you to become proficient."

A dumb grin kept trying to plaster itself across my face, but I didn't allow it. Instead, I hung, waiting for his next words. Maybe the ludicrous things I'd been forced to study—the dancing, the etiquette—had been a test of my dedication, and the real learning was about to begin. We were going on a *mission*—did that mean I'd learn about bomb detonation, or wire tapping, or—

"You need to learn table manners," he said.

"I need— *Excuse me?*" My voice warbled in half laughter, half confusion.

But the look on Alcántara's face told me he wasn't joking. "I'm aware of your . . . *impoverished* background. But where we are going, you will need to be familiar with habits of the elite. Would you recognize a fish knife from a butter knife? Do you know that a charger is not merely a plate? Or where to place water and where to place wine at the table?"

I spoke out of turn, but I couldn't help it. We'd gone from throwing stars to talk of table settings—it was too random and baffling. "If we're going out to dinner, can't I just follow everyone else's lead? It's not as if I'll have to waitress or anything."

"On the contrary, Acari Drew. Waitressing is precisely what you will do."

He did *not* just say that. "Wait . . . I'll . . . be a waitress? We're talking about our mission, right?"

His eyes hardened. "You will spend the following week focused only on manners in an intensive decorum session."

More etiquette. I wanted to laugh, or cry, or something. I would have bet the Trainees weren't made to take a rigorous course in *table manners*. It was frustrating and preposterous. But I kept my expression blank. A girl had to do what a girl had to do, and this girl had to stay alive. "I'll begin today."

He smiled again and touched a cool finger to my chin. "Grace, strength, and now humility, too. You have proven yourself."

I frowned, trying to understand. Had I been right? Had all this bizarre subject matter just been a test?

"So perplexed you are." He patted my chin as he gave a patronizing little chuckle. "I am many hundreds of years old, Acari Drew. Do not think yourself the first girl to receive such a command. Many react poorly to such news, while you have proven dependable, with a maturity beyond the others."

*Take that, Ronan.* Alcántara thought I was mature.

But still, his instructions rankled. With nothing better to say, I said the lamest thing ever. "I'll be eighteen on my next birthday."

He laughed outright. "You are ready, I think."

"Ready?" *What now,* I wanted to moan. *Housekeeping?* Talking to this guy was like riding a roller coaster.

"To hear about our mission. Because I will tell you a secret, *querida.* There are other vampires out there. And they are bad ones."

# CHAPTER TWENTY-ONE

⁂

There were *bad* vampires out there? Like, worse than kidnapping unsuspecting young girls and forcing them to kill one another? *Whaaat the—?*

I was reeling from the bomb he'd just dropped, and I didn't pay attention as Trinity and a couple of her pals passed by, headed into the gym.

Alcántara had noticed them, however, and called, "Guidon Trinity."

Trinity gave me the evil eye, taking in the cozy tête-à-tête between Alcántara and me, and I imagined it was only a matter of time before Masha got the full report. But she was all deference when she jogged back down the stairs to answer him. "Yes, Master Alcántara?"

"Clean this up." He waved a dismissive hand to the target I'd hung on the tree. "I have other uses for Acari Drew just now."

I'd have laughed at the expression on her face if inwardly I hadn't been cringing so badly, because Trinity might as well have moved that target to my back. Her pale eyes crackled with cold fury. Having Alcántara by my side was the only reason I felt safe—in fact, his favor would be the thing that kept me alive . . . if it didn't kill me first.

"Walk with me." He linked his arm with mine in a very old-world-gentleman sort of way.

I'd just inched up the totem pole, and I felt the other girls' eyes boring into me. I forced the thought from my head. I was above them—he'd said so himself.

Etiquette classes aside, it felt good to be treated like an adult—to be trusted, and with such astounding news. Other vampires? *Bad ones?* How could it get worse than *this* lot? The thought chilled me.

Did that mean there was some greater conflict happening in the world, between good vampire and bad? Suddenly, our mission took on a whole other aspect.

Good versus evil . . . It was all so superhero Justice League sort of stuff. A tiny part of me regretted I'd be escaping, turning my back on such a life.

But then I remembered the Draug. I was excited for the mission, but I was even more excited to hightail it off the island. It was only a matter of time before I became someone—or some*thing's*—lunch.

I whispered low, so the Guidons wouldn't overhear, "Where are the other vampires? *Who* are they?"

"We must distance ourselves," he said quietly. "What I have to say is not for curious ears."

We walked to the far end of the quad, to a bench near the

old chapel. The silence wasn't easy as I'd known in the past with Ronan. Rather, there was an energy, a chemistry between Alcántara and me, and it made the silence charged and uncomfortable.

We settled on the bench, and I noted how closely he sat—with the vampires, everything meant something. There were no accidents, and even how and where one sat was rife with meaning.

"What I am about to say to you, what you will see on our mission—these things must remain between us." His intense gaze locked with mine as though he might bond me to this pledge with his eyes alone. "I am confident you will not betray this trust."

"I won't," I said gravely, even though Ronan and Amanda didn't seem to believe it. Unlike them, Alcántara was beginning to trust me. "I can keep secrets."

"That is good, *querida*. Because it is in secrecy that we will be traveling."

I shivered, wondering if I'd wear a mysterious traveling cloak, or carry an attaché. "When do we leave?"

"One week. We shall travel by boat."

I got goose bumps. This was it—our moment was approaching. I'd go on a mission, real good-against-evil stuff. I'd be tested; I'd show myself worthy.

And then I'd make my getaway. Sweet freedom would be mine. I bet I could get any job I wanted once I escaped—I could join the CIA, or be a celebrity's bodyguard.

But then I remembered the whole waitressing thing. "You said I'll need to wait tables?"

"You will be in disguise, *mijita*. These vampires we

infiltrate—the leaders call themselves the Synod of Seven—are a force of evil. They have captured one of our own, whom they would keep locked away for eternity. He is somewhere on their island, and they are starving him, endlessly torturing him for information they think he can provide."

"Who is he?" I whispered, enthralled.

"A vampire by the name of Carden McCloud, from eighteenth-century Scotland."

I heard myself gasp and shut my trap. *I* was being entrusted to help find an ancient vampire. Me. *Annelise Drew.*

The name was familiar, and then I remembered that Ronan had mentioned an elder named McCloud, who'd hailed from the island. I tucked that fact away, images of a kilted, fanged version of Sean Connery flashing in my head.

But one thing stuck in my craw. "If he's Scottish, why did I need to brush up on German?"

"The Synod of Seven members still speak the language of the ancient monastery in which they reside."

I had a nerdy aha moment. "Back in the Middle Ages, Christian missionaries settled on small islands throughout the North Sea. The monks all spoke Old High German—all their books, all their prayers, everything was in that dialect."

"Exactly."

Although I loved being right, the notion gave me kind of a hinky feeling. "So . . . they're priests?"

"No," he said firmly. "They are *vampires*. But they are not like those of us on *Eyja næturinnar*. These are monsters, representing everything we are against. Of this I have no doubt."

I rubbed my hands together, my fingertips gone numb. I

thought of the monsters I already knew, my battered body, the casual evisceration, the sick competitions that turned teenaged girls into gladiators. There were vampires more evil than that?

I still didn't understand what my role would be. I mean, surely Alcántara spoke a dozen ancient dialects. Why bring along a seventeen-year-old who'd only (almost) graduated high school? They trained me hard; they'd taught me how to fight and how to kill. Was it in preparation for this moment? I asked gravely, "Will I have to kill anybody?"

He looked amused by the question. "No, *querida*. You couldn't kill one of them if you tried. If they discover your intentions, you won't emerge alive. Our goal is only to retrieve Carden McCloud. His well-being is our only concern."

Meaning: While my fate was iffy at best, as long as Carden lived, it was all good.

"Why is this Carden so important?"

"They were a ragged bunch, those old Scottish soldiers, but Master McCloud is one of our own, and we stand by our people."

"So we're going to figure out where they're holding him hostage?"

"*You* will figure it out. I cannot risk sending in my men, and yet we must confirm that he still lives, and where they keep him."

My initial reaction was, *But he can risk a girl?* Then the first half of his statement registered, and my resentments faded to the background. I sat up straighter, feeling electrified, energized. "*I'll* figure out where he's being held? By myself?"

I was discovering a whole aspect to life on this island I'd

never suspected. It was so much more than a high school from hell where cheerleaders were killers and the stoners were sociopaths. I was training to be a force for *good*. Soon I'd leave here and could use my knowledge in the real world—maybe be a Secret Service agent, or move to Geneva and work for Interpol . . . whatever that was.

His eyes glinted, seeing my excitement. "Yes, *querida*, working alone, you will determine his location. But then I have others who will join you, and with them, you will do more than just find him."

"We'll rescue him?"

He nodded. "Together, you and I will sail him to freedom. Are you ready?"

All this *we . . . us . . . together* stuff—it made me feel close to Alcántara. And so, despite the intense topic of conversation, my posture, my tone, all of it was at ease. "I was born ready," I told him with a smile on my face.

He laughed then, loud and rollicking. I guess he'd never heard *that* line, though how it'd escaped him through the centuries was beyond me.

And I couldn't help it. I laughed, too, but then I thought, *Oh my God, this is me, bonding with a vampire. Crazy.*

I'd suspected Alcántara had helped me win last semester's challenge, and now I knew why: I was clearly the best girl for this mission. I mean, what other Acari even knew what Old High German was? But now, the way he was looking at me and laughing with me, I thought of another possibility. Maybe he'd also helped me just because he liked me, plain and simple.

The notion made me comfortable enough to ask, "Where does the waitressing come in?"

"The Synod of Seven members have called a summit, summoning vampires from around the world."

I cut him off, astounded. "Around the *world*?"

He tilted his head, looking amused. "Consider it, young one. Vampires only in the North Sea? Truly? We favor darker, colder climes. But why not Russia, or Finland, or Alaska? And so they are in such places, but they are coming here, to a ruined monastery on a private island so isolated, the only ones who give a care to its existence are vampires. These vampires bring with them armies of domestic servants. There will be an influx of butlers, maids, chefs, footmen, and so forth."

I nodded, because that part didn't surprise me at all. Vampires were old-school—they'd have a staff as mannered, uniformed, and extensive as any high-class estate of old. It all clicked—my role, our mission, the dancing, and the table manners—everything became clear. "And you're going to sneak me on the island posed as a waitress."

He gave a displeased wave of his hand. "Stop using such a crass term, *mijita*. Not *waitress*. Let us simply call you an . . . attendant."

"I'm going undercover," I said, marveling.

"Indeed. With all the comings and goings, security will be lax. I hope to arrive undetected, and from there I have a connection who will spirit you inside, clothe you, place you."

Alcántara was relying on *me*. And I wouldn't let him down. I knew I could do it. "Place me?" I asked, eager to hear more.

"You will play dumb, just another pretty serving girl. But all the while, you, *querida*, you will be the brightest star in the room." He stroked my hair, and a shiver ran up my spine, leaving warmth in its wake. Never before had anyone been so confident of my potential, and it was an even greater rush than his tingling touch.

The more time we spent together, the more we talked, the less wary of him I felt, and for a split second, I was a girl and he was a guy, and I leaned my head into his hand. Perhaps a first kiss with a vampire wouldn't be so bad after all. It'd be just the sort of daring fling a woman on a secret mission might enjoy.

I thought of Ronan, and of how we'd shared a few moments. But Ronan had always kept a cool distance, whereas Master Alcántara was flattering, demonstrative, appreciative. It was nice to feel wanted for once.

He stroked his hand down to cradle the side of my neck, and his fingers were cool on my nape. He gave the slightest squeeze. "You will serve their soup and pour their wine, all the while eavesdropping and seeking the clue that will lead us to Carden—if he still lives."

"I can do it." Confidence made my voice ring strong.

"I knew the moment I read your profile, *querida*. The moment I saw your photograph. I knew you were a gift." He took my hand in both of his and began to stroke his thumb in my palm, making slow circles. "Brains, beauty, but such strength and humility, too. You are perfect for this."

Ronan might've been acting cold and distant, but this hot Spanish vampire sure wasn't. The reluctance I'd once felt in his presence faded, leaving only my fascination.

"I feel it, too." It was such a thrill. I'd be James Bond and Lara Croft, all rolled into a five-foot-two-inch frame. My mind went to all sorts of clandestine, sexy-spy places. "It all sounds so exciting."

"Temper your enthusiasm, *Acarita*. Where we are going, if you are discovered, you will know a fate worse than any you have ever imagined."

# CHAPTER TWENTY-TWO

I was going *undercover*. Alcántara's trust made me want to do my very best, and that week I prepared harder than ever. He wanted decorum, and not only did I pour myself into the class, I totally went Martha Stewart on Dagursson's ass. Hell, I could've set a table blindfolded and with one arm tied behind my back if the need arose . . . though, from what Alcántara warned about these new, bad vamps, maybe craziness like that wasn't out of the question.

Exactly seven days passed before we got in that boat. It was seven days of learning how to curtsy, to pour wine without spilling, and to slick my hair into a perfect bun.

I ran into Ronan just once all week, walking across the quad. "Annelise," he'd said, "you must be careful." His voice was intense, but the look he gave me was blank, almost sad. Did he think I was going off to my death, or did he just not like the idea that I was going off with *Alcántara*? Either way,

Ronan was the one with the girlfriend—I didn't know what *he* had to be sad about.

But then it struck me: If I was going to escape—and I had every intention of succeeding—this was good-bye. Forever. Never again would I see him.

My eyes bored into his. I knew a wash of anguish, memorizing those incandescent green eyes. It was harder to let go than I'd thought. The swirl of emotions panicked me till I felt like a girl drowning in the churning waves, battling an undertow that was unexpectedly strong.

I fought it, tossing off a studiously careless reply. "I'm always careful," I said blithely, and when he frowned at that, I added, "In my own way."

"Just remember what I've told you," he said, his own voice gone cool. "Remember to be discreet about the things you've seen."

My twinge of sadness crystallized into anger. Just the notion that he might not trust me made me quivery with a weird cocktail of resentment and embarrassment.

Things had been even worse when I'd run into Amanda. She was so distracted when I'd seen her in the dining hall, I'd wondered what I was doing even sitting with her. I didn't know if they were worried about me, or if it was themselves they were protecting.

So much for the connection I'd thought we'd all had.

It was that mix of annoyance and mortification that fed my response to Ronan. "You mean, don't tell anyone that I followed you to a forbidden part of the island."

His nod was tight, reluctant. "To keep information to yourself is to keep yourself safe."

I crossed my arms tightly across my chest. "Is that a threat?"

"Good Christ, girl. Of course it's not a threat."

"Well, your stupid secret is safe with me. You and Amanda, and your cliff-top hideaway, too. I'll stay shut up about all of it."

He scraped his hand through his hair, spiking it every which way. "For someone who claims to be so smart, you certainly can be dim. This isn't about the cave, or Amanda. I've been doing everything in my power—*everything*—to keep you safe."

"I don't *claim* to be smart. I *am* smart." I stood tall, imagining myself as powerful as my words.

He looked me up and down, and I practically saw the cogs spinning in his head. "Are you drinking more than your prescribed dose of the blood?" Our eyes locked and held, and as he read the truth on my face, his shoulders fell. "You must be cautious. Too much can be dangerous."

"It makes me stronger."

"It makes you volatile."

"I've had only a little extra. To heal my rib . . . seeing as I couldn't *tell anybody*."

He shook his head, exasperated. "I warned them against sending you on this mission."

I bristled, readying for the same old argument. "Because I'm too young?"

"Because you haven't had enough training. Most girls experience their first mission as a part of the final test to become a Watcher. But you, you've been here one term, and simply because you have a facility with language, they're sending you off, where you will quite likely get killed."

"Whoa." I actually took a step back. "Thanks for the vote of confidence."

His words shook me. Would I get killed? I told myself it was only that Ronan didn't appreciate my skills.

But I knew someone who did—*Alcántara*. When I was with the vampire, I felt expansive and full of potential, like a seedling exposed to daylight for the first time.

It was unsettling that Ronan guessed I'd snuck extra doses of the blood. But how could it be a bad thing when I felt stronger than ever? I'd thrown myself into my physical training, working out harder than ever. I'd even mastered those stupid pull-ups. The blood brought me alive with a prickly, zinging feeling that'd put me more in touch with my body and the world around me. I was more attuned to smells, sounds, the sensation of bodies near in space. . . .

With that thought, I sensed them. Emma and Yasuo were approaching. Ever since my little talk with Emma, things had taken off between the two of them, and they'd become mostly inseparable.

I turned, and there they were, walking so closely, their arms were touching. Although it wasn't exactly forbidden, outright PDA would've been pretty stupid. This was the Isle of Night, not the mall, and at the moment I was grateful for it. The last thing I needed was to see Emma and Yas with their hands in each other's back pockets.

But what did his status as vampire Trainee mean for their relationship in the long term? Someday, would it be *Yasuo* who sent us on missions? How would they sustain a relationship then? I thought of some of the other guys . . . Kevin, Rob, Josh. Would they have the right to order us around one day?

Just the very notion rankled. And where was Josh, anyway? I realized I hadn't seen him all week. "Where's the third stooge?"

At the tone in my voice, Emma looked as if I'd slapped her.

*Crap.* Was Ronan right? Was I acting volatile? I'd immersed myself in my preparations, trying to impress Alcántara, but had my excitement about the mission made me lose sight of who my friends really were? Because that sure had sounded decidedly unfriendly. I cut a glance at Ronan, standing there about as readable as a sphinx.

My greeting put Yas on his guard. "Josh, you mean? He's in class."

Ronan hoisted his bag higher on his shoulder. "Which is where I need to go." He gave me a weighty look. "Remember what I said, Annelise. Be careful."

I nodded, uncertain what to say. I'd been angry, but now I was just kind of disturbed. *Was* I too inexperienced, drinking too much blood, in over my head? Was I in danger? Though I had no answers, I was left with the sneaking suspicion that yes, Ronan might actually, honestly care.

My throat tightened with an unexpected surge of emotion. This was it. Ronan looked away, and hard as I willed it, he didn't meet my eyes again.

*Good-bye.*

He walked away before I could manage the word, and I was struck with something sharper than anxiety, deeper than anger. Those feelings seemed stupid now—a silly, childish waste of energy. Was this regret I felt? Because chances were good I'd never see him again.

I'd gotten caught up in the mission when I should've been

warier than ever of Alcántara—after all, he was sending me on an operation from which I might not return alive. My vanity and the vampire's attentions had made me cocky, but I wasn't invincible. Maybe I'd caught Alcántara's fancy, but he could easily tire of me at any time. Tire of me and kill me.

I could never fully trust a vampire, or anything about a system where it was guys and guys alone who sat on the top of the totem pole. I was one of his favorites, sure, but that wasn't necessarily a good thing. Any situation in which there was a high likelihood I'd end up dead was, by definition, not a good thing.

The magnitude of it all overwhelmed me. As did the nagging feeling that I'd messed something up with Ronan. We played for keeps on this island, and I'd taken his caution on my behalf for granted. His advice had been a gift, and I'd spurned it like an unruly child. But it was too late. There were no do-overs on *Eyja næturinnar.*

I faced my friends. "I'm sorry, guys. I think I'm just nervous." My voice was uncertain, and it gave truth to my words.

Emma loosened up at once and gave me an understanding smile. "Of course you are. When do you leave?"

I shrugged. "A few days from now."

"Have you learned where you're going yet?" asked Yasuo.

Alcántara's words echoed in my head: *These things must remain between us.* "I—I don't know what the plan is."

They shared a look, and Yasuo said, "She's lying."

Emma squinted at me and asked with a tease in her voice, "Are you lying, Blondie?"

"Since when do *you* call me Blondie?" I scowled playfully, jerking a thumb toward Yasuo. "*He's* bad enough. Jeez, guys, I spend a few weeks in training—"

"In hiding," interrupted Yas.

I nudged him with my shoulder. "In *training*. I lie low for a little while, and you brainwash farm girl here."

And *boom*, like that, it was all good between the three of us again, as teasing and easy as before.

But afterward, I *did* go into hiding. I couldn't deal with running into any of them, with the pain of these protracted exchanges that only I knew were good-bye. Just as I couldn't deal with the questions cropping up for me.

Like, what did this connection with Alcántara mean for me? What did it mean for all of us that there were evil vampires out there, meeting and plotting?

If I wanted to survive, I needed to focus. So I dug in, and trained hard, and then I woke up one morning, and it was time.

I went to the dining hall for breakfast, and by lunch I was on a boat.

# CHAPTER TWENTY-THREE

W e set off when the sun was at its highest, in a rusted-out trawler that stank of petrol and rotting fish. A couple of fishermen from town were at the helm, and I studied them, taking in their weathered faces and faded overalls. Might *they* be related to Ronan? His family was out there somewhere—a father maybe, or a brother, someone with the same eyes, the same ways, the same habit of raking the hair back from his face.

I scrubbed a hand over my own face. Scrubbed Ronan from my mind. He was a thing of my past now. I had to look forward if I planned to survive what was coming.

I was here with Alcántara, and that should've been the only thing demanding my attention.

The day wasn't bright by any means, but the sky was bleached whiter than usual and sunlight reflected off the water. Looking pained, the vampire shielded himself from the glare, pulling his hood low over his face and holding it fast in the wind.

I eyed his hand, so pale against the coarse black fabric. "So vampires don't like the light after all?"

He cut his eyes to peer at me through the shadow of his cowl. "Curiosity killed the cat, *querida*."

"I thought you liked me curious," I said with a raised brow.

He chuckled at that, and the energy that snapped between us felt like a triumph. "Yes, I confess I do appreciate a keen mind."

He settled lower in his seat, and just when I thought our exchange was over, he said, "You guess correctly—it is no secret that vampires do not relish daylight. We can be in it, yes, but it is very . . . fatiguing. *Incómodo*, no? Uncomfortable."

"If it's troubling, why didn't we wait till later to leave?"

He pulled his hood even lower, but his voice cut clearly through the wind. "Because if it's troubling to me, it will be troubling to others."

"Ah." While I had him talking, I almost asked who the fishermen were, too, but when it came to human townsfolk, something told me that guarding my thoughts would be safest for everyone. I had to put the Isle of Night behind me.

Instead, I passed the time taking in the scenery. There was water. And more water—in a flat, gray, monochromatic palette to match the white light blanching the sky overhead. We passed the occasional island, but each was bleak, and many were more like rocks than any sort of inhabitable terrain.

The chugging and swaying of the trawler was making me dozy, and my chin bobbed down, then whipped back up again as I began to nod off.

There was a low chuckle beside me. Alcántara was watching me, an unreadable expression on his face. "To be able to sleep once more," he mused. "To close one's eyes to the world and melt into dreamlessness. I would trade many things for such sweet bliss."

So, vampires didn't sleep—another new fact under my belt. I met his eyes, waiting to see if he'd divulge more. I felt an errant pang of sympathy, because it *would* kind of suck never to rest again, for all eternity. "It must feel interminable sometimes," I said carefully.

"In point of fact, *querida*, our lifespan is, by definition, interminable."

*Unless a stake gets in the way.* But I definitely didn't give voice to that bit.

He nodded toward the companionway stairs. "Go sleep, little one. There are thousands of islands in the North Sea, and many hours ahead of us. You will need your rest for the work ahead."

I didn't want to go below, but disagreeing wasn't exactly a thing someone did with Alcántara, so I just nodded and headed down the rickety stairs in search of a small bunk where I could nap.

It became instantly clear why Alcántara bore the discomfort of brightness on deck instead of sitting below deck. The stench down there was intense enough to make my eyes tear, and the rattling of the engine was so loud, it filled me, shoving all other thoughts from my brain.

But he was right. If I intended to be at the top of my game, I needed my sleep. I curled onto a thin mattress, preferring the chill to the lone musty blanket, and miraculously passed out.

Abrupt silence woke me. I sat up, realizing the fishermen had cut the power, leaving only the sound of waves slapping against the hull. It was a blessed relief to my ears, which still hummed from the engine's lengthy assault.

I went above to find the men approaching Alcántara. They didn't meet his eyes. Their accents were beyond thick, and they spoke in gruff monosyllables unintelligible to me. "Aff ere, ay ya?"

Alcántara nodded and stood, and I deduced they'd said something approximating *Off here, yes huh?*

I looked around, wondering where we were. It was gray nothingness, with only the hint of a darker gray shadow on the horizon—land, in the distance.

The vampire read my mind. "We'll row from here. We cannot risk being seen or heard."

The men lowered a ratty old dinghy into the water. I'd thought the water was calm, but the small craft bobbed and tossed wildly, and I gritted my teeth, inhaling through my nose. I'd never been seasick, and I hoped this wouldn't be the moment for that to change.

"Come, Acari." Alcántara's tone was sharp, brooking no hesitation.

I had no choice but to follow him, clambering down a rope ladder into the boat. He took the oars, and I sat facing him. His hood hung low over his face, and, looking at him, I felt as if I were in a Greek myth, with Alcántara rowing me to Hades across the River Styx.

As we approached shore, I was glad we'd traveled when the sun was highest in the sky. I made out the silhouette of a creepy stone building on a hill. It was stark and stout, but smaller than I'd pictured.

"So that's the monastery?"

He shook his head. "We'd not dare to roam so close. The monastery is on the far side of the island. That is the charnel house."

I gave him a blank look—it wasn't often I encountered a word I didn't know.

"Where human remains are stored," he said.

"Oh." I grimaced, studying it. And I'd thought our standing stones were creepy.

I glanced back at Alcántara and caught him watching me. He was pulling the oars in a strong, steady rhythm, and it was the little things like that that reminded me of his power. He gave me a smile as if he knew my thoughts—though it didn't take a mind reader. He'd had hundreds of years in which to realize how appealing he was as a male specimen.

He looked back up the hill. Clouds were blowing in from the east, casting dramatic, moving shadows over the stone building. "It was commonplace for monks to keep a charnel house," he explained. "Such things were used to remind them of their mortality."

"Or to remind them of their power," I said.

Alcántara gave me a thoughtful look. "Perhaps."

We landed on the island. *Their* island. And honestly, it wasn't so different from *our* island. We pulled ashore on a tiny sliver of shoreline that I imagined wasn't even exposed during high tide.

I began to clamber out of the boat, but Alcántara was a

surprising gentleman and stayed me with his hand, hopping from the boat and pulling it onto the sand so I wouldn't get wet. He handed me down.

A low cave was barely detectable along the rock face, and spotting it, I said, "Very Batman."

Alcántara gave me a blank look.

"Never mind." I was nervous now, more than I wanted to admit. It didn't escape my notice that he'd held on to my hand a little longer than necessary.

We didn't have to wait long before Alcántara's inside man arrived. We dragged the boat into the cave, flipped it bottom up on a rock, turned around, and there he was.

When Alcántara told me he had a spy on the inside, I hadn't expected *this*. This guy was young, not much older than a Trainee. He was loose and broad shouldered, as if he'd played pro ball and was now considering a career as a bartender. The guy's real name didn't suit him one bit, and in my head I'd instantly dubbed him Buddy.

The two exchanged greetings, and I was surprised to hear his accent was American. Though why wouldn't it be? So many of our Trainees were from the United States—they had to end up somewhere.

Buddy gave me a once-over, his eyes lingering in a way that made me want to punch him. "This little thing is going to find him?"

I scowled. It was such a *Buddy* thing to say.

"Yes," I answered before Alcántara had a chance to. "This *little thing* will do her job."

He laughed a goofy, chortling laugh, and it reaffirmed my instant dislike. I wondered what kind of dirt he had on

Alcántara, or Alcántara on him, that kept him alive and stationed on an enemy island. Too bad I wouldn't have time to ask *that* story.

He stood hands on hips, looking more like he was in a locker room than on an island crawling with malevolent undead. "So, Master Al gave you the rundown?"

*Master Al?* I nodded, mesmerized by his not having full-grown fangs.

"Servants keep their eyes down around here," he continued. "So just play dumb, lie low, and listen."

I'd grown up keeping my eyes down—lying low was second nature to me. "Check, check, and check."

"Find out where Carden is," Alcántara said, taking over the conversation. "That is all. Do not do anything yourself. Do not call attention to yourself. If they discover you, they will destroy McCloud."

*And slice and dice me into Drew-kabobs*, but I seemed to be the only one concerned by that point. "I understand."

But Mr. Football didn't sound convinced. He slid a backpack from his shoulder and tossed it to me. "Here's your uniform."

I peeked inside. It was a *dress*. I frowned. "I guess I can holster my stars under this."

Buddy tsked. "No, *chica*. You've gotta nail this without your toys. These vamps may not be into electric lights or heat, but they sure do have metal detectors all over the damned place."

"I can do my job without weapons," I said with more bravado than real courage.

"You'd better. You're our only chance. We won't get another shot like this any time soon."

I did *not* like being on the receiving end of Buddy's attitude. "What about *you*? Why can't you find McCloud? Seems like you have an in."

Alcántara answered for him. "It's impossible for those who are Vampire to roam through the monastery undetected. Like senses like. They would sniff him out, and once discovered, he'd only raise suspicion. Trainee Lee isn't powerful enough to be a party to the Synod's proceedings."

*Trainee Lee.* I bit my cheek not to snicker at the lame name. Buddy was much better.

"Anyway," Buddy Lee said with a dopey shrug, "I'm only a Trainee. We're like mushrooms, you know—kept in the dark and fed shit."

I raised my brows, wondering where they'd found this one. "Classy."

I could tell by Alcántara's pursed mouth he agreed with me. But I guess Buddy was too valuable to scold. I was dying to know *that* story.

But, instead, I went deeper into the cave, so deep I could barely see in the dark, to change into my disguise. Alcántara was old-fashioned, but still, there were two of them and one of me, and I felt vulnerable and exposed. Not to mention cold. It was freezing, with the wind gusting off the water. I stripped and dressed as quickly as I could, my hands trembling with cold and their clumsily rapid movements.

It was easy enough to sort out the uniform in the darkness, the thing was so simple. Just a flannel dress with a floor-length skirt as loose as the bodice was tight. I had to suck in to zip it up the side—the woman he'd stolen it from must've been

miniscule. Naturally, it was gray, and I wondered what it was
vampires had against color. The finishing touches were a pair
of thick, scratchy woolen hose, my hair tugged back in a bun,
and a white cap on top. A white apron topped the whole thing.
I felt like a Quaker.

But I guess Buddy had a thing for simple, because when I
emerged, he gave me and my snug bodice a cockeyed grin. His
tone was sarcastic, but his eyes were approving. "Hot."

I was about to jump down his throat when Alcántara beat
me to it. The vampire practically flew across the cave to him—
one minute he stood against the wall, and the next he was in
Buddy's face.

When Alcántara stepped away, I saw the Trainee held his
hands clutched over his cheek. Blood was dripping down his
jaw, dribbling onto his collar and turning the brown material
black. "Dude," he mumbled.

Alcántara folded his hands behind his back, speaking
calmly. "*Cuidado*, boy. You will honor Acari Drew. Look upon
her with respect, or the next time it will be your eyes."

I watched the boy wipe blood from his face—me, the girl
who'd just been defended by a vampire.

It was unnerving and frightening, but it was kind of a rush,
too. The feeling I got was that Alcántara *honored* me, in an
old-fashioned, chivalric sort of way.

I held my shoulders back, standing tall. I wasn't an adolescent like Buddy. *I* was on a mission.

Thoughts of my imminent escape faded to the background.
The old Drew shed from me.

I focused on the scratch of woolen hose against my skin,

imagining the feel to be familiar, not foreign. I imagined myself the part. These were *my* clothes. I was a maid. I was invisible.

I looked up to find Alcántara's eyes consuming me. It was one of his epically seductive stares, making me feel I was a blast of the blazing sunlight he hadn't known in centuries.

With a hand on his chest, he gave me a courtly half bow. "You are perfection."

# CHAPTER TWENTY-FOUR

"*Schnell! Schnell!*" a voice shouted at me in German, and I upped my pace. I'd studied etiquette enough to barf, but it turned out real preparation would've been running the fifty-yard dash while balancing trays stacked with teetering plates and glasses. Forget finding Carden McCloud—these guys were a grave-looking bunch, and I feared a broken dish might mean my life.

The darkness didn't help. Old-fashioned was one thing, but did they have to be so freaking authentic? The monastery resembled an old castle, but nothing like anything Cinderella ever saw. It was ancient and freezing, all thick slabs of stone and rats squeaking in corners. I had no doubt there were dungeons—I just hoped the only thing lurking down there was our ancient vampire.

I was pretending to be someone who didn't speak German, so I pasted a confused look on my face and whispered a deferential, "I'm sorry." I kept my chin tilted down, having no desire to catch a glimpse of the older scullery maid I'd just addressed. Her gruff voice suggested a cross between drill sergeant and prison warden.

I scampered away, trying to balance my load and cursing the long skirts that kept tangling between my legs. The trek from the downstairs kitchens, up a winding staircase, to the warped timber floors of the private dining room was made more precarious by the fact that these dudes had yet to embrace electric lights. And though torches burnt everywhere, they weren't enough to cast light in black corners or along the ruts in the floors that kept tripping me up.

I entered the room and slammed on the brakes, cutting my pace from sixty to zero.

A quartet played classical music in the corner, and it could've been a scene plucked from any old book, except the men seated around the table were all pale, all deadly. They really did resemble monks, each wearing the same dark, hooded robe. And, at the moment, they mostly looked like outraged monks, their icy glares focused on a girl, kneeling before them and choking back sobs.

I adjusted my tray, quickly wiping the sweat from my palms. Was I supposed to walk in and serve food or just watch this horror show unfold?

I chose the latter—better not to call attention to myself at this very moment. More important, it provided a great opportunity. Studying every detail, memorizing each face, noting every reaction, were the sorts of things that could save a girl's life later on.

There were seven vampires—the Synod of Seven, I

presumed—with three on each side of a thickly hewn wooden table and one at the head. This guy, obviously the leader, got my most intensive scrutiny. Besides, not only was he in charge; he was also the one currently tearing a new one in the serving girl.

"Are you clumsy," he demanded of her, "or merely a fool?"

Candles littered the place, and long, eerie shadows danced up the craggy stone walls and along the uneven timber plank ceiling. Even the air was different, reminding me of an evening storm in my Florida hometown—I sensed the same sudden cool, the altered light, the air charged with electricity . . . and danger.

"See what you have done. You have spilled Brother Marcus's wine."

She scuttled around on her knees, using her skirts to swab up the spilled liquid, and I cringed for her. Her body quaked too violently, and her efforts were worthless. Her bun had loosened, and wisps of black hair spilled around her face.

Another vampire chimed in—Brother Marcus, I assumed—speaking with an impatient sneer in a thick German dialect. "Yes, and I find myself thirsty."

This was once someone's daughter, now reduced to a pathetic creature who'd likely not survive the night. "Please forgive me," she begged in German. "I'm sorry. I will get you more."

I winced, my blood chilling for her. In her nerves, she'd accidentally spoken the casual *Euch* instead of the more formal *Ihnen.*

The room became utterly silent—silent, but for her whimpering.

"Rise," the man at the head said. As she did, he raked her with a disdainful look. "You overstep."

The girl trembled, wavering on legs too weak to hold her.

"Stand, I told you." The head man grabbed her arm, and she cried out as he pulled her up and shoved her toward Marcus. "Give him aught to drink."

Marcus's mouth attached to the girl's neck in an instant. I'd never seen a vampire feed, and I watched in horrified fascination as he wrenched her backward, his throat gulping convulsively. Crimson pooled in the corners of his mouth and spilled down her skin, shimmering in the candlelight. I couldn't see it in the shadows, but I heard the hideous *plip-plip* of her blood dribbling onto the floor.

Her eyes rolled back in her head, eyelids fluttering. She swayed, her expression either pain or ecstasy—I couldn't tell which.

Two male attendants appeared behind me, and I gave a start. The man at the head of the table gave them a sharp nod, and they grabbed the girl by the elbows, then dragged her from the room.

The leader's eyes found me then, pinning me. I stood there, uncertain. My tray, heavy with plates of meats and breads, felt as if it weighed five thousand pounds. But I couldn't spill; I couldn't tremble—there wasn't room to make a single mistake.

"*Sie bringt die nächste Portion,*" he said, announcing the next course. I just hoped the next *portion* didn't involve me.

I remembered my role—I was a dim, timid, English-speaking attendant. I didn't move, and he beckoned impatiently.

Only then did I step forward, imagining graceful things—ballerinas, cats, flowers in the breeze—delicate things I'd never been but needed to act like now if I wanted to survive. I made my body move in long, elegant movements.

"You may stay," he told me in German, "and see that our cups overflow."

I pretended not to understand. I dared raise my chin just a little bit and widened my eyes. *Pretty . . . I was a pretty, graceful, innocent ballerina,* I reminded myself. I curtsied, whispering, "I beg your pardon, sir?"

He gave me a long, lingering look. I estimated he'd been in his fifties when he was turned, and with a few lines etched on his face, and a head of longish, white hair, he was neither ugly nor handsome. He didn't look cruel, either, but when it came to vampires, I knew better than to judge a book by its cover. *"Solch ein schönes Stück. Und sie spricht nicht deutsch."*

I schooled my features. I was dumb and invisible. I definitely was *not* a genius undercover superspy who hated being called a pretty piece who was unable to speak German.

The other men chuckled, but instead of a jovial thing, the sound was menacing. Candlelight cast them in dramatic light and shadow, and some of their faces were clearly visible, while others were merely shadowy silhouettes, with black holes where mouths and eyes should have been.

One asked with a laugh, "Better that way, is it not?"

"You may stay," he told me in English. "See to it that our glasses remain full and our food plentiful."

"It would be my honor, sir." More deferential whispering from me, another curtsy.

"To the fine wine of Brother Jacob," one of the vampires

announced, and they forgot my existence. They raised their glasses in a toast, repeating their leader's name, sounding like a baritone chorus . . . *Yaa-cub.*

Jacob touched his glass to his forehead. *"Danke. Und herzlich Willkommen, meine Brüder."*

The meeting commenced, and so much for the myth that vampires couldn't eat. These guys *chowed.* And drank. And drank some more.

I supposed eating wasn't just a physical thing—sometimes we ate because we *enjoyed* eating—and if I could spend eternity not worrying about my waistline, you can bet I'd consume my share of Nutter Butters.

I scampered to and fro, ensuring their every need was met and all the while struggling to follow the conversation. Their dialect was old and coarse, and I discovered that reading Old High German was one thing, but hearing it was something else entirely. With no context to work from, I had a hard time parsing discussions filled with disjointed references to conflicts and people I knew nothing about.

Still, I hung on to every word, and it wasn't the urge to save a tortured vampire that drove me—I wanted to get out of there alive, to make my escape. And, if I was to be honest, a small part of me wanted to impress Alcántara, too—to have a moment of triumph before I disappeared into the sunset.

A single phrase popped from the rest, and my heart kicked up a notch. Had I heard correctly?

*"Von der Eyja næturinnar?"* someone repeated.

Excitement zinged through me. I lingered at the table, pouring wine and listening.

Jacob was interrogating a younger-looking vampire who bore a circular bald monk's tonsure on the crown of his head. He demanded, "What of our prisoner?"

"We have him still. We have been interrogating him."

My blood ran cold. Were they talking about Carden McCloud? They'd mentioned a prisoner and the Isle of Night in a short span. I stepped closer, my movements slow, refilling glasses that didn't require it and straining to understand.

A black-haired vampire asked, "Have you learned anything?" He'd spoken in a German so archaic, I wouldn't have understood had I not heard the sentence before.

"No. He refuses to speak."

The head vampire put down his knife and fork. "Then we destroy him."

"As you wish it, Brother Jacob."

"Tonight," the leader added, and then he shot me a glare.

In my concentration, my movements had slowed to a halt, and I flinched back into action, going to put the wine on a sideboard and thinking hard all the while. This was my first—and hopefully last—mission. Failure might destroy my chances for escape. I would not, *could not* fail Alcántara, and Alcántara wanted the prisoner alive.

Carden McCloud was here, and these vampires wanted to destroy him, tonight.

Except I would find him first.

"Have the young female clear these," one of the vampires said in German, clinking a fork against his glass. "I have a taste for your brandy."

Jacob gave me the order, and I went from seat to seat,

gathering the glassware and making room for brandy snifters. As I was clearing, something caught my eye, and I did what was either the cleverest or the stupidest thing of my life.

A pretty, lone steak knife had drifted between place settings, forgotten amidst all the plates and cutlery. But *I* saw it—it was sharp, shining, and calling my name. Its handle was thin and elegant, and with a blade tapered to a fine point, it was balanced, looking eminently throwable.

I dropped a soiled linen napkin over it. I gathered glasses and arranged them on my tray. Then I plucked up the napkin, knife and all.

My ears buzzed, I was so panicked somebody had seen what I did. I was terrified that at any moment claws would grab me from behind and teeth rip into my flesh. But the conversation continued as before, a jovial wine-soaked hum.

I hustled down toward the kitchens, pausing on the spiral stairs, my heart pounding and sweat trickling down my back. The passageway was miniscule, each step just a tiny, triangular sliver, and I leaned against the wall for balance. The stone cooled my damp back, and the glasses clinked on my precariously balanced tray.

Using one hand, I hiked up my skirts and slid the knife inside my panties, along the hip. I flipped it over twice, twisting the fabric to hold it tightly in place.

I smoothed my dress and scurried all the way down, navigating the darkened corridors. Adrenaline coursed through me, and my senses were heightened, hyperaware of every sound and every movement around me.

And then I perceived a slight shift behind me. I was going to ignore it. Until I smelled it.

The unexpected stench of sulfur.

I turned. It was then I saw her. The hair gave her away—even pulled taut into a bun, even in the shadows, that maple hair gleamed, impossibly.

*Lilac.*

# CHAPTER TWENTY-FIVE

I had to concentrate. That was just nerves getting to me, because there was *no freaking way* that could've been Lilac. Lilac von Straubing. My enemy. The girl I'd beaten—supposedly killed.

It was as if the world tilted on its axis, and everything went all melty and surreal, the torches brighter, the hallway darker. I turned again, my heart in my throat.

But the Lilac look-alike was farther away now, trailing some long, lithe, mysteriously hooded vampire like a shadow. They disappeared around a corner.

Was I imagining that she'd shuffled away quickly? That she'd looked nervous? Was my mind playing tricks, or had she stolen one last glimpse of me? I'd know her anywhere—I saw that maple hair and heard the *flick-flick* of her lighter in my nightmares.

But surely it wasn't Lilac. Not only had I killed her; this girl seemed way too subservient to be von Slutling. It was my imagination going haywire under the stress, or maybe it was some bad vampire mojo in the air, making my greatest fears materialize before my eyes. Because Lilac's survival was inconceivable, impossible.

Unthinkable.

Either way, I was shaken. There was no way I could've gone back upstairs to serve brandy with anything remotely resembling composure.

*Upstairs.* The thought jolted me back into the moment.

McCloud was going to be destroyed . . . and soon. *That* was what needed my focus. I had to find McCloud and do my job before I experienced any other hallucinations.

I'd prove Ronan wrong—not only would I survive the mission; I'd make it a success. I'd discover McCloud's whereabouts and report back to Alcántara, who now seemed to offer all the comforts of an old and trusted friend. And then I'd make my getaway, disappearing forever, and Ronan would rue the day he'd doubted me.

One of the head matrons bustled by, and I darted my eyes down, bursting into a brisk walk and trying to look busy. But I caught sight of my apron—it was white, while all the head maids' aprons were black. It gave me an idea.

I scurried into the kitchen and back to the scullery, the small room where the dishes were cleaned. "Ingrid wants you," I told the scullery maid in German, repeating a name I'd heard in passing.

Apparently I'd chosen well, because the girl hustled out. It left me alone. I quickly cleared my tray, darting my eyes around the room. A basket in the corner held a pile of dirty rags, with a black apron balled on top.

I made a beeline for it, tearing my apron off and pulling the black one on. The lap of it was soaked, stinking of chicken broth. I pulled off my white cap, too, shoving it all to the bottom of the dirty laundry. Then I smoothed my hair, snagged seven empty brandy glasses for my tray, and walked brusquely into the hall.

Before, I'd been a wilting, English-speaking maid. But now, in my black apron, I was a bossy, in-charge kitchen Frau.

I stopped the first girl I saw whose hands were empty and ordered her in crisp, perfect German, "Go upstairs. Tell them the other girl is indisposed." I saw by her widened eyes, she knew exactly who was upstairs. I shoved the tray at her. "Serve them brandy. Do not spill."

She stared at me blankly, the glasses tinkling lightly as they jostled on the tray in her trembling hands.

"*Schnell,*" I barked, enjoying it more than I should.

My mind whirring, I stormed on. How to find the dungeons?

I passed another woman in a black apron like mine. The head maids were older, and I was afraid I looked far too young for the part. I felt her pause, assessing me.

I headed her off at the pass, spitting, "*Es ist keine Zeit. Es Probleme mit den Gefangenen.*" No time. Trouble with the prisoner.

Her expression softened, accepting me as a peer. She felt my urgency, though, and nodded down the hallway, where I spotted a shadowy chasm. Another spiral staircase, I guessed, this one going down.

"Carl has the keys," she told me in German.

I gave her an officious nod. Carl was about to meet my steak knife.

This staircase was darker, and foul odors rose from below, damp and rotting. I paused on the narrow stairwell, hiking up my dress for the second time that day, and slid out my knife. Holding up my skirts, I tiptoed the rest of the way down.

Carl was probably the guard—I hoped he was just a Trainee, or better yet, a human man. I wasn't sure how I'd do facing a full-on vampire.

Cells lined the hallway, most empty, a few not, their occupants all catatonic, or worse. I kept my movements fluid and light as I went, repeating my mantra. *I am water that flows. I am Watcher.* Murmuring was coming from the end of the hall, and I walked toward it. The only other sound was the *whip-whip* of the single torch hanging on the wall.

The guard didn't hear me, but the rodents did, and a burst of chittering and scurrying announced my arrival.

*"Vas isst—?"* I heard a German voice hiss in the dark.

I sped up. I was distantly aware of a pale face floating in the shadows, in a cell at the end of the hallway, but I didn't have time to consider it. The guard had turned and spotted me. He was headed my way.

*Crap.* It was a full-on vampire.

No time to think. I stopped short, grinding the balls of my feet to the dirt-packed floor. I readied the knife in my right hand, finding its balance just below the midpoint. I imagined his beating heart—if a vampire's heart did beat—and I threw.

The adrenaline, the ghostly figure at the end of the hall, the vampire rushing toward me—all of these things focused me, and instantly my mind snapped to a different place, one where it was only me and this target, a bright, razor-sharp point where the vampire's heart would be. Like iron to a magnet, my knife flew truly, struck the left side of his chest, and stuck.

He staggered and crumpled. My concentration broke, and I stood there for a second, brutally thrust back into reality. My right side was killing me. . . . I couldn't catch my breath. . . . There might be other guards. . . . That was my only weapon.

And . . . the vampire imprisoned at the end of the hall was staring right at me.

# CHAPTER TWENTY-SIX

The clap of a hand broke the silence, and then another, until it became clear that the vampire imprisoned at the end of the corridor was giving me a lazy round of applause. It was accompanied by the hideous sound of rattling chains—if I could see more clearly through the shadows, I imagined I'd find him shackled.

I looked around nervously, but he stopped me, saying in a voice hoarse with disuse, "Relax. He was the only one."

I squinted in his direction, but his face remained a featureless, pale specter in the darkness. There was only one torch, and even though the drink had greatly improved my vision, it wasn't enough to see clearly through this murk.

"Come into the light," he said.

I stepped forward, tilting my head and peering through the darkness.

"That's it. . . . Come closer. I won't bite." He laughed,

amusing himself, and the sound was a breathy rasp. But when I stepped closer still, he only laughed louder. "My savior is a girl?"

Great, another man to whom I needed to prove myself. I stood tall, making my tone fierce and impatient. "Carden McCloud, I presume."

"A tiny wee thing you are."

Annoyance robbed the respect I knew I should've kept in my voice. "Lucky me. Another Scotsman."

"You've some experience with my countrymen?" Even though his voice was weak, he sounded bemused.

"Unfortunately." Ronan's face popped into my mind, and I shoved it back out.

"Fascinating. Highlander or Islander?"

"Look, I asked if you were Master McCloud—"

"Don't *Master* me, lass." The weakness disappeared, making his tone steely.

"Fine. I just needed to make sure you were down here." I approached even closer, until I could make out his features, and then I wished I hadn't. I'd never seen a starving vampire before, and the sight made me reel. It was a decayed corpse I was speaking to, his face all sharp edges and deep lines, gray and desiccated, with skin as thin as paper clinging atop gruesomely pronounced bones and tendons.

"I'm a piteous thing, am I not?" he asked, guessing at my horror. Metal clinked as he shifted his arms. They were chained over his head, and I saw now how he hung there, barely supporting himself on his feet, some sort of Halloween decoration come to nightmarish life.

"You're starving," I said stupidly.

"And she's bright, too."

I didn't have time for this. "Yeah, whatever. Now listen. They're going to kill you tonight unless I return with help. Master Alcántara—"

"Hugo is with you?" He cut me off, his attitude gone frosty.

"Yes. He sent me to find you." I knelt to retrieve my knife, and it slid from the dead vampire's chest with a dull suck. I patted the body down until I felt the ring of keys tied at his waist. *Perfect.*

I was almost done . . . so close now to freedom. All I needed to do was relay Carden's exact location to Alcántara and I'd be on my way. Bringing the keys would only be icing on the cake for him. Then, when he was preoccupied with his part of the plan, I'd make a break for it. I'd spied several boats docked on this side of the island—by the time Alcántara noticed me gone, I'd be stowed away and en route to someplace populated by humans. Those bigger boats probably made stops in places like Norway or Iceland all the time.

I ignored his intense scrutiny as I cleaned my blade, using my apron to wipe the excess blood clean. I hoped the black material would conceal the stains—it wouldn't do me any good to emerge from the dungeons looking like a butcher— and spent a split second debating the merits of finding water to wash off the stench versus simply hightailing it out of there. I decided to risk it and opt for *hightail.*

I pocketed the keys and gripped the knife, ready for action. Finally, I looked over at him again. "I'll come back with help."

He gave me an easy smile. "You don't seem the sort of girl who needs much help."

"Not generally, no." My reply was distracted, my mind

already in another place. I was *so* close. Close to success. Close to the end of this mission, and to escape.

"So why not unlock me now?"

*Why not?* It did seem the obvious choice. I really looked at him then. "How am I supposed to sneak out a half-dead vampire?"

"You're here with the keys," he pressed. "We can split up. I won't put you in danger. Why not let me go?"

If I wanted to escape, I needed to do everything to the letter. Alcántara had stressed his instructions over and over. *Find out where Carden is. That is all. Do not do anything yourself.* "Because that wasn't the plan."

He gave me an irreverent smirk. "Hugo and his plans."

He'd said it so mockingly, somehow I felt included in the criticism. It riled me. "We can't both just waltz out of here. They'll know the moment you're gone and raise an alarm, and then we're both screwed."

He stared at me for a moment, then nodded sagely. "Of course."

Something about that nod set me on edge—it seemed to imply so much more. "We are coming back for you," I insisted.

"Please leave me now. Leave and forget me." Like that, the cockiness was gone from his voice. "This has been a delightful rescue. You, a lovely champion . . . though I fear you are wasted on Hugo Alcántara."

I stepped up to the cell, wrapping my hands around the bars. "If Alcántara says he's going to get you out of here, we're seriously going to get you out of here."

He gave me a smile, but it was melancholy and knowing, and totally unnerving. "Will you do me one favor?"

The clock was ticking, but this guy was such a mystery. I wanted to puzzle him out, because he was definitely *not* fitting with what I understood vampires to be. "Yeah, sure."

"Tell Hugo I'm dead." He sighed—it was a light sound, yet it seemed to carry the weight of the world. He sagged then, tilting back his head and shutting his eyes. It was a macabre pose, exaggerating the sharp lines of tendons and jutting bones.

"What the—?"

And then, as though to prove his point, his head began to loll. I watched his mouth fall open and his jaw go slack. The bastard was dying on me.

"Dammit." I pulled the huge key ring from my apron pocket. "Not on my watch."

Frantically, I flipped through, trying each key. The padlock on his cell was ancient and rusted, looking like something that belonged on a pirate chest.

I sensed a fundamental shift in the air around me—a sudden silence, or blankness, like a candle snuffed. I was losing him.

"You are *so* not doing this to me." I worked faster. I *couldn't* fail. I had to do what I could to make the mission a success. If I failed, I might never escape with my life.

No, I would succeed, and more, I would make Alcántara proud. I'd make Ronan proud, too—even from afar, I'd make him see.

The key in my hand was rusted—so rusted it left streaks of brown along my fingers. I slipped it into the padlock and jiggled. Though it didn't budge, something about the way it'd slipped into place gave me a good feeling, so I jiggled harder, putting my elbow into it. There was a creak and then the crumbling sound of old metal scraping old metal. The padlock popped open.

I slipped it out and pushed open the door—just a crack, though. The creaking was loud enough to wake the dead—I didn't want to summon them to me, too.

I knelt at Carden's side. He looked even more gaunt up close, but taller, too—taller than I'd realized. His hair, skin—everything about him was ashen. *Bloodless.*

Alcántara wanted McCloud alive. And McCloud needed blood.

I'd never fed a vampire before—never heard of an Acari feeding a vampire and surviving—but I worried he'd die on me if he didn't drink, and fast. I thought of the girl upstairs, feeding the vampire from her neck. I'd do the same with Carden, only from my arm. And unlike the other girl, I needed to keep my wits enough so I didn't pass out.

After a moment's hesitation, I unlocked his shackles, needing to stretch as high on my tippy-toes as I could to reach. I'd just have to trust that, once he regained his strength, he wouldn't do anything ungrateful such as tear me limb from limb. I freed one arm and then another, and his body toppled to the ground.

He looked dead. And not in an undead way—he looked *really* dead. But Alcántara needed him alive, which meant I had no choice.

I took the steak knife and slit my forearm, bringing it to McCloud's mouth. But he didn't move, and so I flexed and wriggled, squeezing blood between his lips. "What is your problem?"

Staring at his red-stained lips, I willed them to move. Finally, I spied the faintest twitch. "Come on, come on," I whispered.

I squeezed my arm harder. A few more drops of blood, and then I saw the tip of his tongue licking at the air. His mouth was stained red with my blood.

And then, like the flick of a light, he was awake, and he *attached*.

I drew in a sharp breath, fighting the urge to shove him away, to protect myself.

His mouth was clamped to my flesh, so strong, and he wrapped his arms around me, pulling me closer. There was an initial prick as his fangs pierced me, and he bit down, sucking harder. A cool, woozy feeling flooded my veins, like a drug seeping into me from an IV.

His eyes had been shut tight. But now they flew open, and he stared blindly, his gaze lit by fire as he sucked even harder.

Panic would not overwhelm me. I would stay in control. I wasn't dizzy yet. I could do this. Just a few seconds more. I needed to succeed; I needed him to live.

His flesh plumped, and it was like watching time-elapsed photos of a growing plant, only *he* was the one who grew. He grew, and his skin became taut with it, until it began to freak me out just how much he was filling out. Even in the darkness, I could see his cheeks become ruddy.

This was no wrinkled *elder*—this guy had been young when he was turned. Vital. Powerful. He sprang onto his knees to hug me closer, and as he moved, torchlight cut into the cell, illuminating him in a shaft of golden light. His hair gleamed strawberry blond.

It was too much. He was too big, too broad and tall and muscular, and it was draining me dry.

I tugged my arm, but it was no good. He was attached. I'd become too weak, and he was suddenly too powerful. I swatted at him, but my efforts were feeble, laughable. I choked back a sob. I wasn't going to escape; I was going to die.

But then he froze. He stopped sucking. And just when I thought I'd black out, he shoved me away.

Carden McCloud stared at me, my blood all over his mouth and chin. Some unreadable thing was in his gaze. Was it fury, joy, ferocity, surprise? And then I gasped, realizing what I was witnessing.

Desire.

And then he kissed me.

# CHAPTER TWENTY-SEVEN

Carden kissed me, and I mean, he *kissed* me. He grabbed me, and pulled me to him, and took me. A thousand flames ignited to life inside me—instantaneous, searing flares—his touch lighting my body from within.

It was a shock. *He* was a shock. He was a stranger to me, his mouth, his touch, so foreign; yet his every aspect was suddenly so familiar. Recognition cut through me, something deep in my core knowing him and welcoming him.

I'd fantasized about my first kiss many times—wondering about Ronan, Alcántara, Josh, even Yasuo. But never had I imagined *this*. This was deep and passionate and hungry, as if he might consume me. Flames danced across my skin, and my woozy head buzzed. I couldn't get close enough.

He nicked himself with his own fangs, and I tasted the familiar tang of the drink. I felt the familiar kick of vampire blood coursing through me. I rose, needing more, and he met me halfway, pulling me to my knees and then up off the ground, fitting my body snugly, perfectly against his.

I pressed closer, twining my fingers deep in his hair, now so lustrous and thick. He growled with pleasure, and it reverberated through me, echoing in my veins, becoming my pulse, until my every heartbeat affirmed this joining, marking, utterly profound kiss.

Until he shoved me back with a snarl.

I landed hard on my bottom and could only stare, my heart pounding, suddenly bereft to my soul. My hand flew to my mouth. My lips were hypersensitive, still thrumming from his kiss.

Confusion reeled me. Why did he kiss me? Why did I feel this way? Something told me I should run, but I couldn't bring myself to. My voice came out weak and confused. "Why did you—?"

"What have you done?" He cut me off, sounding furious, his eyes narrowed to hard slits. "What have you done to us, little girl?"

His words were like waves of frigid seawater slapping me and swamping me. "I saved your life."

"Saved me? You've doomed me."

Despite the kiss, I had to remember he was a stranger to me—a very volatile stranger. And yet I couldn't run; I couldn't fight. I scooted away from him, on my guard. "You're welcome."

But he leapt toward me, keeping close. "This isn't a game, girl." He grabbed my chin and made me face him. "Heed me, because you don't seem to understand. You must never tell anyone what you've done." He gave my chin a little jiggle. "Swear it. Swear you'll not tell anyone that you've fed me."

I flinched from his touch, pulling my chin free. I tried to muster anger, but all I felt was this strange desolation. "Fine. I swear."

"We have to get out of here." He stood, and even though his words had been harsh, his touch was gentle as he pulled me to standing. "Can you make it?"

I nodded. My pride had been puffed up for some time now, and this talking-to left me feeling stupid and embarrassed. I'd thought I was doing the right thing by saving his life. If feeding him was a mistake, I needed to make up for it.

He wiped the blood from his mouth. "I know you and Hugo had a plan, but now there's a new plan."

Breaking from Alcántara's strategy would be a mistake. It was *Alcántara's* opinion that mattered, and he'd be pissed if I improvised. He'd be pissed, and I'd be under scrutiny, and I'd never escape.

But somehow I couldn't muster a care for all that. Somehow all I wanted was to redeem myself in McCloud's eyes. He was staring at me, waiting for my reply; he was so big and powerful, I wanted to lean into him.

I gave my head a shake. That kiss. That *kiss* had done this to me. I struggled to keep a clear head. "What just happened?"

He took my hand and gave it a tug. "Later. There'll be time to discuss this later. We need to escape *now*."

I pulled my hand free. "I'm not budging till you tell me what you did to me."

"Oh girl, it's what you did to me." He stared at me a moment, his expression softening. I expected a different response—something more akin to Ronan's exasperation, maybe. So, when a smile bloomed on his face, it took me aback. The amusement had returned to his eyes; yet that unsettling sadness remained. "We bonded."

I stared at him, wide-eyed. "Bonded?"

He took my shoulders and turned me, guiding me out the cell door and talking as he went. "What happened was this: Hugo sent a dangerously untrained child into the world, and now you've bonded us."

"I'm not a child."

"As you say."

"I don't get it. Are you angry?"

He hustled me along, pushing me gently down the corridor. "It appears that, despite my best efforts, I'm not dead yet. So aye, I'm mad as a wet cat. But we McClouds are accustomed to adversity."

That I'd been the one to piss him off troubled me more than it should have. "Well, excuse me." I stopped short, and he bumped into me. "I can't think of many things more *adverse* than dying alone in a dark cell."

He barked out a laugh.

"What is so funny?" I thought I was being deadly serious.

"My reprieve has been granted at the hands of a wee spitfire, and I find it funny indeed. It's an aggravating thing, bonding to a child." He chucked me on the chin. "But at least you're easy on the eyes."

*Easy on the eyes.* Nobody had ever told me anything like

that before, and it confused and annoyed me. I angled my head away. "I am not a child."

"I was born in 1732. Trust me, you may have a woman's body"—his eyes raked over me, and I felt those flames flicker again in instant response—"but you're still a child." He ran a finger down my cheek. "Shut that mouth before I kiss it again. Now, let's go surprise Hugo, shall we?"

The slow burn in my body was doused at the mention of Alcántara. How had I forgotten Alcántara and my escape? I stopped short. "Is this bonding thing permanent?"

"Not even death is permanent, girl." He swatted me on the butt to move me along. "But if we stay here much longer, that's a theory we'll have the opportunity to test."

Never had I ever been swatted on the butt before. This Carden completely threw me off, and his amusement appeared to rise in direct relation to my aggravation, which of course aggravated me further. "I have a name, you know."

He glanced down at me, his brows raised.

"A name," I repeated, whispering now, close to the spiral staircase. "I have a name, and it's not *girl*."

"Well?"

I stood as tall as my five-foot-two-inch frame would get me. "Annelise Drew. Acari Drew."

He chuckled low. "*Acari*. Such nonsense. Fine then, *Acari* Drew. Hold on." He swept me into his arms and swung me up over his shoulder.

I yelped.

"Hush." He swatted me again for good measure. "We Mc-Clouds have a motto, girl. *Hold fast.*" Guarding my head with his hand, he jogged up the narrow staircase.

I held on, but his shoulder jostled into my belly, and the blood rushed to my head. "Ow . . . crap . . . my ribs." I pounded a fist into his back. "This isn't necessary."

He gripped tighter, speaking in the barest whisper. "I'll decide what's necessary and what's not. Let's call that step one of our new plan."

I hoped his strategy was more complex than that, because I didn't think the vampires would let him just jog out of there, with me slung over a shoulder like his Neanderthal bride. We emerged from the stairwell and made it only halfway down the hall before I sensed another presence. He turned his head, whispering to me, and I felt his breath through my dress, hot on my skin. "Hide your blade."

He stiffened beneath me and slowed but didn't stop walking. "My new feeder," he announced. "It was too much for her."

I went limp, playing dead, but I realized Carden's mistake the same moment he did: He'd spoken in English.

"Shite," he cursed under his breath.

"Such a charming accent—you must be McCloud." I recognized Brother Jacob's voice speaking in thickly accented English. "What a surprise. Leaving so soon?"

Carden adjusted me on his shoulder, his hand a vice grip on the back of my thigh. "I had thoughts in that direction, aye."

"But you must be weakened from your captivity. Or did this pretty snack take care of you?" I heard Jacob step closer. "I sense her blood still pumps. You won't mind if I share?"

"I'm afraid I do." Carden slid me down his body—his long, muscled body—and set me down, shielded behind his back.

Jacob peered around at me, and his eyes lit. "Ah! Why, it's our serving girl."

Carden cursed again, this time in a language I didn't understand. He kept his hand behind him, gripping me firmly.

I steadied myself on his back, but I had to peek around, stealing a glimpse of the other vampire. Something told me if we were going to make it out of there alive, it'd take both our efforts.

Jacob studied me. "Well, young one, I see you're not as dumb as you'd have us believe. But how strange you survived a feeding. Tell me, how is it you can stand on your own? Unless you've been consuming the blood. Is that so? Has someone been feeding you?"

Before I could answer, he was on us. As he hissed like a spitting cat, his face transformed into a feral mask, and he flew toward us. His hands extended like claws, digging into Carden's neck.

Carden brought one hand to his throat and used the other to shove me farther behind his back. He gasped, "Run, girl."

I stumbled backward, nearly falling through an open doorway, and was plunged into a dim, empty room. My heart racing, I dashed in, scanning for a better weapon. Candelabra flickered on a side table. I spotted a piano, a gaming table, a settee. But nothing good—weren't rooms like this supposed to have fireplace pokers? If only I'd ignored Ronan's warning and carved myself a nice stake before leaving. Instead, I slid my knife from where I'd hid it up my sleeve.

I wasn't stupid enough to think I could fight a vampire and win, but I also knew that if Carden died, I was dead meat, or worse. Bobbing the knife in my hand, I inched back toward the door. Ungodly noises came from the hallway . . . guttural, savage noises.

And then the men flew through the doorway, and I skittered backward to avoid them, slamming against the arm of the sofa.

I'd never seen two vampires fight before, and it was epic—terrifying, magnificent. Their fangs were fully bared, gleaming in the candlelight. They clawed and spun, and flung each other through the air as though dancing some gloriously violent ballet.

They slashed, and bit, and hit, two wild creatures battling to the death. Jacob seemed stronger, though, with Carden taking more and more time to recover from each blow.

I stepped forward, gripping my weapon. I was trained. I could do this.

I waited until the two fell to the floor, thrashing. Jacob had Carden pinned. I edged around behind him. I clenched the knife in my hand and raised my arm. *A stake in the heart . . .*

But Jacob was too fast—impossibly fast. He'd sensed me, and he was up and on me in an instant, his clawlike fingers digging into my flesh. He wrenched my arm where I'd fed Carden, and I shrieked in pain. "I smell your blood, fair one. You'll make a pretty dessert."

He leaned into me, slowly, like a lover. His eyes had dilated to solid black orbs, locking with mine, and it was impossible to look away. Baring his teeth, he let out a soft hiss and eased his mouth closer.

I could no longer move. I'd thought I'd experienced compulsion before, but it was nothing compared to this. Jacob had me in his grip, inching his fangs closer and closer to my neck, but I could only stand there, waiting in horror, mesmerized by those huge black eyes that were pulling me in and down.

And then I felt Carden. I didn't have to hear him or see him to know he was with me. That knowledge alone kept me sane and helped me cling to the last shreds of my consciousness. McCloud was there, and I wouldn't surrender. For a single instant—during the span of a single heartbeat—I loved him for it.

He reached over me, seized Jacob's chin and forehead, and gave a sharp twist. I heard the brittle snap of the vampire's neck. Then, grabbing my knife where it'd fallen, he plunged it into Jacob's chest.

He stood and took my hand. "We run. Now."

I let him pull me to the door. "Is he dead?"

He looked up and down, scanning the hall. "He's four times my age. It'll take more than that."

"Why didn't you kill him?"

Looking down, he gave me a cockeyed smile and mimicked the words I'd spoken earlier. "You're welcome."

He snatched my hand and laced his fingers tightly with mine, and we ran, navigating the warren of dark passages. We passed serving women and male attendants, but no vampires. I hoped they were too busy with Jacob's summit to be wandering the halls.

We reached a far wing, and the sound of voices stopped us short. He gestured for me to keep quiet as he inched toward a cracked doorway. I strained, picking up the sound of muted conversation on the other side. And then a tittering laugh trilled through the air.

My eyes went wide. "Is that a *girl?*"

He touched a finger to my lips. "Shush."

He'd touched me without thought, as if he had a right to. And it sure shut me up, all right.

"Wait here," he whispered, and slipped inside. I held my breath, listening to grunts and scuffling, until McCloud emerged again with an armful of clothes.

I let myself exhale, startling when he pulled me into the room with him. A couple pairs of feet poked out from behind the sofa, bodies tucked between the furniture and the fireplace. I drew closer for a look and grimaced. He'd killed them without mussing their clothes.

"I tried to hide them a bit so you wouldn't have to see."

I turned my back on the sight. Something about seeing the woman in her white cotton slip made the death all the more grisly. It made me angry—angry at the situation, and angry at him, too. "She was probably innocent, you know."

He put his finger beneath my chin, his expression soft, and tipped my face to his. "Never forget. Nobody who finds himself on this island is ever completely innocent."

I opened my mouth to protest, but in my heart I knew he spoke the truth.

"We've wasted too much time." He piled a mound of dark purple satin into my hands. "New plan, new disguise."

He went to the far side of the room and turned around to give me some privacy. "If we make it out, there's a wee stream that runs along the eastern edge of the grounds. We can escape that way."

"You want me to cross a stream in a dress?"

"No, I want you to *dance* in a dress. Though, if we're lucky, it won't come to that." Carden stripped off his soiled shirt, revealing a glistening—and very naked—back.

I turned abruptly, my cheeks burning. "Sorry."

"So shy?" He chuckled. "No apology needed, I assure you. Just dress yourself before they find us."

The gown was an old-fashioned thing, reaching to the ground, but having an Empire waist, it looked easy to slip on without help. Still, I was skeptical. "Wouldn't wearing a couple of those brown monks' robes be better?"

"Jacob likes a party. At the end of every summit, he hosts a dance to rival the grandest of cotillions."

"What is it with you vampires and dancing?" I was changing as quickly as I could, and my cheeks burnt hotter as I worried that he might see me in my underwear. Finally, I was wriggling into the dress and smoothing it into place. But when I turned, he was still standing with his back to me, waiting patiently.

"We vampires and dancing?" he asked.

He was acting the gentleman, which was probably what guys did back in the eighteenth century. I studied him. In his stolen waistcoat, he looked the part. The dress clothes made his shoulders seem broader, and though the pants were too short, all in all, I thought he'd pass in the candlelight. "Never mind," I told him. "You can turn around now."

He did, and it took my breath away. He'd combed his fingers through his hair, and it framed a striking face. But Carden wasn't handsome in a pretty-boy sort of way—he was more rugged than that. He was a *man*.

I shook my head. This silly girl crap was just the bond talking, not me.

He walked right up to me, coming nearly chest to chest. "You're a vision, Acari Annelise Drew." When I didn't answer, he tilted his head. "Is aught the matter?"

"Aught's fine," I said, turning from him. "Let's blow this cookie stand."

His hand on my shoulder stopped me. I looked up just as he draped a purple veil over my head. "As much as I enjoy looking at that pretty yellow hair, you'll need this, too."

Normally I hated dresses, but the get-up was so foreign that it made me feel safer, and we walked briskly toward the east wing, Carden peeking into random rooms as we went. "It's no good," he said finally. "The only room with a balcony is the ballroom. So that's where we're going."

I frowned. "Can't we just, you know, sneak out the front door?"

"Too many guards posted there. Jacob will recover and raise the alarm soon, if he hasn't already. There's only one way out." He took my hand and placed it in the crook of his arm. "Fancy a dance?"

# CHAPTER TWENTY-EIGHT

He put a hand at my back and swept me toward the sound of chatter, music, and clinking glasses, and in the torch-lit hallway, scurrying along in my low-cut gown and veil, I really did for a moment feel like a woman from another time.

As we drew closer, though, I got more nervous. Carden sensed it and leaned down to whisper in my ear, "Courage, little Acari. Isn't this what you've trained for?"

He caught my eye and gave me a jaunty smile, as though to say, *I dare you.* His fangs flashed white in the shadows.

Trained for this? *No way.* All the dance classes in the world wouldn't have prepared me for a bond with an eighteenth-century vampire. But I nodded anyway, and with a deep breath, let him glide me into the ballroom.

There were vampires all around, and my heart kicked alive, hammering against my chest. I was prey, and these men around me were predators. Instinct told me to flee, but Carden's firm hand on my back kept me in place. I pasted a calm, detached expression on my face.

"Very nice," he said, and I glanced up to find his gaze intent on me.

I nodded, but I was distracted and darted my eyes away, devouring everything in the room. It was like glimpsing a movie set. The orchestra was playing a Viennese waltz, and couples swarmed the dance floor, the women decked out in elaborate period garb. "Who are *they*?"

"Feeders," he said stiffly.

Only then did I notice how many of the females had scarves tied in elaborate knots around their necks. I shuddered. My guess was, they were concealing more than hickeys.

He took my hand and spun me close, and my body thumped into his as he leapt into a vigorous waltz. "Time for us to leave."

I shuffled my feet to catch his pace, feeling dread that at any moment he'd realize what an abysmal dancer I was. "You don't mess around."

"No need to dally." He glided me in effortless circles across the floor. I'd thought I couldn't dance, but I'd thought wrong. Carden knew how to *move*, and it made dancing a breeze. "The sooner we make it over *there* the better." He tipped his chin toward the far wall and the thick swaths of velvet drapes that I assumed marked the balcony doors.

I nodded. As a dancer, he was a strong lead—I didn't even need to keep count—and for once in my life I was happy to follow. "You've done this before," I said, finding myself a little breathless.

He gave a noncommittal grunt, intent on cutting a diagonal path across the crowd, and we reached the far wall in a matter of minutes. Putting an arm around me, he shot a quick glance around, then ducked us behind the curtain. I was certain we simply looked like a couple sneaking out for a romantic tryst.

The night air was brisk, and it felt delicious on my damp brow. He made a beeline for the stone parapet and vaulted over and down. I hiked up my dress, quick on his heels. I didn't want him to do anything that'd embarrass me, like try to catch me or anything.

It was a low drop. I landed in a crouch and heard the crackle of a tearing seam as I bounded into a run. We made quick progress across the grounds, through a network of squat, stone buildings, and Carden pointed out dormitories, a bakehouse, even an abandoned infirmary. A weird humming cut through the air, and it was getting louder the closer we got to what looked like a chapel.

I slowed my pace. "What's that noise?"

"They still keep the Lauds of the Dead." Seeing my confusion, he clarified. "Some of the vampires keep vigil through the night, chanting for the souls of the dead."

"The dead," I repeated. "Which is . . . *them*?"

He nodded. "They're a morbid bunch."

"Creepy."

I strained to listen. It was a deep, vibrant hum that would've sounded beautiful were it not so disturbing. "So those are monks chanting?"

"Make no mistake," he said. "Those are *vampires* chanting. Old habits die hard."

We cut around the chapel to the bank of a shallow stream and, not even pausing, plowed forward, picking our way over rocks and fallen logs to the other side. Once safely into the woods, we slowed our pace a little, and ten thousand questions popped to my mind. "Some of these guys were priests?"

"Some were. Some weren't."

The notion blew me away. "Jeez . . . Some of these vamps were actual *holy* men?"

"Not holy men," he said. "*Political* men. But aye, good men did live here once—they simply martyred themselves, preferring a one-way trip to their Lord over a life of what they considered immortal depravity."

I wanted to ask Carden if *he'd* had a choice, but I was afraid to know the answer.

"The ones who survived," he continued, "I suppose you could say they're religious. It just happens to be *themselves* they believe in."

I hiked up my skirt as we high-stepped over brush and shrubs, making our way to a clearing in the distance. The woods were shadowy, but there was lighter gray on the horizon—the coast. "How'd vampires even end up here in the first place?"

"There was an attack once, claiming multiple monasteries. All those men, all that wealth, together in a cold and sunless climate—it was irresistible to vampires. A series of quick attacks, and entire settlements were destroyed. Men didn't have a chance. . . . Norse, Vikings, Pagans, Christians, Scots—many on these isles in the far north were turned."

"But humans still live here, too. I've seen their houses, on the Isle of Night."

"Think about it, girl. What do vampires feed on?" He stared, waiting for it to hit me.

"Oh. Ick. They kept people alive so they'd have something . . . to eat?"

"Mm-hm." He gave a rueful shrug. "We must survive. And to survive we must feed."

*We.* I couldn't let myself get too comfortable with Carden McCloud. He was unusual, informal, irreverent, plus we were tied together by this bond I didn't entirely understand. But he was still a vampire. And although something had happened during our kiss that'd blunted my urgency, I told myself I *would* escape.

We'd been walking for a while, and I'd lost sight of anything remotely resembling a trail. "Do you know where you're going? Alcántara is waiting."

"I know how to find Hugo," he said, his voice flat.

But then he stopped suddenly, bristling. He grabbed my arm and put a finger to my lips to shush me.

At the feel of his touch once more on my mouth, I had the most preposterous thoughts . . . that his skin wasn't as cold as Alcántara's . . . and that maybe he'd kiss me again. I glared at him, my eyes demanding an explanation.

"They follow," he whispered. "Make haste now. They may lose our scent closer to shore."

We broke into a run, and glimpsing beyond him, I saw the charnel house come into view. We reached the head of the cliff and scrambled downhill toward the beach.

Alcántara stood in the distance, waiting before the mouth of the cave. His arms were crossed stiffly at his chest, and I told myself it was my imagination that he radiated fury.

"Be warned," Carden said as he handed me down from the trail onto the strip of coastline. "He won't be pleased. Remember what I've told you."

What had I set in motion? I now had a secret from Alcántara. I'd disobeyed him, thrusting myself between two very different vampires. Events had taken on a life of their own, and I was being barreled along, no longer in control.

I looked around, frantic. What about my escape? But the mere thought of it had me tripping over my feet, my movements slowed and my head muddled.

Dread filled me, cold and heavy, because I knew—I could try to run, but as long as we shared a bond, I'd never be able to leave McCloud's side.

We walked down the beach toward the cave, and as we closed the distance, it became clear: Alcántara was furious. I could see it in the way he held himself, unmoving, as though he were seething, barely containing his rage.

I'd disobeyed his orders, changed his plans. Had he really even wanted to save Carden in the first place? Had he truly planned on returning with me alive? Would Alcántara slaughter me for freeing him? Would he sense our bond?

I wanted to reach out and take McCloud's hand, but I dared not. Maybe *we* could escape, together. These two vampires didn't exactly strike me as old friends. "Should we turn around?" I tried to catch Carden's eye, but his focus was only for Alcántara. "We could run."

He paused for the barest second, and in that instant, my hope soared. But then he murmured a reply, his face a stoic mask. "The others pursue us from behind. We have no choice—we must go with Hugo."

"But some of those other guys were monks once," I whispered quickly, desperate now to convince him. The closer we got to Alcántara, the more distant my chances became. "How bad could they be?"

"We're vampires," Carden said under his breath. He met my eyes then, and his were bleak. "We're all bad."

# CHAPTER TWENTY-NINE

lcántara's features were carved from ice. His eyes narrowed on me, pausing, weighing my fate.

But then he turned his attention to Carden, greeting him with chilly courtesy. "What a delight to see you, McCloud. For a man held prisoner, you seem the picture of health. Have you fed?" His eyes flicked to me and back again, and it took every ounce of my concentration to remain composed.

Carden's easy manner was one of the more impressive things I'd ever witnessed. "I killed a serving girl. They keep their feeders well nourished, and she more than sufficed."

"I see our resourceful Acari Drew decided to free you herself." Alcántara meandered toward me until he was right up in my face. He recoiled, his eyes snapping into a hard glare on me. "I smell him on you."

I opened my mouth to speak, but Carden beat me to it. "The girl was attacked." He tugged my sleeve up to show where *he'd* fed, lying calmly. "One of the brothers began to bite, but I stopped him. The girl was too weak—I had to carry her out."

Alcántara pinned his gaze back on me. "Is that so?"

I nodded slowly.

"What else happened? Things must've been eventful indeed for you to stray so far from our plan."

I was so freaked I might accidentally spill the beans about the bonding, I babbled my report. The Synod of Seven. A meeting in a private room. Brother Jacob. The dance. All the serving girls, and black aprons, and white aprons, and feeders in satin dresses.

I rambled, but he only stared blankly, and I heard myself rambling some more, desperate to ease the tension. "And I was pretty nervous after the Synod, and would you believe I even thought I saw *Lilac*?"

I waited for him to laugh, or crack a smile, or something. But if I'd thought his features were frosty before, they just about crackled now, cold and hard as a glacier.

"What did you say?" he demanded, slowly enunciating each word.

I flailed nervously. "I saw a girl, and for a second I thought it was Lilac. Remember, my old roommate who I beat in the Directorate Challenge? Funny, right?"

Alcántara turned from me, shutting me out. To him, I no longer existed. "Ready the boat," he snapped to Carden. "I'll return shortly."

And then he disappeared. No *Good job*, no *Thank you*, no nothing. He didn't even look my way, as if by pretending I wasn't there, maybe he could just make me go away.

It knocked the wind from me. "What just happened?"

I felt Carden appear at my back. "Relax, lass."

"Easy for you to say. You have fangs." I paced the beach. "He knows."

"About the bond? If he knew, you'd no longer be standing."

What had I gotten myself into? "You said you'd explain it all. Does this whole bonding thing mean we're, like, married now?"

"It means we're . . . bonded. It's a thing to be experienced, not explained."

I glared.

"And," he continued, "we are not married. Though we can always enjoy—"

"*No*, thank you." I put my hand up to stop wherever that sentence had been going. I had enough on my mind without going *there* in my head.

To my total consternation, the guy winked at me. "As you wish."

I rolled my eyes. "Look, we need to figure this out before he gets back." Alcántara was scaring me, but could he be as bad as the vampires we'd just fled? He'd said *they* were the bad guys, and what sort of evil creatures killed a bunch of priests, anyway? Maybe he was just jealous I'd brought Carden. "Do you think his mood is some sort of a guy thing?"

"Don't work yourself into a lather. Something about that girl you mentioned upset him."

"Lilac? That's preposterous. I killed her." *Didn't I?* But of course I did. "And I'm pretty sure it was because of his help that I was able to do it."

"I was killed, too, once. And yet here I stand."

I stared dumbly at that. I guess if you lived forever, you got pretty nonchalant about things like killing and death.

"Don't hurt yourself thinking, little one." He scruffed my hair and then wandered up the beach into the cave. When he came back out again, he was carrying the dinghy—by himself. He held it over his head effortlessly, as if toting no more than a giant basket.

I hopped to my feet. "Do you need help with that?"

"From a big, strong girl like yourself?" He smiled. "I can manage."

I scowled. If he was trying to take my mind off things, he was succeeding. "I'm stronger than I look."

"You're but an infant, new to the world." The gleam in his eyes told me he was trying to get a rise out of me.

Unfortunately, his taunts weren't good enough to distract me. I followed him down to the shoreline and sat down, battling the feeling of defeat that kept threatening to swallow me. Shutting my eyes, I tipped my face up, desperate to feel the sun warm my skin. "Sure thing, old man," I said, my mind a million miles away.

The skies had cleared a little bit, and watery light cut its way through the clouds. It should've been shining down on me as I made my escape, sailing into the horizon.

Carden had a boat. Check that. We were bonded—*we* had a boat.

Escape was still an option.

So why was I sitting on the sand? This McCloud certainly seemed as though he'd be game for anything. One thing was for sure—he wasn't exactly champing at the bit to get back to the Isle of Night. In his cell, he'd wanted to *die* before being rescued by Alcántara. Was our bond the reason he stayed with me now?

I realized then that it was more than just the bond that had me lingering by his side. Discovering other vampires—a global community of them—cast a different light on this new world of mine. Yet it hadn't made things clearer. Rather, the true order of things was only now resolving into shape.

Were there others who desired escape badly enough to die for it? Would my friends, even the vampire Trainees, eventually long for such a thing? And that was precisely what kept me there, on that beach, my body already turned back toward the direction of *Eyja næturinnar*.

I needed to go back. I needed to see it through.

Headmaster told us once that the Watchers' aim was to defend, to protect, and sometimes to kill. Did I need to return and one day live up to that motto, except in service to my friends?

I thought of them—the first and only allies I had in the world. Emma and Yasuo. Ronan, Amanda, Judge, even Josh . . . I feared they'd need my help dealing with some greater evil that had yet to reveal itself.

I heard the chuff of sand and shallow splashing as Carden dropped the boat at the edge of the water. I listened as he brushed off his hands, and then there was silence.

I opened my eyes to find him staring at me. His intensity brought the memory of our kiss, burning in the front of my mind. For him, it'd just been a by-product of feeding— not from any desire for *me*. I'd finally experienced my first kiss, and it was no more than someone else's biological function.

And now this daylight scrutiny was making me feel exposed. "What?" I demanded.

"Your hair—it's like sunlight."

I gaped. The compliment—if that was what it was—was totally unexpected. "Excuse me?"

"I've been many long years without sunlight," he said gravely. "A man craves it."

The statement implied a few things, and I didn't understand any of them. It gutted me, making me feel more vulnerable than I had in any fighting ring. I found my tongue. "That's just the bond talking."

He smiled broadly then, enjoying my obvious discomfort. "Probably. But if I'm going to suffer a bond, I may as well enjoy myself."

"Suffer? If it weren't for me, you'd be dead. And if it weren't for the bond, I'd . . ." I petered out, reminding myself to beware of our connection. Had it made me so comfortable, I'd almost confessed my original plans for escape?

He raised a brow. *"You'd?"* His knowing look told me he'd either guessed the truth or felt it somehow. "I think we have something in common, you and I."

"Whatever could that be?"

"We both prefer going it alone."

This was dangerous territory, and I needed to tread carefully. "You don't know me," I told him warily.

"True enough." He looked past me, and his face became a blank slate. "It's time."

I turned to see Alcántara walking down the beach toward us, with some kid in tow. As they got closer, I saw that he'd tied the guy's hands behind his back.

"What the—?"

"Hush." Carden stepped in front of me and called to Alcántara, "We're ready to push off."

Alcántara strode straight to the boat, shoving it into the water. Carden joined him, and I took the opportunity to study our new passenger. He was no more than fifteen, sixteen tops, and his obvious terror was disturbing.

"Hey," I said to him.

He cast me a skittish glance. "Who are you people?"

Who were we? Now there was a good question. "Don't worry," I said, unsure what else to say. "It's cool."

He hopped from foot to foot, shivering. I saw he had a pair of baby fangs, like a brand-new Trainee might. I hoped I was right, and it really was cool.

Alcántara beckoned us into the boat. This time it was Carden who rowed us out to the trawler, while Alcántara glowered silently at the boy. "You are a pretty one," he told him finally. "*Qué lindo.* And a pretty boy like you would capture quite a ransom."

The kid looked ready to pee his pants.

"But I see no need for such crassness," he continued, his tone generous and grand. "I would rather you please enjoy our hospitality. I have many questions about the way of life on your island. You gentlemen seem to have quite the compelling array of female visitors."

My blood ran cold. It *was* the Lilac thing that had him acting this way.

We rowed alongside the larger boat, and Alcántara stood, sweeping his arm as if welcoming the kid onto a Carnival

Cruise instead of a stinky old fishing boat. "You don't mind going for a little ride." It was a statement, not a question.

Once aboard, Alcántara dragged the kid belowdecks, and instinctively I began to follow. Carden stopped me with a hand on my shoulder. We stood frozen like that until Alcántara disappeared down the stairs into the shadows.

"You'll want to be elsewhere," Carden murmured.

My mouth went dry. I remembered the terror I'd seen in that kid's eyes. I tried not to think about it as I listened to his screams.

All night.

We made our way back home, the boy shrieking so loudly I could hear him over the chugging of the trawler. I don't know what, if anything, Alcántara was able to torture out of him. I tried not to think about how he was just a kid like Yas, or Josh. Or me.

He was dead by morning.

# CHAPTER THIRTY

I hustled to the dining hall, needing to talk to someone. I was home again, yet I'd never felt so displaced in all my life. I knew I couldn't tell anyone about the bond, but still, I needed to talk to *someone* about *something*—anything to feel real, to normalize this unsettling and, frankly, invasive relationship in which I found myself.

I skipped the lunch line, grabbing only my allotted shooter of the drink, and made a beeline for Emma. But when she and Yasuo spotted me and flinched apart, something inside me cracked, just a little. They had a real affection for each other, whereas I seemed destined to find myself in disturbing entanglements with vampires.

But then, for the umpteenth time, I wondered what would happen when Yas became a full-fledged vampire. I'd found myself with a front-row seat to their deadly game, and it was all too clear they played for keeps.

I shoved it all aside, though, pasting a pleasant expression on my face. And it wasn't so hard, really. I'd been prepared for good-bye forever, and was genuinely happy to see them. "Hey," I said.

Emma gave me one of her quiet smiles. "Hey yourself."

"Welcome back, homegirl." Yasuo patted the empty seat next to him. "Sit down—we'll celebrate your triumphant return."

I gave him a sly look. "What, no parade? No gifts for the returning warrior?"

"Looks like you got one better." Yas waggled his eyebrows. "Seems your reward is a new vampire buddy."

I stiffened. Had he sensed the bond? What did they know? I searched their eyes; then my shoulders eased. They didn't know anything. And of course they didn't—how could they?

I forced my mouth into an easy smile. "Yeah, Car—Master McCloud is okay."

Yasuo caught my almost slipup and gave me a probing look, wickedness dancing in his eyes.

But his expression was wiped clear when Emma announced, "He's quite attractive."

I gave a casual shrug, but inside I was bristling. Was it jealousy that made my insides feel so jangly? Whatever it was, it was weird, and I didn't like it.

Yas scowled. "Who's attractive? That vampire, you mean?"

Emma nodded.

*"Dude,"* Yas exclaimed with a smirk. "The guy walks around wearing a black skirt."

"It's a kilt," I corrected, my face straight.

He leaned toward me on his elbows. "It's a *skirt.*"

I was on the defensive now, my feelings inexplicably intense and out of control, as if I were PMS-ing or something. I folded my napkin into tiny squares, feigning indifference. "Whatever it is, it's hot."

Emma nodded again, but the playful gleam in her eyes told me all she really cared about was sassing her Trainee boyfriend.

"Whatever," he said, trying his hardest to look indifferent.

It snapped me out it, and I laughed, mimicking him. *"Whatever."*

The moment had passed, but it left me unsettled. Ronan once warned how taking too much of the blood made someone volatile—what happened when a girl drank directly from the source? Because I knew a little bit of Carden slipped into that kiss he gave me.

I changed the subject, making a conscious effort to pull out of this moodiness. "Hey, you should thank me. This island was getting boring, and here I am spicing things up a bit."

"We're still waiting to hear where you went," said Yasuo.

"And what you did," Emma added.

"Mysterious, exciting things," I said, trying to sound aloof, and added with a tease in my voice, "But I bet nothing even happened here."

They exchanged a meaningful glance, and it lurched me back into reality. I *knew* that look.

I took a deep breath. "What?" When neither answered me, I demanded again, *"What?"*

Yas gave Emma a pleading look. "If you don't tell her, I will."

"I'm telling, I'm telling." She met my eyes with a disturbingly sympathetic expression. "It's Josh."

Gooseflesh rippled my skin, and the chill reached deep inside. Had Josh been forced to pay the price for siding with me? I sank my head in my hand. "Oh God."

"Don't worry," Emma said quickly. "He's okay."

"What do you mean he's okay? Okay from *what*? What happened?"

Yas nodded toward the front door. "He can tell you himself."

Josh was limping our way, and relief rushed like a hot wave through me, so strong it gave me a little shudder.

But when he got closer, I saw how he was covered in cuts. *Covered.*

That easygoing, seemingly ever-tanned face was riddled with scabs in angry shades of red and brown and pink. They reached all the way to the neckline of his sweater, and I knew with chilling clarity that what I saw represented only the tiniest fraction of his injuries.

"The fabled Drew, back among us. I'd say *gidday*, but I don't think my body could handle another hit." He gave me a smile, which the thick gash on his upper lip twisted. He eased into the seat across from me, obviously in pain.

"What the hell happened?" My voice came out breathier than I'd intended.

"Good to see you, too." His smile wavered, and he held my eyes for a long moment before morphing into cool-boy once more. "I thought Yas here should get a turn at being the pretty one."

It made me laugh and frown at the same time. "Seriously. Who did this?"

"Random people." He shrugged, and pain made a muscle

in his cheek twitch. "Someone decided I'd make a prime demo dummy for Draug-staking techniques."

"They *practiced* on you? The Guidons?" I sat up straight, scanning the room. "Which ones? I'll kill them."

He reached across the table, putting a hand on my arm. "Stand down, D."

Yasuo tossed his sandwich down, pushing away his tray with a decisive shove. "Don't worry about my man Josh. He'll be the last one standing."

*The last one standing.* It was a long-term game we were playing here on *Eyja nœturinnar*—like one extended Directorate Challenge. The realization gave me a chill. "Stand down? How can I stand down? This is my fault. Oh my God, I am so sorry."

*"Not,"* Josh said in a sharp tone. "So not your fault, so don't even go there. It's just the order of things."

"As much as I appreciate the brave act"—I leaned closer, lowering my voice—"you know things would've been *ordered* differently if you hadn't inserted yourself between me and Masha's hazing."

"It was my choice," he said in an uncharacteristically heavy voice.

I flopped back in my chair, unable to process it all. "Holy crap. I leave for, what—thirty-six hours?—and everything falls apart."

"All is entropy and chaos in your absence," he said with that swollen half smile.

"I'm sorry," I repeated.

"Drop it, Drew. Even if this is some Guidon's idea of retribution, I was not about to watch some dickhead take a leak on you. Seriously. Nonissue." He pointed to Yasuo's tray. "You eating that?"

"Be my guest." Yas handed him an untouched triangle from his sandwich. "Whoever came up with the idea of buttering roast beef should be shot."

"Hey, here's something that'll cheer you up," Josh said over a mouthful of food. "Did you hear? The dance is on."

I swung my head to face him full on—all the better for him to appreciate my signature flat, dead-eyed look. "Thanks. Like I really needed to hear that."

"Next week," Emma said.

Yas added grandly, "To celebrate the end of the Dimming and a return to darkness."

"Oh goodie." So much for normalcy—lunch had been one big dose of *irregularity*, and I had to get out of there. I stood, cramming my rumpled napkin into my empty glass and snatching it up to clear it. "Look, guys, I can't take any more news. I'm outta here before you tell me—I don't know—that I'm going to have to sing karaoke at vampire prom or something."

Josh snorted. "*Fantastic* idea. Really. You'd be sensational."

With a roll of my eyes and a shake of my head, I walked away, not looking back as I raised my hand to wave.

Yas called at my back, "Sharpen those stiletto heels, Blondie."

I was nestling my empty glass in the dish cart when I felt a person standing behind me. *What now?*

I turned to find Ronan and instantly forgot I was supposed to be mad at him. I'd thought we'd said good-bye forever, but seeing him next to me, in the flesh, relief swamped me, enough to bend my mind with a momentarily woozy feeling. I fought the urge to fling myself at him for a giant bear hug.

But then I noticed how very deathly pale he was. "Are you okay?"

"I must speak with you," he said somberly.

As I followed him outside, I had to break the tension and joked, "I bet you didn't think you'd see *me* again."

But he didn't take the bait. Instead, he told me in all earnestness, "On the contrary, Annelise. I am glad to see you've returned safely."

*Wow . . . okay.* "Thanks," I said, and my response was followed by an awkward silence.

He led us down the path back toward the Acari dorm, his face ashen. Finally he stopped, then turned. "Amanda's dead."

It was a total disconnect. "Amanda—what?"

"Your Proctor, Amanda. She was killed. Dismembered. Her body was found this morning."

The grisly specificity was what slammed the truth home. *Dismembered.* Just the word was hideous, unthinkable. The ground dropped away from my feet, and I was falling, falling, although I stood right there, my flesh gone prickly and cold.

I stared at him, waiting for some fluke to correct itself. Waiting for the jarring words to take on meaning and sense. "How did it happen?"

"She tried to escape. And failed."

I tried to armor myself, to muster indifference. After all, I was experienced; I'd seen girls die before. Alcántara had warned me not to have friends—Amanda was merely the first of many I'd lose. And really, she'd been more a kindly Proctor to me than a true bosom buddy.

But the armor didn't work. Years could pass, I might one day get promoted to full-blown Watcher, and I was sure even then I'd still reel from this news.

A million thoughts dumped piecemeal into my head: how she'd taken me under her wing; the way she stirred her tea and ate only plain yogurt in the morning; how she called me *dolly*.

Most staggering of all, she'd seemed such a part of life here, but had she secretly been as unhappy as I was?

She'd been so preoccupied when I'd seen her last. We'd been so disconnected. And now I felt guilty, though I knew that was ridiculous. Still, I had the absurd notion that the fate she'd suffered had been meant for me. That I was the one who was supposed to have attempted escape. I was the one who would've failed. I was the one meant to have died.

I stared at Ronan, looking for answers, but his face remained a mask, frozen and unreadable. My mind raced, wondering what her plan had been, where it'd gone wrong. "How did she—?" But then it struck me: She would've needed help. "That *key*. This has something to do with that key you gave her, doesn't it? *You* were going to help her."

They'd wanted to escape *together*. Jealousy spiked my veins, burning away the guilt with acid. I felt more of an outsider than ever. Ronan never offered to help *me* escape. Hell, he was the whole reason I found myself in this situation in the first place.

"It unlocked a boat dock on the other side of the island,"

he said. "Except Amanda didn't make it. Her body was found at the base of one of the southwestern cliffs. She was tortured, then thrown from the side."

The blood drained from my head. I knew a vampire with quite the taste for torture.

I scraped a hand through my hair. I couldn't let myself jump to conclusions—we were on an island crawling with vamps. "They tortured her because she tried to escape?"

"They tortured her for information."

I blanched, hoping desperately this had nothing to do with my Lilac sighting. We'd gotten back yesterday—plenty of time for Alcántara to find and interrogate her. "What sort of information?"

"Perhaps they discovered she'd taken a lover who wasn't Vampire."

*Ronan.* I swallowed hard. Amanda had once insisted I could succeed on this island without kissing any vampires. Looked like she was wrong.

Ronan was watching my every reaction, the muscles of his shoulders, his jaw, all clenched tight. I imagined it was about as upset as I'd ever see him.

Despite all that'd passed between us, my heart broke for him. I'd miss Amanda, but it was nothing compared to what he must've felt. He'd once lost his sister, and now he'd lost his girlfriend, too. "I'm so sorry."

"As am I."

"No, I mean, I know you two were a . . . you know . . . a thing."

The look on his face was pure astonishment. "Amanda and

me? Never. She was with Judge. She . . . It was always Amanda and *Judge*."

I swayed on my feet, putting out my hand as though I might brace myself on thin air. Ronan and Amanda *hadn't* been together? *"Judge?"*

"Aye, *Judge*. Though her death just proves how impossible such things are when you're trapped on this island."

Amanda and Judge; not Amanda and Ronan. Everything clicked into place. Secret keys, secret looks . . . Ronan had only been the go-between. Did it mean *he* was the one in danger now?

"She was going to escape with Judge?" I couldn't help the stupid question, my tone robotic, me on autopilot.

"Nobody knows about them, and you'd do well to forget it, too."

I glared into space, frustrated, angry, confused, even though it was a waste of energy. Ronan was as helpless as me on this island. My life—both our lives—were beyond our control. Our world was one of secrets and violence.

And then came the biggest secret of all. Carden appeared as though bidden, looming beside us and casting us in shadow. He addressed me but stared at Ronan. "Well, Acari Drew, I see I have some competition for your affections." He'd meant it as a joke, but his smile didn't reach his eyes.

Ronan stiffened. "McCloud. Might I be of service?"

"I sensed some trouble," Carden said. "You wouldn't be bothering our wee Acari here, would you? You see, I owe the little spitfire a debt. Silly, I know. But we vampires tend to stick to the old ways."

Ronan's jaw tightened, something sparking in his eyes. Was it realization? Would *he* be the one to guess our bond, not because he had some magic at his disposal, but simply because he knew me so well?

I found my voice, eager to head off any potential male conflict. "He's not bothering me. I was just going back to the dorm."

Carden casually folded his hands at the small of his back and began to stroll ahead. "I'll walk you."

Once again, I had no choice but to follow. I glanced back at Ronan, and he looked drawn and pale. "Bye," I told him, and I tried to infuse the word with comfort and connection and warmth—my own attempt at a bond.

I followed in McCloud's wake, wondering who this vampire really was and what he now meant to my life, because our bond sure seemed more than skin deep. I'd felt intense emotion, and Carden had appeared, and it terrified me more than any Draug ever had.

Fleeing the island was apparently impossible. Escaping one's bonded vampire felt inconceivable.

THE DAY OF THE DANCE arrived and, as expected, my moment came to dance the Paso Doble. Alcántara held me on the dance floor, leading me, shooting me wicked grins, and calling me *querida* as if nothing had happened, though, of course, something had.

Like, things *really* had.

I felt Carden's eyes on me. I sensed him from all the way across the room where he was leaning against the wall with a sort of amused disdain, as though he knew a secret nobody else did. He was easy with his smiles, and Guidons swarmed him like a bunch of cats eyeing an open can of tuna.

I told myself the jangly feeling in my belly wasn't jealousy.

I'd helped save him—I should be happy. Mission accomplished. I was a company girl now—an agent in the fight of good against evil . . . or at least evil and a worse evil.

So why wasn't I happier?

I should've felt triumph. Word had gone around that my mission had been a success, and the Guidons were giving me a wide berth. Another girl in my circle had died—this time a friend—and once more it hadn't been me.

Yet the only thing I felt was alone. I was rudderless, at sea. And I couldn't help the nagging suspicion that the vampires who'd trained me weren't entirely what they appeared.

Read on for an excerpt from

the next Watchers novel,

# BLOOD FEVER

Coming from NAL

in August 2012

H is lips.

Not quite full, not quite thin. Just the right shape for an easy smile. They hitched up at the corners when he got that *look*—that look that said he was thinking of doing something reckless.

I'd move closer, and he'd part them. His eyes would drift to my—

"Acari Drew."

The stern voice brought me back to myself. *Crap.* I was doing it again. Thinking about *him*. The vampire. *My* vampire. Carden McCloud.

"Are you paying attention?" my teacher asked. Thankfully it was just Tracer Judge and not one of the vamps. Daydreaming in class when a vampire was your teacher was high up on the list of Stupid and Possibly Deadly Things To Do.

Just after bonding with a vampire.

As I'd bonded with Carden McCloud.

*His lips.* A glimpse of fang, shimmering. I'd felt that fang, an accidental slip, a hot kiss. . . .

"Acari Drew?"

"Yes, Tracer Judge," I said automatically. I gave a quick shake of my head to clear it.

*Focus.* I was in class. Combat medicine. It was actually kind of cool. I wanted to focus.

I wouldn't call myself a teacher's pet, but I was the smartest thing they had going around here. My brains were what made me stand out. But it'd been my abusive, deadbeat dad who had hardened me, who had landed me on the Isle of Night.

Generally, every girl here had been an outcast in her former life. There were girls who'd called juvie home. Druggies and gang girls. Bad seeds. We were the sorts of girls who'd never be missed.

Only the most elite eventually became Watchers, so vampires recruited only the strongest, the most ruthless. The best among society's bad girls. But training was lethal, and survival demanded *more*. Something extra. Something special.

In the normal world, my genius IQ had made me a loser. A social reject. But here? Here it made me an object of fascination. Someone with possibilities. In a place that valued secrecy and cunning, smarts meant potential.

We all had talent, but all too often these were things like a proclivity for knife play or an inability to feel pain. (My pyromaniac, maybe-dead/maybe-not former roomie-slash-nemesis, Lilac, came to mind.)

*Roommate.* Now, there was a topic to consider.

As in, where was mine? Fall classes began last week and there was still no sign of Lilac's replacement.

Rather than seeing the empty bed in my room as a good sign, it freaked me out. There was no way the vampires were letting me have a double room all to myself, and it did *not* bode well that something was holding up this new roomie.

Had she already been selected? What would *her* gifts be? And would she view me as a freak, as Lilac had?

But, most important, would I be able to hide my relationship with Carden from her? Because this blood bond was proving to be . . . immersive.

I couldn't get him out of my mind. And believe me, I tried. But I was drawn to him, his touch, his eyes. *Those lips.*

Kissing those lips, I'd tasted the vampire blood I'd been drinking since my arrival on the island. The difference was, from Carden, it hadn't been some refrigerated dose in a shot glass. It was hot and pulsing from the source, ringing with his life essence.

A tug of desire pulsed at my core, as though he was summoning me.

I scrubbed my hands through my hair. *Must focus.* I would *not* think about Carden's blood. His blood had done something to me, altered me in a way I didn't understand.

Things I didn't understand made me *intensely* uncomfortable. And this was one thing I couldn't ask anyone about. Carden's warning echoed loudly in my head. Nobody could know about our bond.

"Answer my question," Tracer Judge said with a peculiar note in his voice. He sounded annoyed, testy. "Preferably sometime today."

I gritted my teeth and brightened my smile. A *whoops-sorry-I-zoned-out* sort of smile. "It's a compelling question, Tracer Judge. Perhaps you'll rephrase it for me."

Judge didn't smirk, though. Normally he would've smirked. Tracers were hard-core enough, ruthless enough, to do what it took to find and retrieve girls like me to this bleak rock. Some of them were decent, though, deep down. And Tracer Judge fell into that category.

He often let me stay after class to do independent studies. He taught topics in science—infiltration, forensics, combat medicine, the cool stuff that I loved. He was okay, for a Tracer.

Except these days there was something fundamentally *not* okay about him. Not since his secret love, Proctor Amanda, had been killed.

Though *killed* was a pretty tame word for what had happened to her. Ronan had given me details I was certain I wasn't supposed to know. She'd been tortured. Dismembered. Flung from a cliff.

I suspected that Master Alcántara had been responsible for Amanda's death. On our mission, I'd gotten a peek into the Spanish vampire's interrogation techniques. They weren't pretty.

Amanda had been going to meet Judge so they could escape. *Together.* And I was *so* sure I wasn't supposed to know *that* bit.

I have no idea what Judge would do if he found out I knew. Kill me? Who the hell could guess? I'd learned not to trust anyone on this island. People—and I used that term loosely—played for keeps around here.

I still didn't understand why Ronan had confided in me.

For a Tracer who'd sneakily relied on his hypnotic, persuasive power of touch in order to get me here in the first place, he sure did act like a friend sometimes.

But as I was constantly reminded, friends were a bad idea. Friends could die.

Enemies, though . . . I had those crawling out my ears. There were any number of girls, Acari as well as the older Initiates and Guidons, who wanted to see my ass in a sling. Especially Masha and her pal Trinity—they were Annelise Drew Enemies numbers one and two.

Just the thought sent a chill creeping along my flesh. *I'd* wanted to escape. That could've been *me*—tortured, mangled, discarded.

When I'd taken the assignment to go off the island for a mission with Alcántara, I'd thought it would be my chance to make a break for it. To run as far away from *Eyja næturinnar*, this Isle of Night, as I could get.

Should I have tried to escape when I'd had the chance? There had been a moment on our mission when I could've fled. Would Carden have killed me if I'd tried?

Somehow I knew he wouldn't have—in the same way I knew I couldn't go far from his side even if I tried.

All I'd wanted was to free myself, yet I found myself more entangled than ever. What I felt for Carden, this sensation in my body, was beyond thirst. It was a yearning. An emptiness that only Carden could fill. And I didn't want that *at all*.

Except part of me really did. Want it.

Want him.

"Earth to Drew." It was my pal Yasuo, sitting next to me. A tall, cute vampire Trainee, he had the bluster that came with growing up in L.A. and the sensitivity that came from watching his Japanese gangster dad murder his mother. He sing-songed under his breath, "Drew and McCloud sitting in a tree . . ."

Yas could be such a *guy* sometimes. At the moment, his real damage was probably that he'd overheard Emma—his girlfriend and my *best* friend—mention how cute Carden was.

I stared ahead, hissing into my fist, "Shut up." But I forgave him instantly. All I knew was that Yasuo had my back, and in a place like this, that was all that mattered.

Tracer Judge silenced both of us. "Is there a problem?" he said with uncharacteristic sternness.

"No," I told Judge quietly. "There's no problem."

Ever since bonding with Carden, I'd been scattered. Fragmented. Unable to pay attention. Aware only of this itch I needed to scratch. It was like experiencing the surliness of PMS, a parched thirst, a fevered chill, and a deep-down wiggly boy-wanting feeling all at the same time.

I was *off*, and whenever I tuned in to the feeling, asking, *What is my deal?*, I'd remember: Carden.

Master Carden McCloud, ancient Scottish vampire, was my *deal*. I blamed *him*.

But I could never admit to that, so instead I lied. "It's my fault, Tracer Judge. I let my focus wander for a moment. I apologize."

My formality seemed to mollify him, and the glare in his tired eyes eased a bit. "I repeat: What is the basic difference between combat medicine and emergency medical technique?"

Inhaling deeply, I used my breath to sweep my mind clear

of Carden. Amanda and Ronan, any once and future room-mates, every conceivable friend and enemy . . . I relegated them all to a tiny corner of my brain.

I sat straight in my chair, attentive Acari Drew once more. "The primary difference is that the EMT is the *first* responder, whereas, on a mission, if someone gets injured, the Watcher is the *only* respon—"

The door opened, cutting me off. I was ready to scowl—I'd assembled quite the pretty little answer in my head. But then I saw who stood in the doorway.

It was our headmaster. Silence smothered the room, sudden and complete.

Headmaster Fournier rarely made an appearance in the classroom. This was unprecedented. Unheard of.

He didn't bother with niceties; he just dug right in. "A girl has been discovered," he said, only a hint of his French accent detectable. "A *dead* girl." His tone showed that he found such a thing distasteful. "Someone killed her, without permission. *Someone* on this island bled her dry."

I had thought it was already quiet—until we all held our breath. This was shocking news. *Nobody* on this island acted—or killed—without it being somehow sanctioned by the vampires in charge.

Killing without permission . . . Did that mean someone had actually granted *permission* for Amanda's death? I shuddered.

Sure, deaths happened all the time. In a combat ring. During hazing. At the hand of a bored vampire merely wanting to teach a lesson. But random, anonymous slaughter? There was no such thing.

Most of all, there were no abandoned bodies. Every corpse was repurposed for some other grisly means. Nobody killed and left the body to rot.

Nobody crossed the Directorate.

For Headmaster to stoop to a classroom visit meant this death had upset them. It meant this was a mystery. No surprise that vampires didn't appreciate mysteries.

Headmaster Fournier's shuttered expression made me nervous. But then he pinned that icy stare on me, and my nerves became nausea. "The question is: Who among us would want to see Guidon Trinity dead?"

Like her heroine, **Veronica Wolff** braved an all-girls school, traveled to faraway places, and studied lots of languages. She was not, however, ever trained as an assassin (or so she claims). In real life, she's most often found on a beach or in the mountains of northern California, but you can always find her online at veronicawolff.com.